SKINNY
DIPPING
IN THE
LAKE
OF THE
DEAD

Skinny Dipping
in the Lake of the Dead

❖

stories

❖

Alan DeNiro

Small Beer Press
Northampton, MA

Small Beer Press
176 Prospect Avenue
Northampton, MA 01060
www.smallbeerpress.com
info@smallbeerpress.com

Distributed to the trade by SCB Distributors.

Library of Congress Cataloging-in-Publication Data

DeNiro, Alan.
  Skinny dipping in the Lake of the Dead : stories / Alan DeNiro.-- 1st ed.
    p. cm.
  ISBN-13: 978-1-931520-17-1 (alk. paper)
  ISBN-10: 1-931520-17-8 (alk. paper)
  I. Title.

PS3554.E5325S56 2006
813'.54--dc22
                                          2006004977

First edition 1 2 3 4 5 6 7 8 9 0

Printed on 55# Recycled Paper by Patterson Printing, Benton Harbor, MI
Text set in Minion 11

Cover art © 2006 by Ellen Klages and Jupiter Images.

CONTENTS

Our Byzantium   1
Skinny Dipping in the Lake of the Dead   15
If I Leap   39
The Fourth   49
The Centaur   59
Cuttlefish   63
The Caliber   69
The Excavation   87
A Keeper   93
Fuming Woman   109
The Friendly Giants   115
Quiver   123
Child Assassin   145
The Exchanges   155
Salting the Map   161
Home of the   183

For my parents.

OUR BYZANTIUM

In your absence, the Byzantines infiltrate our city. Several circumstances give the Byzantines a tactical advantage. It is a college town, relatively small, away from any significant airport or interstate, nestled in the Allegheny foothills. It is early June; most of the students—the only real hope for able-bodied defense—are in their hometowns. Finally, a hot azure hangs over the squat buildings of the town, making clear and rational thinking nearly impossible. It was easy for the Byzantines to send a contingent by riverboat and mountain road and assume control.

Where are you?

Yes, you reside in this story, even if you never appear.

You are in Pittsburgh, visiting Todd, your almost ex-boyfriend. I say *almost* because, although Todd has been cheating on you, you don't want to cut the cord. On a Thursday night, he called. Unbidden yet compelled, you decide to drive up to the city of three rivers, to unleak the damage that hasn't already burst through. To fuck and fight until the two are indistinguishable. You'll come back to the city with more questions unanswered, to hash out with me.

On that night, after your phone call, you leave my apartment (my efficiency) without giving me a sigil or sign to work with. The moon is a barn owl's face smoothed over by warm wind. Five minutes before you leave, I am already waiting for your return, feeling sick for you. Can I hear the armies coming?

Move backward a few hours, before you storm out. We are

naked; it is five minutes before midnight, we make Pop-Tarts. You are already in exile from yourself.

Though we have showered, we didn't touch or wash each other during our showering, though I imagine that technically, water ricocheting off your shoulder and hitting my breast—or a thousand other discrete packets of skin—would constitute *washing each other*.

That water, however, would have been unintentional, a "cognitive misunderstanding." Similar to the penumbra, or glisten, that surrounds you. This is literal; don't construe this as a metaphor. The literal halo rests about two to three inches from your naked body. Your nipples are still hard. We haven't had sex in actuality, yet, or ever.

At this moment, I can hear the canter of horses descend from the foothills and green caves. Eating, I see pasted on my kitchen wall a picture of a mosaic of Empress Theodora and her attendants. Faces in gold and taffeta gazing at us like court stenographers. You tore this out of a *National Geographic* and gave it to me when we first started pawing and not-fucking, told me that I needed a moral compass.

"I'm going back to him," you say, and your back sags, and the canonized light around you creaks with it. I have come to accept these minor miracles of yours, drive off my own doubts, keeping angry at myself for entertaining doubts.

Theodora, pasted above me, doesn't look amused.

"But we were going to go hiking tomorrow," I say. A simple task, involving putting one leg in front of the other. I have the intense desire, always, to climb with people. For people to climb me.

You don't reply. In the archaeology magazine that I took from your apartment (why do you have this again?), there's an article about Byzantine bathhouses around Jerusalem, where they found scores of infant skeletons, dried dung, coins. Prostitutes used the bathhouse sewers to get rid of their baby boys—girls were sold into prostitution. This excavation caves into me.

You would have been comfortable there, among the laughs of anklets, or am I being cruel without measure?

After finishing your cigarette—which I didn't know you started until you finished, you say, "I need to sort all of this out."

"We've been talking about this until our lips are blue," I say. Todd, in many ways, is with us here in this university town. All of our discussions are permeated with him, and your relationship with him.

"We can't do this," you say, and pull down your sweater, fold and stuff your bra in your back pocket. No, we can't, but we are. No, we make…love? No, you make as if to leave, and feign the kiss. I'm the tired shrinker, I live inside the jade of protocol. My door opens from your hand. There are other doors, somewhere. You walk out of one of them.

Empress Theodora follows me inside many places, orifices. There are limits to what I can say and act upon, but I can't speak for my capillaries, my skin. They dance their own dance. I wish you luck and hate that bird of luck that might, that will, put its talons on your shoulders (a false luck). Whatever rests there and guides your glide—I want to raise hands against it, to strike the breeze out of its skull. And then blow the breeze back. This is awful. The terrible mouth speaks its own shape into another's throat.

Everywhere I am (I am useless, I could fuck a telephone book), you aren't there, and I hate you for that.

Thinking of you.

The next morning, fat plumes of smoke rise in many directions. The summer heat and the smoke combine to form a kind of incense that I try to cough out of my system. The mountains surrounding our little, compact town are very Balkan and friezed with morning fog. The sun is a mosaic in five hundred puzzle pieces, golden pottery shards that no heavenly hand has bothered to reconstruct.

Driving to work (answering phones at a hospital, a job inherited from you) I see what the commotion is. Men on horses block the road. They're forming a roadblock.

They are cuirassiers (I find this word out later from Jerilyn).

3

ALAN DeNiro

Their shields have gold and blue owls on them. Their helmets are
maroon along the edges. They start quizzing me, in a language I recognize as Greek. After my helpless looks, they move to Latin. One of
them, with a heavy nose, becomes disgusted by my lack of classical
training and jabs a broad swordpoint near my face.

The night before, the dull ebbing of you and I, has left me numb.
All of my terror was spent after I came on your breasts (not making
love; it was more like dissecting it).

Another of the cuirassiers, one with blue feathers on his helmet,
leaps off his horse and forces me out of my Tercel. He goes around
to my back windshield and smashes it with his elbow. The glass turns
into spiderwebs. My first interrogator halts him and points up the
road. In the haze, I don't notice the car graveyard until he points out
the acres of confiscated cars, many of them halfheartedly bruised like
mine. I also see the shuffling of commuters, now on foot. Some walk
in the direction of their original destination, some stumble back to
town, taking off their suits or fast-food hats. There are new rules; no
use for trappings. A few try to plead with the soldiers but are severely
beaten.

Nearly everyone accepts their fate. I walk the mile and a half to
the hospital. The hospital is in flames. Soldiers—from the irregular
ranks—throw wheelchairs out the third-story windows. For the
moment, there are no people strapped into the wheelchairs. These
ragtag soldiers don't seem concerned that the hospital is burning.
Loot is loot. I return to the checkpoint and explain my predicament
in hand gestures, and I'm given a red wooden chit as some kind of
passport. I'm allowed to return to town. A long line of us return to
our homes, to see if they still stand. A convex of a pilgrimage.

A heart is a tetrarch of chambers, blood rushing in and out like syco-
phants in a court. Coming in exhausted, coming out replenished.
The heart has no use for emotion or allegory. You have a heart a
cannibal would love—broken, fixed, or perennially lukewarm.

❖

4

Home. I still have my efficiency, though someone has scrawled a word in Greek on my third-floor door, and the center of the door is caved in slightly. I try to call Pittsburgh information; you told me Todd's last name in a drunken stupor once when you tried to suck my dick but your mouth kept missing, and you muttered his name instead, calling him "Emperor Todd." But the phones are dead. Severed.

When we walked home, a woman on the road kept yammering about how the National Guard would save everyone, the president would be on his way to assess the damage.

"Bullshit," said another man, who I recognized vaguely as an unemployed actor/employed bartender (the breed was plentiful in town). "We're past saving. If the Byzantines are here in the first place, then there's only fate to deal with. Our armies can't kill fate."

I sweep the kitchen floor, trying to remove any trace of you, your detritus: hair, skin, etc. I wash the plates of their Pop-Tart sprinkles. For every dish I clean, there are five more that want to be soiled considerably. I scrub the counter, which has a faintness of your rosemary perfume. The scent might have been called Artifice. The power still works, for the moment, so I turn on the fan and sit in the middle of my hardwood floor. My hands feel cold, like permafrost, after the cleaning. I'm suddenly afraid that I wiped clean any trace of you, and that memories will come undone next. I'm afraid I won't remember if your hair is jet black or has strands of brown mixed through, like a well-shuffled deck.

Someone's chanting in Greek into a loudspeaker down the street. My efficiency is close to the university's school of law. I'm afraid to see what the Byzantines will do there. The Byzantines love to make weapons out of law.

I must have fallen asleep in the middle of the floor, dreaming nothing. When I wake, it's dark and hot—eternally hot—and someone is knocking on my door. The fan has expired, my neck and back have a film of sweat, like chrism. The knocking is insistent and iambic. Afraid of soldiers, I fumble in my pocket for the red chit, as if ready to gamble with my life.

5

ALAN DeNiro

Through the peephole, I see Jerilyn, wearing a shirt of purple cashmere. Opening the door, she eases inside, her head down. Her cheek is scuffed with a bruise and her shirt near her shoulder is torn. She's on the edge of tears and moves to my bed, lying down. In my refrigerator, the orange juice is still somewhat cold, and I pour her a glass and find some Neosporin, which I daub on her cheek with a tissue.

Jerilyn and I grew close after we had similar experiences with semipartners, "ether people" she called them. (My holding patterns. This means you.) She's tall, perfect hazel skin, eyes glinting white-blue. Scores of men in the town, in her academic program (she was getting her PhD in classical studies) have lusted after her body and mind, and she has found herself, over and over again, in disasters of relationships, Superfund cleanups of sex. Though I recognize her great allure, with her mind large as an empire, I have had no desire for her to be anything except my friend. I didn't understand this (when we first met, I was almost afraid of her beauty), and I don't think she did either, which was why, I think, she trusted me.

"Soldiers," she says. "Armenians, I think." She begins to babble in Greek and then snaps out of it, saying, "They took my thesis and told me I wasn't mystical enough." Her breathing slows, and she appraises me, sitting next to her on the bed, under dark eyelashes. "This isn't how I thought it would work out."

Jerilyn knows Greek and Latin well; she was the daughter of an English consul of Turkey and spent much of her childhood in Istanbul, receiving a living education in dead languages from ancient tutors, as calls to prayer washed over the city.

"What the hell do we do?" I say. She leans her head back against the wall, exposing her flushed neck. "They'll settle down, I think. They're trying to prove a point, banish idolatry from our minds. But they'll settle when they see we're harmless." She sets down the empty orange juice cup and thanks me for it, and then she asks where you are. You and Jerilyn are uneasy acquaintances; she knows too much of your dirt.

"She's in Pittsburgh. With Todd."

"You deserve better than that whirlwind." Jerilyn considers you a Theodora, a woman who tried to gain control of her life after a maelstrom of a childhood. Empress Theodora wasn't afraid to kill, either. "I doubt she'll come back," Jerilyn says. I involuntarily flinch. Why do I put myself through the convolutions of broken love when it never was fixed in the first place? When it isn't even love? This is not your fault.

Outside—orangutan smoke, fires and shouts, the blowing of golden horns.

"Can I stay here?" Jerilyn asks. "I'm afraid to go home. They were starting a procession right next to my apartment, in the stadium. Saying mass. Installing icons."

I nod. Processions, for saints I don't recognize, pass by the window, more or less spontaneously. Maybe the Byzantines gain converts.

Theodora, when she was a prostitute in Constantinople, fourteen or so, would lie on the stage naked and servants would pour grain over her breasts, onto her inner thighs and vagina. She was a Leda. Geese, representing Zeus, would be released and peck at the grain. The patrons of the banquet would watch with thin detachment.

In five years she would lure Justinian, they would fall in love. She would become empress. The daughter of a bear-baiter would outshine everyone.

Jerilyn and I creep out at dawn, looking for water, and...others, to see if others we know lived or died. We only see others skirting the edges of our vision; no one approaches us. Jerilyn has a blue chit, the same size as mine.

When I woke up, my skin was olive colored, matching Jerilyn's, as if I'd spent three weeks vacationing on an Aegean island. The page torn out of the *National Geographic*, of Theodora's face, was now ingrained into the wall, a mosaic calcified there. I don't conceive of this as strange.

7

There isn't the same frenzy of the last two days. Years have fallen out of the sky and buried themselves in the soil, on my wall.

"Do you think you'll be able to write about this?" Jerilyn asks me, taking my hand.

"Not yet," I say. "There isn't seepage. It's all so sudden; I can't process any of it."

Jerilyn laughs. "That's a poet's answer if I've ever heard one." Jerilyn is shy. Jerilyn is not-you, and I don't know why I didn't, couldn't, can't love her. This is an inscrutable mystery. We climb the steps up a garden terrace—the air is cloud covered, and slightly cooler—and she says, with amusement but also great measurement, "You have an epic poem in you, somewhere, about this. This town. But I imagine that she's filling your mind, your pores…" There are few other pedestrians. At the top of the stairs there is a menagerie of tents pitched on the tree-peppered central quad, where just a few (dilated?) days ago, students and tourists played Frisbee golf, sunbathed, necked. There are soldiers in formation, drilling in less orderly fashion than I thought they would. They bark laughter when on relief and smoke Kools and Camels.

I don't see you anywhere—do I expect you to land next from the heavens, dismiss Jerilyn, tell me how much you missed me, truly missed me? An assumption?

A few of the soldiers leer at Jerilyn, but she ignores them. "Well," she says, pointing, I expect, at an actual *well* in the middle of the quad, but instead on the steps of Old Main there is a long trough. The attendants are gruff but give us a ration of water, about a half a canteen. We sit on the steps and watch the renovations. Already, I can see changes. The Byzantines prize learning. They have begun piling the textbooks, chandeliers, flower arrangements, toilet paper, chalkboards, chalk, and globes onto the quad—not necessarily in that order of importance.

Jerilyn stiffens, cocking her head slightly at the soldiers bantering behind us, as they pore through a crate of calculus textbooks.

"What is it?" I ask.

"What color chit do you have?"

"Red."

She grabs my wrist, as if checking my pulse. "We need to get you out of here," she says in a low voice. "People who received red chits are going to have 'piercings.' I can only imagine that that means that they'll pierce your tongue. Make you mute."

"What?" I remember the times that you talked about piercing your tongue, and also how you liked to kiss my inner thigh, because that was the most innocent place on my body; it made me seem like a woman. "Is that what the Byzantines used to do?"

"To many of their enemies. Yes."

"How will we leave?" On one hand, the Byzantines seem lackadaisical with security. What they intend to do to the town: erect a few crosses, use our departments of ancient learning to enhance their own, Christianize us, nothing much else cruel. On the other hand, I doubt they would hesitate to kill, whimsically, anyone who provides the least resistance.

"I'm a poet," I say. "Why don't I get a blue chit?"

Jerilyn squints at me, growing somewhat impatient. "The Byzantines don't care about poets, really. Name one Byzantine poet. They were mystics, soldiers, and historians."

She stands up and I follow her. "So you're going to save me?"

"No," she says, "I'm saving myself. I'm leaving with you."

But I haven't made the choice to leave yet, though I know I have to, have to. It is clear that you have no intention of returning to me.

Part of me thinks this is all your doing, that you beckoned the Byzantines to take the town for their own.

"All right?" I say, making a decision, leaning closer to Jerilyn. "Lead."

Later that evening, I gather my things at my efficiency. Across the alley, eye-level with me, a woman vomits coins into a saucepan. The coins sizzle. Once when we were drunk you tried to stick a pinky down my throat, telling me to hush. Hush.

What is left to discover here?

⚜

It is possible that the Byzantines were sleeping in the hills for hundreds of years, waiting for the precise moment for you to leave. It is possible that in 1453, at the fall of Constantinople, there were two ships of Byzantine exiles fleeing their ruined city. One captained by Venetians heading to Venice. The one we all know about, that history teaches us carried the only survivors. What about the other ship, though? The secret barque, with a plain sail (no cross emblazoned; that would only tip off the Ottomans raping Constantinople, guarding the Golden Horn), piloted by eunuchs, might have kept sailing west, west past the rock of Gibraltar, west dodging the sea serpents and krakens dotting the maps of terra incognita, laden with the last relics and knowledge of the empire, arriving on virgin shores. Then, burning the ship christened *Artifice*, they would trek, burdened with the stores and firmaments of their lost empire, away from ocean into the juts of the Finger Lakes and into the recesses of the Alleghenies. Like golden, resplendent bears, they would find caves at the center of the low mountains and sleep.

This is only a theory, similar to the ones delineating Theodora's arc from the stage to the throne, or the time when you said you loved me, and I tried to theorize why you had said that, because I knew you would silently recant in a few days, and you did.

No one would be hurt, you assured me. A body grasping for another body would mean overcoming obstacles and would also be fun. The naive legion in me retreated and tried to surge forward, thought it could save you. You were a reliquary in the middle of a city besieged by…I don't know, let's say besieged by Hungarians, or Genoans. The relic is a knot of sainthairs in a golden cross box, hidden in the robe of an acolyte's cloak, hanging in a cedar closet (the acolytes themselves are not hanging; that would occur later). If this box of holy hairs is, in fact, you, and the armies hoping to capture this are animal/vegetable/mineral invaders, made of dismembered imps, hoping to raise the dead by desecrating and wearing the lyrical relic, then I'm the boy with the arrows made out of bones, on the turrets, hoping to defend you, barb and poison those who would demonize you. You are my sometimes patron saint. I spit antiprayers on the shafts and tip, tighten/cock the bowstring. Patron saint of inconstancy and the whirlwind face. I will become angry if I can't defend you, defend this metaphor.

What I don't (declamations of weakness, flagellations and schisms, socks undarned) realize is that the armies, already wall-storming, are your own legions. The press of my defense only makes irate what I think I'm saving. You don't want to be saved, you don't want to be a city. There should only be ruins—and the saint's lock of hair is really a noose, slithering out of the altar boy's pocket and into the sacristy, into the monstrance where the Eucharist, the body of Christ, lives, and then you disappear from any further hint of allegory.

Jerilyn hotwires a car outside of my apartment. A Pinto. At first, I don't like my chances. Incense still hangs heavy in the air. We're shooting for the interstate thirty miles away. I didn't want this to be a car chase. Jerilyn only received her license six months ago, which gives her driving acumen a recklessness that I like.

The twilight gathers the hills together and says, *All right. Stop the escapees—*

(I requisition your real name in my back pocket. I smuggle it out. I have no idea how it got there.)

I try to breathe with some regularity. The skin under my fingernails bleeds, and I don't know why.

The Pinto's chassis, however, hasn't collapsed. For that I'm grateful. Jerilyn drives along a dirt road along Ravenna River.

We drive through the final outposts of the university town, past a strip mall and a video store nestled in a gully. Jerilyn holds out her middle finger at the stationary horseman of the cataphracti. Arrows glance off the car's chrome. The Pinto has taken on properties that I didn't know a vehicle of Henry Ford could obtain. With Jerilyn at the helm, licking her lips and pinpointing the exact back roads for escape, the vehicle has taken on a kind of obscene sainthood.

She bangs the radio hard with her flat fist. We receive words, at last, over the airwaves. At first there is a Dairy Queen commercial, with the obligatory bad jingle, where I'm potentially treated right. Past the tail end of the commercial, a not-so-smooth transition into "Sister Christian" by Night Ranger. Even as a teen, I knew Night Ranger was White Lion on a bad day. Jerilyn suddenly gets flustered, punches off the radio. "I am not the Dairy Queen," she says quietly to herself. "No, I don't think you are the Dairy Queen," I say measuredly, "we still have a democracy—"

Jerilyn waves me off. She's speaking from the side of a page, the secret text at the spine of the book. It is her but not her. Perhaps, more fully her. "No, Dairy Queens are everywhere, recombinant, bovinal." Rolling down the car window as we pass a flock of small children with ashes on their foreheads (it is not Ash Wednesday), driving through rich rocky scrubland she shouts at them—really shouts at them—"I am not the Dairy Queen! I, too, am the Night Ranger!"

Her hair, usually brown, contains flames at that point, at the roots.

Yeats had it wrong. This is a country for old men, armies confusing the decadent with the mystic (maybe they are the same; Theodora certainly thought so). The hills compress. Jerilyn grows more stately and regal as she drives east, because she isn't afraid of anyone. I remember my old fear of her, and my illusion that you were a soft pillow, ballast of the next state, and that you were only away in Pittsburgh to gather strength to eventually *comfort* me.

What bullshit.

Instead, Jerilyn is real and when I first started to write this I thought that it was supposed to be about you, but maybe I was wrong. Maybe the dichotomies seduced me. It's been known to happen.

Jerilyn's eyes leak blue in the darkness. We have found the interstate and we're driving due east, along the edges of the lakes. But there is flatness to the east, and further east, the ocean. I can almost hear the salt spray. She has a friend in Binghamton we can crash with.

At a rest stop, after I piss, Jerilyn has placed four votive candles on the dashboard and lit them. Their flames are little phoenixes. She says she doesn't know where the candles came from; she found them in her duffel bag. There is a relaxed and plaintive look that the candlelight and the glow from the vending machines gives her, as if she's stepped out of a moonlit bath.

"We're safe," she says, unbuttoning her tunic. I hardly know what to say. On each inch of her skin is a song of Solomon. Why can't I, why don't I love her? Why is part of me with you?

"Don't you see?" she says, drawing me close with her wide, smooth fingers. "You're my love. My Byzantium. You."

Jerilyn is my Theodora. Yes. No. In the Pinto, I'm still afraid of her. Of you. I kiss her nipples, her aureoles (no penumbra or halo; only nectar and sweat), and then press my face between her breasts, sighing, hating that I'm paralyzed.

"What is it?" she says, but as soon as she says it, both of us know. I don't want to speak for her.

"I don't know why," I say. Her breastbone is like a supernova. "You're a kiln, but not my kiln."

After ten seconds, the soft salt of her tears tangles in my hair, and drips to my forehead and then my cheeks.

"Who is she?" she asks me at last, not cold, but not warm, either. "Where is she?"

"I don't know. I don't know."

It is not you. It is not Jerilyn. Years from now, I will be able to remember how to unearth a person who will help me to recognize myself. But not yet. Pain, of telling this to Jerilyn, that I only want to be her friend, shoots through me. "I'm sorry," I say at last.

"Don't," Jerilyn says. She buttons her shirt and restarts the car. Gelid wax drips across the dashboard as we enter the interstate again and keep driving east.

If you don't mind—though I still think of you, sometimes with fondness—I'll exile myself from you. I'll stay, ballast myself with Jerilyn, as long as our friendship can hope to last. We carry our Byzantiums in flight. I take Jerilyn's hand with great suddenness as she drives and passes a semi. Jerilyn smiles and interlocks her fingers with my fingers. As I hold her hand, the landscape around us liquefies into tunnels of light the color of whalebones. We, all of us, are mosaics of venoms and balms.

Driving in the dark, though we move through the forested flatlands, we see olive trees instead of pines and oaks. Next to a strand of olive trees there is an illuminated woman whose hair is like your hair. She retrieves diamonds jutting from the ground and places them in her tunic, but the minute she stops and looks up at me, rushing past, her hair is like someone else's hair.

—

SKINNY DIPPING
IN THE LAKE OF THE DEAD

Once upon a time I lived in Suddenly,[1] a suburb bordering the Lake of the Dead,[2] which used to be Oil City. Oil City used to be important hundreds of years ago, but it's underwater now. Now

1 Population: 2544. Chief natural exports: country music, video footage for the Library of Congress, microfilms. Mayor: Charles Browbridge, age 16, a real prick. Religion: 24% Ideological Atheism (Reformed), 22% New Life Gnostic, 17% Coptic Christian (various denominations), 17% Bahai, 12% Mahanaya Buddhist, 8% undeclared/other (Source: *Suddenly Happy Times*, yearly logbook, 2276).
2 Oil City used to be the petroleum capital of the world; Colonel Drake discovered the world's first exploitable petroleum deposits there in 1842. But the oil boom slowly ended, and the nearly abandoned city was flooded in 2136 to make room for a recreational lake. Five years later, Pennsylvania dissolved into its Five Nations, and when the Gnostic New Life Party took over Pittsburgh city government, they cut nearly all traditional recreational funding.
The reason?
Information dumping, mainly in the form of 60,000 metric tons of archaic "floppy" disks from both the University of Pittsburgh's graduate schools and surplus disks from the long defunct Able's Online Services. These were sealed in flatbed trucks and scattered throughout the empty streets of Oil City days before the valley flooding. The information dumping, patently illegal, caused a Superfund cleanup committee to be formed in Pittsburgh City-State government, where the problem was promptly ignored, since no one lived in a 20-kilometer radius of the lake. But one year later Suddenly was founded by Damian, age 14 at the time, because he "hated taking out the fucken trash" (Source: Damian, 11). Sometimes I get off on history. Well, not get off. You know; you can escape science, sometimes, but never the past. My dad used to tell me that, before he left for Greenland.

15

there's just Suddenly, a teenaged commuting station for Pittsburgh, about one hundred miles and an hour away on the new srails. There are also the deaders,[3] who live on a twenty-story parking garage set in the middle of the lake.

I didn't like Suddenly much and did my best to get by. Here's one reason why, for starters: I didn't like the gold tinting they implanted in all the buildings, or the hieroglyphic billboards either, whose strobes were supposed to impart psychic wisdom on passersby. But when the New Life Gnostic party won city hall, I guess there was no stopping them.

Don't worry, I've just begun.

What else? At the time this story—all true—took place, I lived with my best friend, Owen, in a mid-rent bungalow down a shady lane. But they were all quiet, shady lanes in Suddenly, so I guess that's not too descriptive. Owen sang lead for a country band, Messenger Ash,[4] which had a joint contract from Federal Express and Billboard to record two hits, guaranteed Top Fifteen annuities. Have you heard them?

The story I'm going to tell takes place just this last April, when I was still in school. It begins when everything was still the same. Stories usually happen that way, don't they?

But I imagine you want me to answer the question: *How did you first meet a person who changed your life? Why did this person change your life?*

All right.

I met her for the first time at the Teenage Wasteland Emporium; she was Owen's new date, and I was to meet both of them there. Owen dated often, usually a girl a month. In the queue it smelled like Bibles.

3 No one knew too much about the deaders. Many of the New Life Gnostics appeared to be interested in trade, but the interest was not reciprocal. When we were kids, we were, of course, fascinated by them. But after a couple years, when puberty hit, the parking garage became just a part of the Suddenly scenery. Once in a while you would see them grocery shopping, not really talking to anyone else, making sharp hand signals to the vendors. But everyone grew used to that, too, and ignored them.
4 Name drop.

A crowd of Coptic Gideons in black suits did their best to press square black books into all of our hands. Standing in queue for the Emporium was strictly a hands-in-pocket affair. Peering around, I could see that people weren't just from Suddenly, my hometown; they ranged from all over Greater Pittsburgh, marked and clanned. There were guppy-hairs from Bradford and pricklers from Greensburg and basilisks costumed in rare, crinkly vellum from Erie.

Owen snuck up behind me. She moved beside him.

A girl, about our age, with sharp blonde hair and slender cheekbones. Her clothes looked ancient[5] and gray, but her skin looked slightly damp in the tinted glass of the Emporium windows shining on us crimps standing outside. She looked back and forth between Owen and me.

Introductions were made. Her name was Jane. Jane.[6] She was a deader, the first I'd ever met.

"Hey," she said. Her tone didn't lilt, like I half expected. Children in elementary school always mocked and imitated deaders by lilting

5 People tend to flip around the word "ancient" like a beer burger. Please note that all of this tonal exposition of the deaders is meant, in the long run, to be countered with an amorous adventure, which I can't wait to write about.

6 "You're going out with a deader?" I asked Owen three hours before, back from school, passing around a joint in his room. I remember the room to be strewn everywhere with recording equipment, bongos, and banjos.

"Why don't you relax?" he told me, inhaling. "It's just a girl." I sifted through his new songs logged onto his computer, which I liked to do sometimes. I guess he didn't mind, and in fact, I had just found a rhyme for him: Geoffrey Chaucer and flying saucer.

"Does she live on the parking garage?" I was desperate for a scrap of information, since I hadn't dated anyone in six months, but he played it very understated.

"Of course," he said. "She has really beautiful blonde hair. I think if I move to L.A., I'll bring her with me." I didn't know at the time that he had only known her two weeks; I assumed from his tone that more time had passed between them.

He finished the joint and tossed it in his garbage pile. "So do you want to go tonight or not?"

Otherwise, another slow night at home, so I nodded. We arranged to meet in three hours at the Emporium; he had to meet Jane at the pier. I would have to bother him later, I thought, if he even made it to the parking garage.

their accents, but I realized in one of those fits of casual revelation that nine-year-olds generally have no idea what they're talking about. More like the soft rural twang that Owen approximated with voice implants when he sang his to-be-hits.

Jane and I small-talked a little while waiting. I asked her how she got over to Suddenly, and I hoped I didn't phrase that too awkwardly. She smiled easily; even though her teeth were a little bit brownish, I think I started to fall in love with her, just at that moment, when she lightly touched me on the shoulder. "Well, we have boats, you know." She squinted at me; whether from the dimness or from wanting to stare into my naked soul, I couldn't tell.

"Good to hear that. No man is an island," I said, hoping a reference to an old poem would impress her.

"I'm not a man," she said.

She sure as hell wasn't. After that exchange, Jane held Owen's hand, so to kill time I watched the tandoori chickens of Awful Arthur's across the street, the spice-pak hens frenzied and bumping against the cages in the restaurant window. And I ought to mention as well the Gnostics of an intense vegan subsect who, every night around nine, threw paint bombs against the outer wall of Arthur's restaurant. Patrons on the balcony clapped at the spectacle.

Thankfully, we whisked through the queue slightly faster than normal because of Owen's blooming superstar image. "I think I'm going to dance a little with Jane, then talk to the DJs," Owen told me, handing me my pink wrist tag. "Why don't you see the wrestling match or something and then we'll catch up to you?"

"All right," I said, sighing. I thought Owen was all right, the closest thing I had to a best friend, but he always had one compartment of his brain in the "biz." He had worked too hard to get his break to stop. Music from five different directions pierced my eardrums at the same time. "I guess I'll hang around the wrestling match a little."

"Wonderful," Owen said. "Catch you on the flip side." Whatever that meant. Jane looked around, devouring the interior landscape with her eyes, distracted, and the two of them drifted away.

I climbed the staircase two flights to the upper floor to the square circle, in a medium-sized attic with a high ceiling. I looked at the card; only a very minor match, Savage Chicken versus Electrocution Solution. It wasn't to begin for another fifteen minutes. I took my seat in one of the upper rows. Both the floor below me and that below the ring were transparent; dim white flares flickered on the dance warehouse below. I could see scores of people my age going through the motions of any other Sunday night—slithering in pairs to a new Arabian tango, groups of four lurking in candlelit corners, and couples rubbing opium patches on each other's inner thighs.

The bell rang, and the other dozen wrestling spectators mildly clapped their hands. Savage Chicken, bedecked with his razor and rubber wings, clucked his way into the ring. Phosphorous flecks raced off Electrocution Solution's arms. The screen above the ring gave essential biographical material; Savage Chicken, for example, had a PhD in paleoanthropology.[7]

The two wrestlers locked arms, Chicken nicking the bicep of Solution. They untangled. Solution let off a bolt of electricity, which Chicken dodged; the bolt dissipated against the invisible energy soakers of the ring.

As the match droned on, I grew more and more bored. I cradled my head in my palm and looked down.

I could see Jane languidly dancing, alone. She kept staring up at me. She waved, looking mildly pleased with herself. I waved back. Owen was nowhere to be seen. Two seconds of cowlike staring was too much. I stood up and made for the stairs, just as Electrocution Solution bounded onto the corner ropes and was about to pounce elbow first on Savage Chicken's skull.

I could have sworn that Mr. Solution gave a wink of good luck to me just before he dived. I dived, too, into the fray of the music and

7 It turns out that Jane, who used to study paleoanthropology at Penn on a full Rural Indigenie scholarship, knows Savage Chicken's body of work quite well, and she tells me that she plans to do a paper on his Maori Cycle any day now.

the crowds after I bounded down the stairs and then dived into the dancing crowd, looking wildly around for Jane.

I saw her closer to the opposite side of the hall. Everyone drifted around; dancing in place was not to be heard of. I finally pushed and flowed to her side.

"Where's Owen?" I asked her, at the top of my breath.

She gave a sphinxlike shrug and didn't answer. Instead she said, "How was the wrestling match?"

"Bad. Incredibly bad." A silence came between us. She pirouetted a half step closer to me.

Cacophony from the speakers; no song particularly began, or ended, but they flowed into one another. The music had picked up; after a few seconds I realized it was a remastered, double-time version of one of Messenger Ash's ballads, "The Trouble with Trouble," complete with the new, two-hour-old lyric that I helped to coin:

Honey, your love makes me feel like Geoffrey Chaucer
Stuck without a tale on a flying saucer

Owen must have just uploaded it to the DJ. The sound of my own words (with Owen's voice) blaring into the dance space with people actually dancing to it made me smile. The Balinese backbeat and slide guitar kept the song thrumming. While we danced, I told Jane that I wrote part of the lyrics, but she didn't seem particularly impressed. A mix of contradictory signals and signs, I thought to myself.[8] I saw Owen in the DJ's box briefly as I passed by, hunkered down over the instrument board. A breeze of perfume—orangeish, maybe, or oleander, or marjoram, or all three together—wafted from the ceiling, in spray mists.

And Jane, when she bumped next to me, smelled lightly of honey.

8 I swear that I read this on the urinal wall when I went to piss, two minutes later, before leaving the Emporium's dim doors: "Take it from me. Take a piece of string. Swallow it. Let it digest. Now, you are that string. For a year, a lover will be able to tether herself to you." A Net number followed.

"The Trouble with Trouble" ended and slower chant-dancing began.

"I hate slow music," she shouted above the noise.

I looked at her. She looked at me, calm. We had both stopped dancing. What could I have done in this situation? If I had only known what "this situation" was; I could only see "this situation" around the edges, the scrim.

"Let's wait outside for Owen to finish," I finally said.

Owen didn't catch us; he might not have cared. We walked out the exit; I noticed I was shaking slightly. Awful Arthur's had closed, and the Gnostics had to take the last srail back to Pittsburgh. The cool April air stung my skin. In the calmness, Jane looked like a blonde ambulance, or a bright ghost.

So we sat on a bench advertised with a parent-swapping agency, and we began talking. It's funny how a face is nothing like you remember it from the first gaze. Yes, she still had the high cheek-bones and green eyes that I remembered from forty five minutes before, but seeing her up close was illuminating. My memory, the first time, got it all wrong. A shift and inflection in her features that I wasn't able to explain. It was like postcards you buy of, say, Angkor Wat or the Disney Ruins looking nothing like the places you actually visited.

"I like it here in Suddenly," she said, looking up at the clear sky poked with stars.

"Spend more time here and you'll sour." I tried to make it light-hearted, but I'm sure it came across with a bitter tinge. "What do you do on the lake?"

She shook her head. "Not much. Watch the sky a lot. Go swim-ming. Read. Do you like to read?"

"Sometimes, though it's hard to find good books." I leaned back on the bench, feeling more comfortable. Maybe I was a little drunk on her honey scent and her closeness. "Do you go to school?" I asked her.

"I used to." A confusion passed over her face, but only briefly, before she regarded me with an amused squint. "I studied in paleo-anthropology."

"What's that?"

"It's the study of preliterate cultures through archaeological records. Human origins. What happened in the hundred thousand years after we fell out of the trees, so to speak." I guess I nodded a lot, even though I didn't understand at that point much of what she mentioned. But that was my fault, not hers. I was beginning to learn how a person's mind could be like a nipple or an earlobe, how a person could fall in love with a person from what they say instead of how they look. Or maybe, when the two intertwined things really cooked.

"It makes me sad," she continued, "to think that so many people and places have disappeared. So many vanishings." She rummaged through her handpurse and opened a pack of cigarettes, Malaysian. She tapped the end and the tip lit. "Do you want one? Wait, I'll give you another one for good luck."

I had smoked pot before, and opium, but nothing as taboo as a cigarette. My hand shaking, I reached for the two Jane had already offered me and sucked in the smoke, putting the second cigarette in my vest pocket. My tongue tasted like bacon bits, but at least I didn't cough from the smoke. She held her cigarette balanced between her left index and middle finger, shaking it slightly to clear the ashes from the tube. A threesome ran past us in sync, holding the Belgian flag between them, probably to the Suddenly hostel. Jane peered around.

"Look, it doesn't look like Owen will be joining us tonight. Why don't we get out of here?" Her question had been entirely foreshadowed yet was completely surprising at the same time.

I finished the last of my nic-stic and stomped it out with my sandal. "Sure. Sure." Standing up, I saw that underneath the bench someone had arranged two crumpled female condoms to stand upright, like two bunny ears. "Where to?"

She turned around and walked backward slowly for a few steps, swinging both of her arms and snapping her fingers. "The Lake. All right?"

So we walked to the Lake, about two minutes, the other end of Suddenly from my bungalow. Owen's bungalow, too. In a couple of minutes we reached the edge of town and the lake shore. The water looked particularly smooth and dark, like my hair, and foggy like ... well, fog was fog. Out in the distance in the lake, I could barely see a few hazy lights from the upper levels of the parking garage, where Jane and the other deaders lived.

"Do you love Owen?" I blurted out.

Jane started laughing. She spun away from me a little, kicking up the grainy sand, holding her arms around her shoulders. "Owen? I've only known him a couple of weeks. I have a bunch of Messenger Ash discs. You can't force yourself to love someone, no matter how good it may be for you. You don't expect it where you expect it, anyways. Do you know what I mean?"

"I know what you mean." I didn't. A pair of white-bellied augmented chickens dived and skimmed near the water close to us.

She leaned closer and took my hand. Her skin felt like cool milk. We stood there for a couple of seconds in silence, hands interlocked. She leaned over and whispered, barely, "I have to go now. It's time for me to go back." I could feel very slightly her tongue touch my earlobe.

I nodded, the hurricane whirl of the past hour catching up to me.

"Can we see each other again?" I said.

She nodded. "Here, around ten-ish or so?" When I said yes, she said, "I feel like I've known you for ages already. In a way."

I nodded, not quite understanding. "How are you going to get back?"

She pointed west. "Oh, my boat's over there a little ways. It used to be a carnival ride boat. Leaky but fine. I'll see you then." She gave me a quick peck on the cheek and walked west.

I walked myself up the shore and didn't go home right away. I sat on a dingy dune and watched the fog, watched the lapping waves, and most of all, hoped to watch Jane's boat drift to the vague outline of the parking garage. But I saw no boat, even though I waited for twenty minutes. All I saw was a slightly larger wave that appeared to be moving backward, against the normal current of the lake, receding farther and farther away from me.

I finally got back to the cream-colored bungalow, with all the other little bungalows of parent-free teenagers in neat little rows on Value Street. Tomorrow was school. I looked at the Date, Time and Temperature Channel transfixed on our TV. That and the Aquarium Channel were the only two we had. Incredibly, it was barely midnight. Still an hour or two to get homework done. I entered the shower.

"Hi!" the shower said. "What water temperature would you like today?"

All I wanted was peace, to sift through the thoughts in my head like a kid would sift through shells in sand. Instead I got the talking shower. I mean, I was eighteen; I wasn't a kid anymore, right? I had a responsibility to my own introspection or something like that.

Owen didn't wake me up in the middle of the night, or secretly slit my throat, but when I woke up I found a sticky note stuck on my room's doorknob:

"Hey fuckhead! Read your mail."

Sure enough, the THANK THE GODDESS, YOU HAVE MAIL button flashed on my console, so I popped open my mailbox and started poring through Owen's message:

"Quo fucking vadis? Why didn't you wait for me? Why did you take off with JANE? Did you know that I was nearly done in the DJs booth? Could you show a little bit of compassion for the fact that I made your lyrics a part of the song? JANE is my girlfriend and I'm so upset that you might have been sleeping with JANE or holding her hand that I have been forced into writing a letter. Extremely passive aggressive behavior, isn't it? I reckon so. INsincerely, OWEN."

For some reason, in any correspondence he had to all-capitalize people's names. I had to get ready for school, so I peered around the door of my room. No sounds. I tiptoed into the kitchen. The bungalow was empty, and I started prepping for school, eating a can of Scallion Medallions for breakfast.

Not that I was going to get that much done, anyway. Jane flooded my interior monologue, my subconscious digi-recorder, or whatever else psychologists like to call it. Love is stupid, I said to myself walking to school, my face feeling hot. High school was set on the old Pitt extension campus, from before UPitt annex moved out to Vladivostok. Since there were only four hundred students or so left, there was a lot of room; rolling hills and glades and all that nature. We even had squirrels, which our main rivals, Upper Saint Clair Christian Reformed, didn't have. And squirrels are their mascots, even. The teachers are mostly in their seventies, and used to be communist academics way back, who all flooded to the Pittsburgh suburbs en massé when the New Life Gnostic Party took over. They try to push weird, farty music on us kids.

But I didn't want to be in school that day. First of all, I had this very university-application essay looming over my head, which my guidance counselor was forcing me to do.[9] For English Etc. class we acted out *The Tempest* in improvisation. I played Caliban and hobbled up onto the sound stage surrounded by firs.

"Do you feel Caliban's pain?" Ms. Volanda called out to me from beside the stage. "Be Caliban." The rest of the class peered at me and took copious notes on their handpads, everyone so well behaved.

"Ummm…" I said.

---

9 The "imppointment" (a Very Important Appointment) with the bastard went something like this. "Agribusiness," he said. "No," I said. "Hmm. Geology," he said. "Hell no," I said. "Literature?" he said. He was obviously grabbing for straws, and I called him a chump.

"Well," the counselor said, leaning back, mimicking me, "what are you interested in, then?"

"I don't know. Computer science maybe."

The bastard actually took off his vellum sneaker and threw it at me. "What kind of loser do you want to be? There's no future in computers. In ten years all the software will be self-replicating. All the important cognitive AI work is being done in

"We need a Miranda," Jules, the teacher's pet, said.

Ms. Volanda gave me a scathing look and scanned her class of twelve for good Miranda candidates.

"Leigh. You're Miranda. Do you think Caliban is attracted to you?"

She leaped onto the stage, unfortunately a born thespian. "Of course he is. I'm beautiful." She was, in her immigrant Mooner kind of way, but she wasn't the girl; I felt uncomfortable, made so in equal parts by her acting and her frankness.

So I decided to actually do my best to play the part.

I cackled. I peered wildly at Miranda-Leigh. "So you think you're my better?" I said in my best Caliban voice.

"Good!" my teacher said.

"Scum," Miranda said. "You're supposed to do what my father says, at all times."

"I don't have a father," I blurted out, before I realized it was me, and not Caliban, who was saying that. That jolted me, but no one else appeared to notice; the note-taking became furious, palms flashing. By the time Ms. Volanda told us actors to freeze, I already had. I mean, inside.

I hated acting because it made you too real.

Plus I'd known a lot of actors at high school who were very pretentious.

I droned like any other drone through the rest of the day, peeking my head around corners in some places, looking for Owen. He

biotech. You'll go the way of the blacksmith and VCR repairperson." I'm not good at computers; I just like to work with some of them, but I kept my mouth shut.

"The corporate-campus recruiters will start swinging by our school in the next few weeks. We need an essay from you." Probably just to fill his quota.

"An essay?"

"A composition. For the recruiters. Write an essay about how you met one person who influenced your life, and why." He looked at me with a glance that he probably thought was very amused. "Has anything interesting ever happened in your life?"

That, in itself, was an interesting question.

P.S. His office smelled like cough suppressants.

might have been at his agent's recording studio, or whisked away to the FedEx offices. I don't know what he saw in Jane, or what Jane saw in him. Probably, less than each realized. But that was easy for me to say.

The 3:10 whale call boomed into my math classroom;[10] the end of the day. As the entire school streamed out, about two score of adults stood there at the foot of escalators; almost all held animated placards. Some of the kids leaped off the half-story into some bushes, rather than going down the escalator into the throng of adults; most likely, some of the high-school students' parents srailed up from Pittsburgh. I half expected Mom to be down there. Mom was—and still is—deputy secretary of state in Pittsburgh, and eighth circle in the Gnostic Congress. But she didn't live in Suddenly, and didn't want to live in Suddenly; not many older people did.[11] Thankfully, she wasn't down there, although I recognized a few of her friends in the crowd.

"Join us! We want you all to join," a thin, graying woman said, grabbing my shoulders as if she wanted to press me against her chest. "We're trying to petition Pittsburgh to clean up the lake!"

10 The blue whale, in the nation of Pittsburgh, was the Animal of the Month of April. One in Pittsburgh often saw whalemobiles—little scooters shaped like, well—whales, darting and skipping in and out of traffic all around Pittsburgh's Golden Triangle. It all made me incredibly ill.

11 Here's my last rant, hopefully:

Most people in Pittsburgh pretend to be very sophisticated and jabble on about how awful the new suburbs are, places like Suddenly and Anabasis and I Would Go Here If I Were You. But it boiled down to veiled complaints about the people who lived there; namely, people like Owen and me.

The people who whine, their business suits are crisp and recently downloaded from a designer in Osaka. The absolute worst places to live would be those older suburbs anyway, the ones we slid through on the srail, the few times we needed something in Pittsburgh. Cutesy names like Mt. Lebanon and Applewood and Huckleberry Heights. What the fuck is a huckleberry? The people from those places wore their lacquered badges on their lapels, as in "Say Hi to Me! Be Nice! I live in Huckleberry Heights!"

Suddenly doesn't need badges. It's an antibadge kind of place. Even though I hate Suddenly, I have to give it credit for that.

"And develop it as a whale park," someone else behind her chimed in. I saw their pixel signs, all of which involved whales of some sort frolicking in the open water.

I tried to press through the crowd, and many other students did as well. The school administration usually cleared the steps of the school with mercenaries when this kind of mess happened, usually about once a week. But our principal must have accepted a large bribe or blowjob or something. "Clean it up?" I said, hoping the barest modicum of conversation would set me free.

The thing that pissed me off most was that her face looked so fucking concerned, as if I hadn't been taught a Very Important Secret yet. "Don't you know about the floppy disk crisis?"

"No."

"It's awful," the second woman said. "All the information disks at the bottom of the lake have been leaking corrosives. It's killing all the plants and marine life."

I don't think I'd ever seen marine life in the lake, except perhaps for the passing high wave right after Jane left. "Disks don't leak. They're not batteries." A thought struck me. "And what about the deaders, then?"

The woman—who I remember helped my mother with her channeling exercises a few years back, when I still lived with Mom—shook her head slightly, as if she were saddened by something I'd said. "You don't understand. The deaders will have to understand how important their lake is to the preservation of endangered species."

I pulled out the cigarette Jane gave me and held it out to light it. The crowd of adults gasped; even some of the students gasped, as if I held up someone's finger that I'd gnawed off. I didn't bother lighting it,[12] but walked through the thinned crowd more easily. "By the way, have fun salinating the lake, okay?"

Leaking disks and whales. Dear Goddess. At least my mom was a little bit intelligent and showed more tact before spewing off suppositions. It was a wonder anyone ever wondered why teenagers

---

12 If my principal had seen the open, lit cigarette in passing from a school window, I might have been thrown into prison for five years anyways. Tempting, but I didn't want to risk it.

would ever want to move out on their parents to Suddenly.

Back at home, I took a nap. I knew I had to write the university application essay, even though I'd never had real intentions of going to university anyway. What would I do instead? Hadn't the slightest.

In my nap I dreamed a pretty messed-up dream. I usually dream of water, but this time the dream took place in a desert city. I was the city's lone remaining alchemist, and my penis had transmuted into lead. I wandered the city aimlessly in search of Jane to change it back—if not to skin and bone, then at least to gold. I never found her, though; the city was nearly empty. Elks wandered among the adobes. A few times I thought I saw Jane from the corner of my eye, naked except for a pirate sail wrapped around her midsection. I must have spent a half hour in what felt like real time, slogging around the city with venomous deadweight for a dick.

Nothing resolved itself, but things rarely resolved themselves in waking life for me, either, so I didn't mind too much.

When I woke up it was dark, crickets humming all around the bungalow. Still groggy from the dream, I went to the kitchen, fixed some coffee, and looked at the television. Fifteen minutes until meeting Jane.

Walking out of the house, I peeked into Owen's room. He lay on his bed, head propped up on a corduroy pillow. He was naked except for his cowboy boots, and a naked woman with black hair was sprawled on top of him, moving down on him with her mouth, her back to me. The room smelled like asphalt, probably her perfume. For three seconds I thought it was Jane—my mind didn't register the color of her hair. The scariest thing was Owen's look—glassy eyed. And those eyes locked straight onto me, a mix of numbness and smugness and satisfaction. He lay perfectly still as she moved, and for about ten seconds my feet locked in place. I couldn't break his stare. I wanted to break him. At last I stumbled away.

Three days later I was told he had moved to L.A. for good. But that's his story, not mine. Except that he never gave me a piece of royalty for "The Trouble with Trouble," the bastard.

Groggy from that encounter, my head clearing only gradually, I left the house and took the long way to the lake, past the Teenage Wasteland Emporium, pushing through the usual throng of Gideons, and down Theory Avenue, where all of my teachers lived. A dark night with only a crescent moon to speak of. I went down the embankment and to the place where I had talked with Jane the night before. The lake itself loomed there; perhaps it was a trick of atmosphere, but the lake appeared larger and vaster than I had ever seen it before.

She was there, waiting for me, sitting on a fluorescent pail that a child must have left behind, smoking a cigarette and staring out into the water. The closer I came to her, the more careworn her face looked, and she didn't notice me approaching until I was right next to her. She wore gray jogging shorts and a gray T-shirt and gray sneakers. Everything about her was gray.

"Hey," I said, sitting beside her on the sand.

"You startled me," she said, flicking out orange ash. She looked at me once, then continued looking far into the Lake. I put my hand on her shoulder, and while she didn't pull away, she didn't pull closer either.

She sighed. "Nothing. Everything." She dropped her cigarette to the ground and stomped it with her sneaker. "I don't know what to do. I don't—" She stopped in midsentence.

"What's wrong?"

She took a deep breath. "Do you want to go out there?"

"Where?"

"The parking garage. I want to take you there."

I hadn't considered that, ever. "But people from Suddenly never—"

She waved her hand sharply. "I know, I know. Things have to change, though." She slid her arms around me and kissed my neck. "Please."

Whether I was passive at that point—something I had been accused of by many guidance counselors throughout the years—or more active than at any other moment of my life until that time, I couldn't say. I wanted to run forward and in place at the same time. I gave her a yes and asked her where she docked her boat.

"I don't think we'll be using a boat. I mean, I didn't use one before. I didn't want you to think I was a freak or anything." She stood up, walked to the edge of the water, and looked back at me.

"Do you mean swim?" I said.

"Yes. It's good practice anyways."

Practice? "But the water's cold. I won't be able to breathe—"

"You'll breathe. Don't worry, I'm with you." Her face, so young to my eyes yesterday, gained an extra slant to it, fierce and sensible. I started thinking about *The Tempest,* about how Caliban must have felt if Miranda had asked him to dive into the water without his knowing how to swim. Sometimes literature can screw up my head like that in crucial moments.

Before I could drift off too much, Jane started to take off her clothes, and she told me to do the same. "The clothes will just weigh us down." The matter-of-factness of her request probably freaked me out more than anything. But I pulled them off, dumping the sand out of my boots, and putting them in a neat pile. The wind felt sharp against my skin.

"What if someone steals them?" My back hunched over; Jane was obviously more used to this than I was. Her body looked like a pale blade cutting the sky.

She handed me a vial with a milky fluid inside. "Breathe this."

"What's in it?"

"Science juice," she said, laughing. "Seriously, it's a long story. But it will let you breathe the water, and protect you against hypothermia. You might have to be careful, though. You might go into temporary memory shock. Just stay close to the surface and you'll be fine."

"Where do you want to take me?"

"Home."

The thought of a home soothed me and scared me at the same

time, since I'd never had a home. Too old for mothering, too young for the cities myself, I chose a purgatory by the name of Suddenly instead.

I held the vial to my nostrils and breathed. Jane did the same with her own vial, tipping her head back. It smelled like cloves and magnesia. Jane began stepping into the water, and I followed her. The water gave off crazy reflections of our bodies, ripples bouncing off each other, making our silhouettes look almost intertwined. A warmth shot through me, then a hotness in my lungs.

"Now remember to breathe normally," she said. "And the water will be fine. It won't last as long for you as for me, but it'll be enough."

She slid into the water and began to swim. And I saw her transfigure as the water splashed onto her skin. Her body became gray, the color of the clothes she left on the shore. The thin moonlight made her look like a cloud diving into the water. She submerged, her face popping up a hundred yards out. Then she waved to me.

"Come on."

The water felt icy and piercing, and yet my own chest burned from the vial liquid, and all of my limbs tingled. The sandy bottom gave way under me; so I kicked my legs out and churned my arms outward, like the swimmers I always saw in condom commercials.

I mean, what did I have to show for a crush at that point? Skinny dipping in the Lake of the Dead, that's what. And maybe drowning.

"Are you ready to dive?" she asked me, when we were about a quarter of the way out into the lake. I kicked my legs up, trying to keep the water out of my mouth at all costs.

"What's down there?" I gasped.

"Oil City. The city." Her gray face was clear and composed, and her green eyes looked like two miniature Neptunes. "I think I love you," she said. I leaned over to kiss her, and she took my tongue in her mouth. I kissed her neck, her earlobe.

She still smelled like honey, and her skin tasted faintly of honey. "What's happened to you?" I asked her.

She managed, while floating, to wrap her legs around my calves. "I want to talk about it with you when we get home, all right?"[13] she said. Now I want to show you the bottom." She took my hand and squeezed it. "Trust water."

"How will we see?"

A sly smile. "I'm light."

And she didn't lie. She kicked her body down, and I felt my body sinking. She didn't lie, because I could see her body translucent in the water, luminous capillaries flecking her skin. Her grayness became alabaster, and I rushed to follow. I felt that the vial gave me strength to kick further down than I would normally have thought possible.

What did I see? I could see the faintest hint of a smokestack top five meters away from me, and below that, a roof with MAIL POUC (what is a pouc?) painted with large white letters on the tar. My head began to feel light, with rings in the periphery of my vision the color of jellyfish. Jane careened below the smokestack and to the level of the underwater street. Duckweed tickled my calves. I moved closer to Jane to see the landscape more closely. We both skimmed the bottom; buildings arose around us like concrete ghosts.

A smaller building came ahead of us, squat and metal monochrome; I could see a tiny lamplike light in the window. She entered the front door sideways and motioned for me to follow her into an airlocked chamber. She closed the door behind me. The water seeped out of the anteroom, and I felt my lungs fill out with actual air. I gasped a few breaths while Jane held me by the waist.

"There, there. Try to breathe." After ten seconds I caught my breath, though I still heaved.

13 Probably not too much needs to be told on this point, but the essence is this: the deaders were unwillingly affected by a nanovirus when Oil City was flooded to make the Lake of the Dead. That was why it was flooded in the first place; one of the oil magnates, latched onto a dying petrochemical industry in a dying town, invested most of his money in biotech; specifically, tech involving epidermal grafts from dolphin DNA. Jane was a second-generation deader and received the same treatment as her parents. She told me all of this, more or less, the next day, when we sat on lawn chairs and sipped cape teas, talking about our future and our pasts. As promised.

"Hey. We're home." She gave a small, wry smile. When the last water trickled out, she opened the door into the main house. "Most of us live under the parking garage itself, but consider this guest quarters of some sort."

Inside, I felt as if I'd stepped into an antique store made of rain. The lamp I'd seen from the distance was set in the window, giving off blue, hazy shapes all over the room. A hammock was tied from wall to wall. Someone had scattered papers, dolls, china sets, miniature soldiers, and toy oil drills on ledges and tables set along the walls.

"What are all these things?" I asked her, moving toward one of the tables, sifting through frail, nineteenth-century newspaper clippings from the *Erie Daily Times*.

"Debris. This used to be the historical society building, but we've kept it up the best we could. I try to archive the items, whenever I get the chance."

"You've studied it, right?"

She laughed. "It's not exactly paleo, but close enough. There's a lot of ghosts here." She looked at me curiously. "You're not wearing clothes, you know."

It was a strange sensation that I felt on the tips of my fingers, the breeze coming from an overhead fan. Strange, as if the world were slowing down a little bit. I didn't know why my stomach felt so heavy. I felt like I was just beginning to wake up from a long dream, teetering on some thin line between sleep and the living world.

Without knowing why, I burst out laughing, and we moved to each other.

In many ways, this was just a beginning instead of an ending. But you can say that about any story. I don't think Caliban's story ended when Prospero took off from the island.

And besides, this is an essay, not a book, right? There were probably some gaps I couldn't remember. There's all of Jane's family to speak of, the deaders. They were paradoxically disgruntled and yet comfortable to be around. They, too, deserve their own story.

People always say that one event should naturally progress to another, and then another.

Life almost never works like that, does it?[14]

They like to think that, in Suddenly, at least.

What's next, then?

I live on the parking garage now, sort of, on the fifth floor. I say "sort of" because I feel that I'm not ready to go under the gene therapy to give me the gill skin. At least, not yet. And maybe never. I can't say at this point. The other deaders treat me well enough, I suppose, but I really don't know them well enough to feel a part of them. There are sometimes misunderstandings between Jane and me as well, but they are, as they say, workable. For now, it's good enough to help wire and program the parking garage for the Net, using equipment they throw out at the Suddenly high school.

All over Suddenly, they talk a good game. They're always throwing things out, as if there's no tomorrow. And a lot of the Gnostics make peeps about wrecking the parking garage and making the lake *sparkle* again with whale songs. I've started to go to the town meetings once a month, to give them tooth and hell, and I was even interviewed by the Town Hall Channel once. Maybe I'm following in my mother's footsteps. Maybe I'll run against her one day or another.

For now, though, it's good enough to watch Suddenly from a distance, with binoculars, from the top level of the parking garage.

And for now it's good enough to drink the temporary nanovirus vials and go diving with Jane, help her dredge up Oil City. I love

14 Here's a story about the next time I went deep swimming, recounted by Jane:

"You kept mumbling something about oysters, and for a little while I figured that I would have to use lifeguard training or something."

"What's a lifeguard?" I asked her.

"It's not important. The point is that I was afraid that I would have to carry you, and I was afraid that I wouldn't be able to make it. I guess I didn't realize how close we were to the parking garage. But anyways, to keep you swimming, I told you a story about oysters. I don't know, it was kind of a cadence I said to myself, even though I knew you couldn't hear me."

"What kind of story about oysters?"

"An oyster with a pearl for a heart."

watching her face when she tries to reconstruct ancient scuba-diving equipment or a camouflage pup tent. And just yesterday I pledged my love to her by sticking my hand in an antique waffle iron.[15] I think she thought it was kind, bizarrely kind.

And so I sat down and wrote this essay, with much coaxing from Jane.[16] That is, I'm writing it now. My past has finally caught up to my present. I suppose that since I have no intention of going to university for a long, long time—or even trying for an apprenticeship on a station—it won't matter to any administrator what I've written here. My guidance counselor will probably hate me for this, because it's blowing my "chance," but it was always his chance rather than mine, wasn't it?

So if you're reading this from a university—still reading this—then I hope you understand why I won't be attending your fine school, whatever it is, in the near future.

But then again, now that I think of it, maybe these words mean something to me now, and to my lover, because it's the story of—our story.

---

15 It wasn't on. We couldn't find an antique adapter.

16 "You know," Jane said to me just about fifteen minutes ago. "This isn't bad. Loopy, not exactly an essay, but not bad. Are you sure you want to be a computer scientist?" We were in the historical society, the place where I liked to go down and write.

"What do you mean?"

"I think you should give up everything vaguely involving computers and write."

"What about politics?"

"Screw the politics. Even if you have to leave the Lake and Suddenly and everything you've ever known to accomplish it."

"What about you?" With the lake breeze against my face, I looked down into the lake. I could pretend it was my future: vast, unknowable, deep.

She set the manuscript in my lap and put her hand on my knee. "I'm going to write my book too, remember. The history of Oil City. The oil magnates. The town's death. The flood. Us. You. Everything leading up to this moment. When that's done we can go anywhere. And besides," and she said this taking her time, "it will be tomorrow soon, and tomorrow for a long time after that."

I mean, I'm eighteen, and this might be a facile thing to say at this point in my life, but I love her. I really do.

And that's my composition.

There's one last thing I forgot to tell you. My name. I guess I'm ending with something that I ought to begin with. Names are important, right?

My name is Gregory, a name taken from the Greek, which Jane tells me means to awaken.

If I Leap

The good-bye girl sits at the picnic table watching the boy fall from the sky. He wears a yellow jumpsuit, and she has nick-named him Chicken Little. She sips her ginger ale. In the center of the park, an Eastern Orthodox priest gives away toothpick cru-cifixes next to the fountain. He doesn't appear to notice the boy's plummet.

The boy completes his fall from the Georgics skyscraper, hits the pavement, dusts himself off, and walks over to talk to her.

"What are you doing?" she asks. Two weeks ago her parents threatened to kick her out of the house because she didn't want to spend any time at home with them. So she sits in the park in her summer vacation and eats her brown-bag lunch of baloney sand-wiches and Fritos. Next year she will be a senior at Pency Prep. He gives a crooked, beaky smile.

"Practicing."

She finds him fetching.

The next day she gathers the nerve to touch his arm as they sit on the picnic table. It isn't feathers attached to his body. But beneath his jumpsuit his skin has a yellowish tint, the color of lemon Jell-O. The skin is soft. "You're not normal."

He doesn't argue. He can't remember much except his name and the urge to jump off buildings. "Chicken Little," he repeats. He grew up in Nebraska.

"The sky was huge there," he said. "Dark wheat and deep blue sky." He shakes his head slightly. "All vaguer than a dream…"

No one else in the city appears to notice him. It's a private show for her. She doesn't mind, because the boy certainly breaks up the monotony of the lunch hour, and her lunch hour breaks up the monotony of the day.

One day, while watching him fall, she realizes that her life has been incredibly unhappy. The velocity of his descent doesn't change, yet she can see him in mindless, excruciating detail, like a slow close up. She stands up from the picnic table, body awash with sadness. Looking more closely, she sees that Chicken Little closes his eyes when he falls, a slight smile, his tawny hair whipping.

The good-bye girl realizes he's in ecstasy. She drills him about this later, not about why he doesn't die when he hits the pavement (and at the same time she doesn't want to know, she doesn't want to know). He gives a bright, easy laugh. His body is lean and taut, and the yellow jumpsuit is almost baggy draped over his narrow bones.

"You flatter me," he says. "Nothing makes me happier than falling, nothing."

"But why do you do it?" she asks. She wants to touch his hands, his soft, saffron fingers.

He laughs again. "Why do you watch me?"

Because you're beautiful, she wants to say. Instead, "I'm bored most of the time. I have enough money to live but too much time to force me to spend it." She offers ginger ale and he accepts, tipping the entire aluminum can back. "I have work to do," he says finally, after drinking. "I might not be back for awhile." He points to the top of the skyscraper, thirty stories high. It used to be the headquarters of a long-forgotten financial institution. Now the building houses minor telemarketing franchises, art students, and carpetbaggers. The boy keeps pointing to the top of the building.

"Yes?" she says, trying to see the exact spot where he points to.

"I have to remember these tiny falls for when I do big ones." He arises from the picnic table and glances back. "You'll see me soon. Keep an eye out."

And he's gone before the good-bye girl knows to say good-bye.

It's two weeks before there's any more sign of him. Time slows for her, like it must slow for Chicken Little as he falls off the skyscraper. But this slowing, she realizes, doesn't *give* her anything. The slowness makes her miss him even more.

She sees a poster for a fiction writing workshop in the basement of a Greek Orthodox church—apparently run by the priest who's always in the park—but she figures it would be a bad scene to really write what she would like to write in public. She keeps a journal instead, where the thoughts pour out like hot wine. "The wings, I want the wings to take me cool as a feather, because I want him to be my feather-boy…"

Such thoughts cannot bring him back or help her contend with her parents. The house is not actually a house but an apartment, but she likes to pretend. Her room resembles a monk's cell. She has to sleep somewhere. White walls, a few magenta candles littering the windowsill, a trigonometry textbook on her desk. She carved the book out to make a safe, where she keeps her lockets.

"Oh, for Christ's sake, Marlena," her father says to her mother. "She's moping around for a reason."

"Am not," the girl shouts down from the top of the stairs, from her room, where she can hear anything she wants to hear.

"I think she's in love," her mother mutters to her father, amused.

The girl stands on the bed. "Fuck you!" she yells. She can almost see her father rising out of the rickety chair, and then holding his hands up in a supplicating gesture.

"See what I tell you?" her father says to her mother. "Look what we have to put up with."

"I know what we put up with," the mother says, sighing.

The girl closes her eyes and hops off the bed. Her knees buckle and she nearly lands on her dresser.

"What was that?" her mother calls up.

"I'm coming up there after I eat supper," her father says. The girl has scraped her knee and doesn't bother to Band-Aid it or swab the scratch with cotton. "Damned if I'm not going to come up there." She hears him sit.

That night, she bolts out the door and wanders to the park. It's not the safest place in the city to be at night; the empty streets chill her. The pigeons sleep in secret coves. Even though it is July, a brisk air has entered the city. She holds her thin, violet-colored jacket close to her.

The girl stares up at the looming skyscraper. There ought to be gargoyles there. Or him, perched on someone's window. Maybe to watch TV. But then she thinks that maybe he's too sophisticated for TV. She walks across the street to the entrance foyer but the door is locked. A security guard has a booth adjoining the vestibule inside; he watches TV, and his unclipped cardboard badge rests on his desk.

She knocks on the door. "Closed," the man says, turning back to the set.

"Have you seen a boy?" she begins but then realizes it's hopeless. No one has seen him. She squints at the television, through the grainy glass of the foyer. A disaster has just struck in a South-East Asian country whose name she can't pronounce. Some terrorist tried to blow up one of the new, hundred-story high rises. The shards of glass glitter on the narrow street in what must be afternoon on the other side of the world. As the security guard turns away, the live camera shows bodies carried away on makeshift stretchers made of sailing canvas.

She opens her mouth and stares. One of the men in the blurry camera's eye, rushing a bloodied man away to an ambulance, is Chicken Little.

Next week he returns and falls off the skyscraper again, and the girl tells him what she saw. "Cat's out of the bag?" he says.

"Way out." She crunches down on an apple. "I'm somehow intrigued by this double life of yours." She's pissed at him, for being away for so long and not telling her why, or at least dropping her a postcard.

"It's really hard to talk about," he says. "But I'm here for a reason. I have important tasks."

"Whatever," she says, crossing her arms. "You could have told me."

He begins laughing, not unkindly, and her face flushes.

"Falling is a gift for me," Chicken Little explains. "I get presentiments about disasters that might happen. These dreams, these images of terrible events come to me only during my falls." He shakes his head. "I try to save people afterward, if it feels right, but it doesn't always work."

"What do you mean?" Here, she takes his hand, and he doesn't pull away.

"Five times out of six I'm wrong. It's hard work having these dreams while I'm falling; I'm improvising this as I go along. But I have to."

The priest next to the fountain sees her and turns his head away, hands jammed full of toothpicks.

"This is strange," she says. "I don't understand how you can do this."

"If you don't understand, I want to make you understand." He sits up from the picnic table, still holding her hand. "Come on."

It takes them about fifteen minutes to walk the dusty stairs all the way to the top, silent except for their footfall. The stairwell smells like old taffy; she sees his old footprints crisscrossed on the tiled stairs.

All of the footprints lead up.

When they reach the top door, she gathers her breath, slumping in the hall. He doesn't look particularly tired, but he waits for her. When her breathing calms, he creaks the door open and they step out.

The platformed roof of the Georgics skyscraper could be the roof of the world to the girl. Barren, blistering, hardly an atmosphere between her and the sun. She clenches his arm for support.

A few pigeons linger and hop, but they're lean and look more like ravens than the fat cooers she's used to in the park.

"Come here," he says, and walks to the edge. Vertigo hits her; her legs want to buckle, but he keeps her steady. "Look down there."

She looks. The street, the park, even the black trash bags sagging on the curb, all appear microscopic and pristine. "It's beautiful," she stammers. She's scared out of her wits but continues to look.

"Hold my hand before I go, all right?" he says.

"Are you scared?" She wants to hold him close and tell him not to jump.

He kisses her neck; she puts her arm around his and notices an extra softness there, like goose down, or extra-fine tissue paper. "Scared?" he says. "I'm always scared." He touches her sandy brown hair and leaps.

She crouches to the edge and for an instant wants to follow him, to see what would happen if she follows him, to let the air kiss her slowly. She stays there and watches him land, though since the ground is so far away she can't see the exact details. Pigeons dart next to her and then scuttle away.

An hour later he opens the ancient door. His narrow face looks tired but purified.

"Anything?" she asks.

"Maybe. It's too early to say." He sits beside her, and their legs dangle off the edge. "It's always too early to say. I'll have to sleep on it."

"Sleep with me," she says, and she can barely believe the words streaming from her mouth. "I mean," and he slides his arm around her waist. "Where do you sleep?"

"Here, on the roof. Don't you have a home to go to?"

"Not really," she says. The thought of her parents milling around the kitchen fills her with dread. "I want to stay here."

That night he discloses blankets in a corner of the roof, with a heating duct providing warmth from the wind. They huddle together as the long darkness comes, as pigeons flutter around them.

"You're shaking," she says in his ear, running her fingertips along his thigh. She has never wanted to do this before, like this.

"Yes," he says, moving on top of her. "Shaking."

She opens her legs. As he moves inside of her, deep guttural sounds come from the back of his throat. The noise arises from a place inside of him that she hasn't uncovered until now. He comes quietly, and she not so quietly. She holds onto his soft neck for dear life.

Weeks pass. The girl makes perfunctory visits home to eat and gather her things. When her parents ask her where she is going, where she has been, she makes up an elaborate story about a Nostradaman named Amanthar she shacks up with on the east side. The entire thing is a fiction; she considers what the Orthodox priest would think of her story. The story keeps her parents arguing long enough about what to do about Amanthar that she's able to slip away, after her parents move to the basement to fight. She tells Chicken Little nothing about her family and home, wanting to keep those two worlds as separate as possible.

Yet school will be starting in a month. She can't imagine classrooms, desks, the mundane world she used to know.

The fifth time they make love on the roof, it is afternoon, and she notices that the color of his semen, which she wipes from her with a box of tissues stolen from home, is a milky blue color.

"Should I even ask about that?" she says, tossing the Kleenex into a ventilation duct.

Chicken Little doesn't say anything at first. Then, after they've put on their clothes, and he jumps and returns to the top of the roof, he says, "You know I'm different."

"Yes, but—" She wants to kiss him again and does. "It makes me wonder what you're made of."

"The sky." It takes her a few seconds to realize that he has answered completely seriously.

A week later, she notices that the sky begins to cool. The slightest hint of Indian summer is around the corner. That morning, Chicken Little looks worried.

She knows what he's going to say next. The girl has been dreading it for ages.

"Something awful is going to happen," he says. He slumps down on their mat; the nest, she used to joke with him. I can't tell you much more, but I'm going to have to leave."

The color drains from her face. "Like before?" She sits next to him but he's either too distracted to hold her or doesn't have the strength.

"Yes. Something like before." He rests his head on his knee and wraps his arms around himself. "Part of me wishes I wouldn't have to go through this. If I could, I would live normally, like you."

She laughs. "I'm not normal either. I'm with you, after all."

"You're right," he says slowly. "Maybe you're not normal anymore."

That night they sleep together, but apart. She doesn't say much or touch him, even though that's what she wants more than anything else in the world.

School begins and he doesn't come back. The summer begins to seem distant to her. Though she doesn't like it much, she's forced to reacquaint herself with friends she doesn't care about, with classes she grows bored with after the second day. The thought of college nauseates her. She sleepwalks through the halls, through the house. There's no reason to get angry or depressed, she tells herself. I'm a high school student. At the same time, the girl knows that something is different inside of her.

She scours the newspapers for signs of disasters: floods, earthquakes, terrorist attacks, of which there are many. There are no signs of mysterious strangers in the grainy photos. Not too many people saved, either. What if he's always too late? she thinks to herself. I'm a morbid bastard.

On a Saturday in the beginning of October, she goes back to the park. The trees have all turned their colors, their pelts. The

Orthodox priest still plies his trade, although there are even fewer passersby than in the summer. He gives her a frigid look and for some reason seems terribly afraid of her. This surprises her. "I wish I would have taken your class," she calls out, lying, but he pretends not to hear her.

She looks up. For the first time, she sees the Georgics building as a small building, not a vast superstructure but a normal, old skyscraper in a forgotten neighborhood of the city. She pries open the stairwell door and begins the walk up. Someone has cleaned the stairs of all the dust, and she begins to cry. "I don't even have his footprints anymore," she says.

At the top she kicks the door open. The sunlight bursts upon her, but the air chills her deeply. The autumn must have driven the pigeons away. The roof is empty; even their careworn blanket is gone, probably thrown away by the same janitor who cleaned the stairs.

Trembling, she steps to the edge. The black frock of the priest looks like a tiny crow below her. The street is empty. She looks at the sky, the sharp blueness, the cirrus clouds stationary there. "I want to be there," she says, unafraid, and with her toes quivering, she jumps.

At first the girl imagines that she has only fallen off her bed in the middle of a bad dream, instead of a thirty-story building. Then she is nowhere, and her mind slows, taking its time sifting through the sensations around her, relishing the rough breeze of her plummet. Her hair dances in front of her eyes. She doesn't need to close her eyes to see what she wants to see, what she has been craving and fearing since Chicken Little said good-bye.

The falling disappears. Sounds drown out into silence. She sees Chicken Little in a small jet plane tilted in a weird angle. Downward. The passengers, about ten of them—mothers and businessmen and small children—wail. A stewardess tries to walk through the chaos; she has an airline insignia on her lapel that the girl has seen on many commercials. All these views are crystalline to her. But Chicken Little is there, and from his under-the-seat compartment he pulls out—

efficiently, as if he has been training for this his entire life—a huge bag, large enough that he must have smuggled it on board. She sees smoke come from the wing and she wants to cry out, but she can't cry out. All she can do is watch as Chicken Little pulls parachutes from the bag, about ten of them, and distributes them. A couple of passengers rush toward him crazily, but he gives them a fierce look, and they calm down. The plane starts to shake and blur, and the last image the good-bye girl sees is Chicken Little looking at the crooked window of the jet, in the middle of the disaster without a parachute. But of course he has none. And he looks worried. She realizes that he doesn't know if he can make this jump, so high in the air, and still land on his feet.

Then she finds herself falling again, the freeze-frame loosening. Nothing in her life has ever felt like that descent, gravity sweetly calling her down. The ground comes closer and closer, and she rotates her feet forward. She lands, knees bending but not breaking.

She places her palms flat on the cool sidewalk and appraises the landscape around her, like a cat. The priest, who had been watching her fall, rushes to her, dropping his toothpick crucifixes along the way.

When the priest comes within earshot, sweat beading on his face, she says, "I've seen the future tense. There's still time." Time to find the airline, the flight number, and track him. To save him if he needs to be saved.

The priest looks at her as if she were a ghost. "You've cut yourself on some glass," is all that he can manage to say.

She turns over her hand. A shard of clear glass has lodged below her thumb. The blood trickles down her palm. The blood is the color of the sky on a clear day.

THE FOURTH

A t first, Indigo McCarthy hadn't realized that an agent from the
Department of Agriculture was shadowing him. But he soon
learned. The pursuit started at U.S. Postal Service Station No. 4245.
The Ag agent was a mole in USPS who'd requested a transfer to
Vermontville, the tiny hamlet bordering the resort lake. A lot of
middle managers from the city spent summer weekends there with
their families. It was the weekend of the Fourth. At the post office,
the Ag agent found that he liked sifting through other people's
mail, particularly when the mail had the potential—the energy of
activation—to contain harmful animal or vegetable products. Such
secret parcels threatened the nation.

In Indigo's case it was a manila envelope with no return address
and a Berkeley postmark (itself suspicious), which contained three
small packages of Kool-Aid powder: Lemon Punch, Fruit Cocktail,
and Wacky Blueberry. Oh, Indigo McCarthy must have been up to
something, the agent knew.

In the tiny post office break room, he blew his nose on a standard-
issue department handkerchief, a wheat stalk embroidered on each
corner. He double-checked the pump load ammo in his wrist gun,
and resealed the envelope with a glue stick he'd picked up from the
Ben Franklin store in town. None the wiser. He grimaced. The field
office in Milwaukee had the wherewithal to give him a wrist gun, but
a ninety-cent glue stick was apparently out of their league.

A few men and women in trim blue uniforms were coming into

the break room from the Secret Break Room that even the infiltrating Ag agent dared not venture into. The aggie hurried. Any one of them could be a plant, he reasoned, from any agency. It was best to be too careful. Indigo knew none of this fifteen minutes later, as he yanked the envelope and two postcards from his PO box and walked away. How could he have? Professional spies were on the scene.

As he drove his cherry-red SUV from the post office to the lake, past a series of dales and abandoned hobby farms, an Immigration and Naturalization Service official in an SUV followed him. Star-spangled rectangles of cloth rippled on every street corner. The air exploded with toy explosives. The INS agent's SUV was white and didn't blend in well. She'd been working this case for a few days, and it was finally coming to fruition. Suspicious packages always portended something suspicious. The INS agent had Indigo's credit report on the front seat, as well as a Xerox of his recent international itineraries to Canada and Mexico. For "business." The agent chortled. Indigo had two girls. His wife was a pharmacist. The wife waved at him as he pulled up to their time-share lake cottage. Clean white stucco, worn in, peonies obscuring the cobblestone path through the front yard. But in a pleasant way.

The INS agent sped on, but not before a metal strip adhering to her passenger-side doorknob took several photos of Indigo's hand, which held the postcards and envelope. The photos were uploaded to a satellite and then down to a processing station in the basement of a Miami funeral home.

Unbeknownst to the INS agent, the ghostly afterimages of the photos were intercepted by a Department of Transportation agent hiding in some shrubs across the street, holding something akin to a laser pointer. She uploaded the images and started running away from the SUV, toward the nearest airport, where there was a Cessna waiting to take her back to Duluth.

"Who are those from, honey?" the wife, Marsha, said. A quick hot peck on the check. It was hot outside. Their marriage was on the rocks. (One didn't need to be a spy with advanced training to see *that*!) The two girls, Esther, five, and Miranda, seven, were in the lake, splashing, adorned with life preservers shaped like smiling killer whales. Below the submerged black fins and the legs kicking out, an Alcohol, Tobacco, and Firearms bureau agent waited with scuba gear and sonar implants, listening. Like Virginia Woolf, he had stones in his pockets when he jumped into the water. He'd learned that through a debriefing of "great American subversives," and won a certificate for the idea, which hung over his desk back at the Cedar Rapids headquarters. He was quite proud of both the certificate and the desk. The girls giggled. A trout was brushing against their toes.

"I don't know," Indigo said. "I haven't really looked at them. It's probably just junk." It's all junk, he thought. "I need a beer."

"Get it yourself." Freeze, retreat. Snap, Indigo opened the screen door and got a beer, postal cargo still in hand, snap, a wide-angle lens captured Marsha's backside as she walked down the cobbled sandstone path to the lake. The sandstone was imported from France. *Super* suspicious, code red. Snap again, the cobblestones and her ankles, for good measure. Not everyone was honorable.

Within the lake's circumference (it was shaped like a pill bug, twitching, ready to curl up), other children played, but in a desultory fashion, as if they knew something unpatriotic was going on in the McCarthy household. Speedboats sped by in front of their cabin a little more slowly. In a few hours they would be angrily shaking their fists, assembling in the town hall, shouting "Burn down the stucco! Burn down the stucco!" If the Forest Service agent hiding in a stand of trees had his way. He couldn't get close to the house without blowing his cover, which was that of a middle-aged man who had just lost his consultancy job, masturbating amongst the trees, and that was all that could be said about him, except for the pictures he took, three-fourths of which were of Marsha's behind. Forestry espionage was hard, especially since it was department policy to deforest, which left very few trees for hiding places.

Indigo sank into the inviting folds of the sofa with his beer.

Before he sipped, he set the beer down on the coaster. The coaster released a pheromone undetectable by the human nose. Indigo moved toward the blinds to draw them—a cold chill brushed against his neck, the kind of primitive but still efficient "first strike" response that Indigo's ancestors had used when hunting for giant elk in the Pictish highlands. Most of the time they didn't succeed. His wife went into the bathroom to make a call and masturbate. The vibrator was hidden in a carved-out copy of *The Prince*. Not that little fellow who planet-hopped and got his ass handed to him by a snake; rather, the no-holds-barred paragon from Florence, back when Europe mattered. The pheromone drifted out of the living room and underneath the front door, to a badger waiting in the brush five hundred feet away. Upon detecting the scent, the badger rose to its hind legs to get the circulation going and scurried around the perimeter of the lake through the brushy, as yet undeveloped lot adjoining the McCarthys'. The badger was much more nimble than his species profile; a strict Department of the Interior training regimen ensured this. He also had a small but deadly explosive charge wired to his cerebral cortex, with plasticine wove through his underbelly, but his superiors hoped it wouldn't come to that. The secret logo of the Department of the Interior was the badger. Screw the docile buffalo, content to chew prairie grasses on the *official* stationery and apparel of the department. (What happened to the buffalo? Buffalo Bill happened to the buffalo, that was what.)

"C'mon, little buddy," the badger handler of the DOI said, waiting in a pickup truck on a road on the other side of the lake, listening on headphones to the badger's labored breathing. But then the breathing stopped.

"Honey, do you smell something funny?" Indigo said, calling out to his wife. She didn't answer. The packages of Kool-Aid still rested unopened next to Indigo's elbow. Trembling in the air conditioning. The daughters in the lake were listening too, in anticipation. Children had intuitions about perfect summer days, that they could disappear at the drop of a hat. It was a survival tactic.

There was a soft, but still distinct, explosion a couple of lots over. A man screamed: "I'm on fire, I'm on fire." Forgetting his cover. But what else could be expected from a Health and Human Services agent who had no experience with badgers in the field? Explosives-laden badgers at that? The HHS agent—who'd convinced himself through several seminars that his work was to protect the McCarthy children, always think of the children—saw the wiring running underneath the badger's belly and then pounced from his hiding place in the marshy scrub. He had attempted to take the badger by the tail and club it to death against a rock. But the nearest rock was barely within sight along the lake path, a good two-minute walk away, which required hauling the badger by hand. The animal wasn't human and therefore didn't require health or services. For all he knew, the badger could be a double agent for those nasty Belgians. The badger, then, sacrificing everything for the good of the department, exploded.

Screaming ensued. Indigo, startled, sat up. The Interior agent began crying and sped away, the mission lost. The ATF agent at the bottom of the lake chucked all of his stones at once and began to surface. Indigo called out to his wife again, who again didn't answer. The screaming stopped. All was still, pleasantly so. Fishers cast their rods. Sunbathers, pale as groupers, turned over on their floating rafts in syncopation.

Indigo couldn't decide what to do next. He needed backup, 911. He needed a fire marshal in his corner. He picked up the phone, but the line was dead. Marsha had his cellphone.

"Marsha?" he called. "Kids?" He went to the bathroom door and tapped on it. No answer. He rattled the handle in that special push-pull that only he knew. Marsha had locked herself in before.

The bathroom was empty. The window was open, letting in a breeze that felt much too cold, too much in the throes of autumn. Too much autumn. The lake would close and board up in autumn, leaving the residents of Vermontville to waddle between snowbanks en route from car to church or bar. Which was what they probably wanted.

They wanted to be left alone by people like Indigo, sophisticated to the point of having agents after him. He looked out the window and saw no one in the yard or the black, quiet lake. He started yelling *Marsha, Marsha,* veering back to the living room. Sitting in the chair he had recently departed was a man in a black suit. He was wiry thin, and his pianist's hands were tearing into the manila envelope. Beer frost was on his lips. He had drunk from Indigo's beer, an outrage somehow more vile than his very presence. Indigo stood there, too afraid not to speak, but lacking words to adequately express what was now in front of him.

The agent ignored Indigo and tipped the open package down into his lap. The three Kool-Aid packages slid out like origami. The agent carefully placed the manila envelope onto the coffee table and made a stack of the Kool-Aids. Indigo could see, with the motion of hands, the shine of pearlescent gloves.

"Who are you?" Indigo said.

"The members of your family are being held as enemy combatants." The agent didn't look up. "I imagine you want to know about your family. Families are important."

"Who are you?" Indigo asked again. And then, "Enemy combatants?"

"Stop asking so many questions. It's clear you hate your family. Since you didn't ask about them. So let me ask the questions, buster." The agent stood up. "What do you know about these Kool-Aid packages?" He shook the lurid colors.

"I don't know—I don't know who sent this—"

"Let me give you a hint. Bad people. People are either good or bad."

"I want a lawyer."

The agent snorted. "Listen, I told you. Your family consists of enemy combatants. They are thus exempt from the Geneva conventions as well as U.S. jurisprudence. Let us not speak of them again."

"My daughters—they're just kids." Indigo considered rushing the man, or rushing away. He couldn't decide. It seemed like an important decision. He wanted it decided for him.

"Children enjoy Kool-Aid. This is natural." This statement was simple enough that Indigo suspected a trap. "But as I advised you before—"

Indigo cocked his head. "What's that noise?" There was a noise. He wasn't paranoid, not really. It was a sound like a video game, pixels chiming and exploding, a player raking in a high score.

The agent put a hand to his ear. For the first time, panic filled his eyes. He straightened his spine. "Fuck," he said to himself. "It's too early." Then he realized that Indigo, a noncommissioned citizen, was his audience. "There's a Blackbird coming," he said. "A drone has been launched. Your cottage—" The firework sounds increased. Yes, it was the Fourth of July, a holiday designed to remember the Declaration of Independence that several wealthy planters and shippers had made against a king. But the screeching sound was different, from the sky, plowing down like the future instead of the past. The future always came from the sky.

The agent got up and ran, ignoring Indigo. The Kool-Aid packets were still on the coffee table. Indigo could hear the agent screaming on the lawn, running toward the lake. For cover. The boom was fast and deafening. Seconds passed. Indigo scooped up the packets and dived under the coffee table. He didn't quite fit there, but then again, the imitation plywood would afford little solace from the detonation of a smart bomb anyway. So Indigo was not worried. *I have a stomachache*, he thought, as the sleek chrome object hit the surface of the earth. Bomb-shelter position as he learned in Catholic school, hands over head, orange-juice light—

Not exactly the surface of the earth.

The surface of the lake turned white and horizoned. The window steamed and then shattered, letting in the hothouse air from the outside. Indigo slid out from under the coffee table, clutching the Kool-Aid to him. His whole body shook as he stumbled out of his house, toward the hot lake. The grass on the water's perimeter was scorched. No one boated or cavorted. The sky, it seemed to Indigo, as he began running toward his car, ought to have been splotched with gray, ready to rain. But the weather never tracked anyone's interior state—the sky was jewelry blue.

Something white and light landed on his shoulder, and he flinched. Something landed in his hair. He fished it off. A leaf-let. Leaflets falling everywhere: "Your locale has been targeted for subversive activity. Please vacate the premises and contact proper authorities." The too-late leaflets began to snow around him in ear-nest. He couldn't see the source; there wasn't a plane in the sky.

He opened the door of his SUV and entered the cool vinyl cave. His wife was lying on the backseat. His children were lying on the backseat behind the backseat, curled into each other. They all slept. He didn't want to disturb the moment so he started the drive into town. Opening the window, he tossed the Kool-Aid packets out, one by one. He touched the button; the window sealed shut like a guillotine.

The silence in the car had no precedents, no antecedents. The silence was a vehicle with four bodies in it. Indigo didn't want to disturb anything. Close to town, the abandoned farmhouses encroached on the newly built super–Wal-Mart. Or was it the other way around. At any rate, the farmhouses loomed with doorless thresholds, sagging floorboards, gutted ovens. He didn't want those abandoned places. He didn't want to be abandoned. At this point in the game, watching what he said appeared the best way to achieve that goal. Marsha snored, beginning to wake. He would not tell her about the agent. He would not ask about the package or let on that he knew about her affairs. Probably she had affairs. All he wanted was to drive into town, and then his family would wake, and once in town there would be a parade to attend—patriotic clowns on stilts, the VFW marching with their scarecrow uniforms, cheerlead-ers throwing sparkled batons high in the air. The batons would fall into hands. And later, when the sky was dark, fireworks would burst upon the public square. Marsha opened her eyes. She sat up and yawned, stretching her arms. It was unclear whether she had a care in the world.

"Indigo," she said, still half-asleep, peering down at their children. He clenched the wheel until his knuckles whitened. "Indigo, the kids don't have their seat belts on. But they're lying down. Should I wake them? Are they safe?"

THE CENTAUR

Once a man was shot in the leg during a battle. Fear of gangrene
compelled the field doctor to unlock the leg from the rest of
the body. The doctor sawed off the leg and stitched on a fairy tale
in its place. The man lay in his cot and stared at the tattered tarp
above him, listening to the grapeshot thudding into phalanxes over
the ridge. He couldn't tell who was winning. The sky was on winter's
edge, threatening either thunderstorms or snow squalls. The scent
of gunpowder and rotting straw made him woozy. Birds with heavy
purple feathers and scimitar beaks landed on the ash trees outside
the makeshift field hospital. They skittered off when the cannons
discharged. He missed the light, airy birds of home.

After the operation, when he had regained consciousness, his
nurse kept saying that he was lucky, lucky to be alive and full of
future possibilities. The nurse had azure eyes. When the soldier
asked about the doctor, the nurse—who'd held his hand during the
amputation, and bit her lip as if she were the one who had been
shot—told him, with a sad face, that the doctor had been killed in
his sleep by a wasp. He was allergic, who knew.

While the soldier slept that first night, he had a dream about a
knight who was trying to get back home after a long, unsuccessful
quest. The knight had forgotten what his quest was in the first place.
Now he was trying to cut his losses. He had a wife in his mountain-
side manor, and a young son whom he had not yet seen. He was gone
for two years, and his family no doubt thought him dead. The journey

ALAN DeNIRO

home required traversing a dense forest. The forest had no trails;
he had to cut through the thickets with his sword, which bore an
emblem of his family's house, the squirrel, on its pommel. After the
first day, during which he traveled only a few miles, he lost his sense
of direction. Every tree looked tall and old. With night approaching, he decided to rest and gather his bearings in the morning. As
he slept, a fog rolled in, and with the fog came a troupe of dwarves.
Only days before, the dwarves, masquerading as jugglers and clowns,
had approached the knight's manor, performed a confused show,
and killed the wife and young son. They were capitalizing on the
bog's cover to evade the authorities. However, they didn't have
much to worry about, since the jaegermeister was at that time on
pilgrimage in a faraway land to cure his gout, and the fairie queene
of the forest, nominally its protector, was preoccupied with a game
of correspondence chess with a naiad and could not be disturbed.
The dwarves, far from home, on a secret mission, and desperate for
commodities they could transmute into liquid cash, preserved the
dismembered remains of the knight's family in mountain ice and
cloudfox flowers. They nearly tripped over the sleeping knight, and
a few, at first, were eager to slit the knight's throat. Their leader, however, was edgy about the whole failed expedition. He didn't want to
press their already frayed luck. He made it clear to his compatriots,
in elaborate hand signals, that the knight was not to be disturbed
under any circumstances.

One of the dwarves, adjusting his heavy pack on his small shoulders, let the wife's right leg slip out onto the moss and leaves. He was
too afraid to stop, and within minutes the dwarves were far out of
reach of the knight. When morning broke and the sun discharged
its smoky light, the knight woke up. He had had a wonderful dream
about his wife. In the dream, he courted her on the ramparts of
a ruined castle. In the rolling fields below them, sheep ate bright
golden barley, and men in hobbyhorse costumes played jaunty songs
on flutes. His wife leaned toward him, stroked his hair, and told him
that she would never leave him, no matter how far away he might

be or perilous his station in life. She smelled like apricots. When she leaned forward to kiss him, he awoke. Sitting up and stretching, he wondered about how he would find his way home—he had forgotten for a few minutes that he was still quite lost—and perhaps whether it was worth risking a campfire to cook bacon. When he saw the foot at his feet, he thought at first that it was a dead bird or vole. When he crawled toward it and bent his head closer, he recognized at once the silver buckle set into the shoe. He pressed his fist into his mouth. Unsure of whether he was still in a dream or cursed, he touched his wife's heel. He never grew clearheaded enough to seek revenge or to supplicate the fairie queene for mercy. Instead he left his sword and pack behind and plunged into the thicket, cradling his wife's leg, never to be seen again.

A crash woke the soldier up. The shrieking clatter was loud and close enough to touch. For a few seconds he was deaf. Dirt clouds filled his vision like a locust swarm. He jolted and tried to fall out of bed and run away. But his leg, his fairy-tale leg, had fallen into a deep sleep. It tingled but wouldn't move. The fairy tale, it turned out, was cheaply constructed and poorly suited for sudden movement. The tarp blew off, and he saw soldiers approaching the makeshift hospital from the far ridge. He could tell that they were local irregulars—his country had made frequent incursions amongst them—from their ragged uniforms. Some of them carried pikes instead of muskets. They had harnessed their few stout horses to cannons, which bullied the artillery along the broken road. In an instant, he knew that the front had surged forward, and the medical corps, no doubt under orders, had retreated, leaving the invalid and hopeless behind. A man on a cot next to his called out for his aunt. The soldier looked around wildly for his nurse, whom, he realized at that instant, he had fallen in love with when she held his hand, which seemed ages ago, even though it was had only been yesterday. He loved her, even though he had seven children and a wife, his family, awaiting word from him, hundreds of miles away. He didn't care. Squinting, he saw her. The upper half of her was in one of the leafless ash trees. She was cut into two. The explosion that had woken him must have killed her and vaulted her into the tree. Her eyes were closed. Vaulted into the branches below her were the hindquarters of a horse, a sorrel. The hooves still twitched. The rest of the horse was nowhere to seen. He wiped the dust from his eyes and squinted at her. The nurse looked like a centaur, ready to leap out of the tree and gallop away from harm. Sinking his head down on the straw pillow, he closed his eyes and listened to the soldiers' song, bellowing over the ridge, coming closer. The song was a heroic ballad, a plea to defend the motherland from its enemies. Hail the size of frog eggs started raining down, drowning voices. Once in a while, the nurse in the tree said to him, there is something beautiful in our mistakes.

CUTTLEFISH

There is a young boy on the pier's edge breaking apart cuttlefish with a sharp rock. It is Genoa; the sun is just about to set. The boy will sell the broken bits of the cuttlefish's internal carapace to his only friend, the bird merchant, for a few potatoes, or other fare, a shell. The boy has no use of money, the metal of his surroundings. The bird merchant will feed the cuttlebone to the canaries and place the remnants of the cuttlefish into small vellum bags, which he will sell for a tidy sum. One bag to a brass cage.

But this is only the beginning of a chain of events, of bodies.

The bird merchant will sell the canaries to miners' foremen, arriving in Genoa by boats of all fashion, or leaving in the same boats, taking recruits and canaries to distant mines. In these mines, the canaries will most likely die: from wayward sparks; from asphyxiation; from lack of limestone, when the vellum bag runs out of cuttlebone. They most likely will die—but not without shrilling first, not without saving human lives deep in the earth's vertical veins.

Bones feeding bones. Limestone is built on dead bodies, and each fleck has a voice. It becomes easier not to hear these voices because these are, technically, inanimate objects. The bones of the dead? Too many, no room for relics. No room for the billions of Calymene or Griffithides or Montlivaltia. No room for the countless corals or the mammoth tusks arrayed like scimitars in the Siberian permafrost. There are too many minerals to extract from the mines, too many deals to be plied. Hands touching minerals means over-coming obstacles—the most tired story of them all.

The boy, however, hears. He can't stand the voices of the cuttle-fish, and so he kills them. Hundreds each day. Even when he crushes them, even when the cuttlefish are in the belly of a canary, he hears them, puckering.

One says: *I'm in a mine in "Virginia." It's dark. There is a bird screaming.*

How does a cuttlefish know Italian? Irrelevant. The cuttlefish knows Italian. The boy, halfway around the world from Virginia, pauses to cover his ears. His hands have become splattered with the cuttlefish ink, a protective measure used to confuse predators. Not protective enough. He begins working again. He catches a few by hand, but sometimes he finds the cuttlebone washed up on the mud-died shores just outside Genoa, with the mountains burning behind him in viridian. Whenever he finds them, he likes to take the shells to the pier to crush them. Water on three sides, pier sticking out like a wooden tongue. A reminder of water. The terminus.

Genoa, itself a city crushed by the batterings of other European powers, understands the boy. This month, the French flag ripples over the battlements. The next month—who knows? Genoa has lost its place, like a rock skipping across water, which halts its forward progress and sinks into the sea.

Genoa is a city of sojourners, and the boy is no exception, with his cuttlefish proxies.

The harbor chaplain would like to save him—incense peppering his hair as a prostitute from northern Liguria kneels in front of him in the sacristy—but doesn't know how.

The dock workers think he is crazy and feed him bits of bread, like a gull.

The boy doesn't think he is crazy enough, knowing what he knows, hearing what he hears, the continual semaphore. Knowing that the waves lapping against shores have barely anything in com-mon with the girth of the sea, deep in the waterbowels. Even the most terrifying waves are droll compared to what keeps in the unspeakable depths.

A cough startles him. He looks up; he sees the bird merchant at the foot of the pier walking toward him. This is rare. The merchant usually likes to dwell in his office, counting and grooming his birds. He's fat; he wipes his face with a handkerchief, out of breath.

"Someone's come for you," he says. The bird merchant thinks the boy is a curious specimen; the boy never speaks to him, never makes threatening gestures, only deposits his week's bones on the table.

The bird merchant averts fear by taking minute care in placing the cuttlebone flecks into the bag. He inherited a scale from his father—who had ventured to India to find a rare specimen of grackle and never came back. Weighing the cuttlebone relieves torpor. He dreams—each night after an encounter with the boy—of vast ocean caverns. In these dreams, his eyes become bright torches, shining light on flowers and corals with all the wrong colors: ochre yellow, cobalt red, every imaginable inverse of a rainbow.

The sky and the sun are both lies compared to the sea.

If the bird merchant suggested that the boy has sent these dreams to him, the boy would shrug. Waking and sleep ebb into each other. Neither one is a dry shore.

Standing up, brushing the bits of cuttlebone off his torn smock, the boy nods to the bird merchant. The boy leaves the slippery cuttlefish corpses, fifty of them, at the pier and heads with his pail to the bird merchant. The air is tangy.

Walking, the boy hears more voices. A cuttlefish off the Rock of Gibraltar scurries away from a dolphin in a stream of ink, *help help help*. The dolphin is wayward and will probably die soon, but not before a meal. Climbing into the heart of the city, the boy doesn't hear the women shopping for blood oranges titter at him. The bird merchant hears, and he puts his arm around the boy, protective. The boy has no odor, which is bizarre. Beggar boys ought to stink like swamps. A dog in the eaves of a butcher shop devours the last feather and bones of a chicken without a head. Cuttlefish arc along many shoals. When cuttlefish are old, they want to find a good place to die, just like anything else. Anyone else. They try to escape. Heads swirl from the heat. The cuttlefish's eight tentacles pucker, streaming away from the dolphin.

Raise the sea, the boy says. *Do you read me?* Down the maze of alleyways, the boy quickens his pace, and the bird merchant struggles to keep up. Someone hisses passages from the Bible in the Vulgate.

More cuttlefish: in Korea, a warlord crams seven cuttlefish into his mouth. They are still alive, and their suckers attach to the roof of the warlord's mouth. The vacuum created is a pleasing affect to the taste buds as the cuttlefish struggle to free themselves. The boy squirms as they squirm. Below the dolphin, the sea floor stirs. Earthquake. The boy elbows into the rotting shop of the bird merchant, the smell of white dung everywhere. All manner of macaws, parakeets, cockatoos, canaries, staring at him from their cages. A prism of wings. They don't trust him.

He sees and hears another *help help help:* in London, there is a collector of aquatic curiosities plopping a giant cuttlefish—large as two fists—into a large jar of poison, a poison that will preserve the cuttlefish against deterioration. The boy nearly freezes because of this one cuttlefish's death. Worse than death, worse than the ague of the collector who himself will die in a few days from accidental poisoning. This lone cuttlefish in a jar won't calcify, decompose, blend back into stone. It will remain separate, probably for centuries, buried on a high shelf with separate jars of rare giant mollusks and squids, right behind the secret shelf containing the skeletons of infant Siamese twins.

The boy shudders. He pours his cuttlebone on the table from habit. The bird merchant, coughing, shuffles around, delaying going into the back room. The warlord crunches into the cuttlefishes' skeletons. His gums bleed from the sharp edges but he doesn't care. The dolphin is startled by the outcropping of rock moving below him, toward him. Anemones swirl, displaced from their territories.

A cuttlefish is not a fish. It is important to understand that. A groundhog is not a hog, a jack-in-the-pulpit doesn't scream invectives in a summer field, and a boy who breaks apart cuttlefish is not a boy. Not, at least, one who has known a bed, because he doesn't sleep; or a forehead kiss from a mother right after birth, because he never rested for a time in the swell of a womb.

The boy circumvents. Who circumvents? Which vulture among men? *All are vultures*, the cuttlefish, if polled, would probably say.

After a few seconds, with the boy's eyes piercing his back, the bird merchant relents and pulls open the curtain.

The curtain ruffles open: there is a wooden table. There is a half-eaten bowl of pasta—risotto smothered in pesto—and on the opposite end of the table there is a vampire squid. The squid is harmless, really. Although it would look ravenous and spectral in ultraviolet light, now it looks frumpy, like an expensive woman's hat a century out of fashion. It can't breathe air, but that problem is rapidly being solved, as seawater rushes up from a wide hole in the corner. The tunnel eventually leads to the Mediterranean, a few miles west of Genoa.

"I have no idea how this hole got here," the bird merchant explains. "I went to the front room, and the hole was there. I found this creature on the table."

Tide. The water rises. The squid on the table raises a nearly invisible eye to the boy. Birds in the other room chirp in staccato.

I know why you're here. The cuttlefish I've killed, the boy says without speaking to the squid, *is the last. I'm going to find the voices. Killing them hasn't made them go away. I hate that I have arms with hands. Don't we hold kinship?*

The vampire squid skims an aureole on its backside, jet black and purple, upward. Consent, or indifference toward the child, its kin? Irrelevant. The boy splashes toward the hole in the corner, knee deep in the cold water. Crouching down he hears a vast churning. In all the world's oceans, millions of cuttlefish dip and sway, each of their eight tentacles aligning straight out, perpendicular to their bodies. A sign that even the boy, who has already shucked away his form, can't decipher.

This phenomenon goes unrecorded in human history.

The boy slides into the narrow passage. His knees are warm, and then he no longer has knees. The bird merchant lets out a hiss, an astonished cry. The boy undulates downward, pushing hard against the tide, pushing to eventually find the most unfathomable trench in the ocean. The squid tries to flop off the table but isn't successful, so the bird merchant steps forward and takes the creature into his hands, like an important parcel he must deliver. He gently sets the squid down in the already receding water, and with a squish, the squid scurries into the tunnel. He stands there for a few minutes until the room drains, leaving a few salty puddles.

What to discard, what to save?

The bird merchant stands in the corner, hands folded in front of him as if he prays. How does a bird merchant remain so calm at the sight of a vampire squid? How does he resume his business, ignore the veils of limestone shrouding the world? Onto you, reader, this question is entrusted. Keep it fast to your body. Wear this question around your neck like a scapular, a sacred heart over your heart. In the middle of the night, an answer might storm upon you. Like a flock of birds coursing above your house, fleeing a body of water, it won't be in any grammar you recognize.

Dot, sky, dot, sky, dot.

THE CALIBER

When Shelby was a senior in high school, her uncle Jalen was put on a second-tier Most Wanted list by the FBI. It was because of his cult. In Jalen's world view, people who made over a million American dollars transformed, literally, into a different species—the blood of the wealthy turned a copper color, and they communicated with each other by bouncing their thought patterns off sunspots. The wealthy also had vast banquets—he instructed his fifty family members, his new family, in the Allegheny Forest in Pennsylvania—at which etherized human servants were served. Jalen never failed to send a postcard to Shelby every other month, about which Shelby had mixed feelings. She liked the pictures of exotic locations but had a hard time sympathizing with the diatribes inscribed on the backs of the postcards. The pictures beat out the words, however; she kept most of them.

Before Jalen's family was accused but never charged in the killing of a lumber magnate, the FBI's interest in Shelby had been, as far as it was known, zero. That dramatically changed when Jalen's mail was first being sifted through, a few weeks after the "accident" with the lumber CEO, a few weeks before the start of senior year and the start of football and cheerleading season and everything else sickening.

On the first day of school, the principal summoned Shelby to his office. The pattern of his overcombed hair was like the sigil of an Assyrian scribe.

"You, ah, Shelby, will be having a companion," he said, folding his hands and leaning over the desk.

Shelby simpered and put her backpack in her lap. She refused to make eye contact with the principal. Shelby had fairly gray eyes. "Companion? Is this in regards to failing physical education? Or one of my 'special needs'?"

The principle chortled, to convince himself he had rapport with even the most quizzical of his students. "No, it's, ah, in regards to your uncle. It's for your *protection.*"

"In other words, they're spying on me. I'd like to have a discussion with a lawyer."

Ten minutes later, Shelby was slinging her backpack on and crossing her arms. "This is *high school*," the principal told her. "It's not as if you have rights."

Her agent waited for her in her first class, Calculus. He wore the black suit, black tie, and sunglasses familiar from many movies, and sat in the back row, stuffed into a desk so old that it still had a hole carved out for an inkwell. Shelby rolled her eyes but didn't say anything. Everyone in the class stared at her anyway.

During roll call the man was ignored, but he dutifully took notes in a yellow legal pad and copied down the homework, even though he hadn't been assigned a book.

Throughout the entire day, the agent kept a "comfortable" distance from her in both the classroom and her treks between classes. The only problem was that, for Shelby, no distance was comfortable in high school.

It wasn't that she was too ugly, or too smart, or too graceless, or even too average. And yes, there were a few in the school (her trailer park being the only nonmansion housing in the school district) as poor as her. Yet this was not the crux of her loathing. It was that she considered the entire idea of high school to be flawed; a bad, yet lucid dream.

I have a shadow, she thought to herself in the girls' restroom, burying her face in her hands. She could hear the echo of his breathing outside the door.

Without knowing why exactly yet, the usual suspects didn't catcall her, didn't even look and sneer at her.

"Huh," she said to herself. She walked home along the berm of the state highway. The mansions in the subdivisions of the gated communities—Ficklespring, Westforest Grove, Threnody Terraces—shone in the distance. Their white marble fronts could have had pennants and pinafores, for all she cared.

Inside her trailer park, she opened her mailbox, one of twenty-three other boxes stacked like purple martin houses, or hives.

The agent came running behind her, waving his hands. She stopped with her hand on the mailbox lid. Nearly out of breath, he said, "Allow me, ma'am."

Ma'am. She snorted as he opened the box and gingerly poked his hand in, as if there might be a nest of vipers in there.

He had a nice voice, actually. The hayseed twang was mostly weeded out, but it kept some of that backwoods lilt that Shelby herself possessed.

The only item in the box was one of the postcards from Uncle Jalen. The front was a picture of a Cancun beach. The agent turned it around and around, balancing the corners on his fingers.

"Give me that," she said, snatching it out of his hands. She peered at the back. It was the usual block print of her uncle. Handwriting experts, analyzing his careful anonymous script, would have no idea just how crazy Jalen was.

DEAR NIECE SHELBY, it began, as it always began. CANCUN IS BEAUTIFUL IN THIS TIME OF YEAR, IF YOU CAN STAND THE PEOPLE. WHICH I, UNFORTUNATELY, CAN'T. WHEN ARE YOU GOING TO VISIT YR UNCLE AND HIS FAMILY? CALL AND I'LL HAVE SOMEONE GET YOU. A scratchy number—not in Jalen's hand—followed. LUV, JALEN. PS BEWARE OF THE CALIBER OF PEOPLE YOU

There wasn't any more room on the postcard, so Jalen had stopped.

The postcard had Mexican stamps but a Bradford, PA, postmark.

The agent had his arms crossed and he scowled, as if Shelby had somehow been the author of this message. She shifted from one foot to another, trying to dodge guilt by association.

"I have homework to do," she said. She started walking the two hundred yards to her yellow-vinyl-sided trailer.

"Are you aware of your uncle's theories?" the agent said, keeping stride with her.

She raised one of her shoulders, a half-shrug. "Kind of. He's a loon. He keeps sending me these postcards."

"We know." *We* was said in hopes to scare her, placing the force of a vaster network behind his words. "And you happen to be the only person he keeps constant communication with, besides certain gun manufacturers and a 'Rusty' in Spokane, Washington."

Pirouetting around and walking backward, she said, "Rusty?"

"Exactly. Do you know him?"

"No," she said, exasperated. She could already smell the chili her mother was concocting.

The agent gave a stiff smile and entered a note-to-self on his legal pad, right underneath the homework assignment for World Civilizations.

The front yard of the trailer had ceramic ducks and gnomes. Every time Shelby came home, she expected their positions to change slightly, like planets orbiting the sun. They remained motionless. And anyway, she reasoned, the planets were actually moving very quickly around the sun, so the whole metaphor was shot to pieces.

The agent put a hand on her shoulder. His hands were incredibly warm. Shelby could hear, as if through a funnel or a conch shell, her mother in the kitchen shuffling around, stirring things, oblivious to her daughter's mortal peril.

"Your uncle harbors and teaches ideas that are dangerous to the state," the agent said, in a low voice. "He believes that people transform into inhuman creatures when they reach a certain level of wealth. He isn't afraid to act on these ideas. He is a terrorist."

"Well, you're a terrorist, too." The agent stepped back at this volley. "You're causing me a certain amount of terror."

She bounded up the steps and slammed the screen door in his face. Mercifully, he didn't pursue her any farther but instead sat, a few paces back, on a log pile.

Her mother didn't notice the agent, and ditto with her dad when he came home wearing his Wal-Mart uniform. She looked out the kitchen window before they sat down to dinner. The agent had disappeared, chameleoned himself, which she reasoned was probably for the best and probably what he was paid to do.

Shelby had never showed her growing collection of postcards to her parents. Jalen had never asked her to join them before. Observing her parents scarf down chili, Shelby considered them highly normal people. They weren't rich but they were devoted to the modesty of their lives and treated her father's brother as if he wasn't alive. But Shelby knew he was alive; he hovered, when she closed her eyes, on the edge of her sight.

Later that night, as she finished up her Western Civ homework, she heard rustling outside. It was the agent, holding a slender government-issue flashlight, poring over the notes he had taken. He didn't appear hungry, upset, or tired. Merely studious.

He had delicate, piano-key hands. He still wore the sunglasses, though it was dark.

With a struggle, she opened the window. Quietly, so her early-to-bed parents wouldn't hear, she said, "Do you want to look at my gun?"

"Okay."

He crawled through the window and stood in her low-ceilinged bedroom, the walls replete with quotations from Nietzsche and Groucho Marx. The agent rotated his body, noting the surroundings, as if he found himself on the other side of the looking glass.

Shelby wasn't afraid of him. He was like weather, or the memory of an old lover (she was too young to have an old lover, but not too young to dream of having one). She realized there was no way to dissipate him.

From the cigar box underneath her cot, padded with baby socks, she produced the .38 caliber pistol. The silver gleamed, even in the poor fluorescent lighting.

"May I?" the agent asked.

After a second of hesitation, she handed him the gun. He held it up to the light.

"It's a fine gun," he said, handing it back. She quickly returned the gun to her cigar box. Her cheeks were turning red from her revelation.

"Did your uncle give that to you?"

"No," she lied. "I bought it through the mail."

The agent stood up and smiled. "Still, I think your uncle would approve. It's important to be careful with a weapon like that."

"It's not like it's even a weapon. It's more of an idea. An idea I have sometimes under my bed." She leaned against the bed, stretching her toes. They stood there with the sounds of crickets, TVs from other trailers, the scurrying of raccoons. At last she said, "Is your job to protect me, scare me straight, or frisk my life for information?"

Already he was disappearing from her room, retreating out the window like a movie in reverse. "You're pretty fucking clever, you know that?"

The profanity somehow didn't seem a curse, and his question didn't invite an answer. The words stung her as she stood in front of the window, watching him disappear into the shabby woods, but they were neither angry nor kind words.

They were just words.

The fall stumbled on. An extra layer of coolness and distance fell on her. *I am a disaffected character* she wrote on the second stall in the ladies room, right below the toilet paper dispenser. Two weeks later, her words were scratched out with *Who has a big dick? Who has a big dick?*

The agent kept close to her, and the students and teachers grew used to this. In a way—though Shelby would have never known this—it afforded her a certain level of celebrity. People assumed she was dangerous. When the quarterback on the football team called her a psycho, he was found three hours later with his head in a toilet stall, shit staining his neck, with the worst swirlie ever known in that lavatory, which had seen many swirlies in its thirty-six-year history.

She continued to receive postcards from her uncle. Siberia. Hawaii. Brussels. Each message was more urgent than the previous. WHY DON'T YOU COME VISIT, I DON'T WANT TO PRESSURE YOU OR ANYTHING BUT

There never seemed to be enough room for what Jalen wanted to say.

One crisp October morning, one of the wide receivers of the football team (which was well on its way to a third consecutive win-less season) approached her. He gave a backslapping grin. His shirt was an Armani rip-off and he was named Jerry, or Jesse, or something like that.

"You interested in a party?" he said, shuffling his feet. The agent was somewhere around the corner, out of sight, but watching her.

"Yeah," she said. "Sure." There was illicit pleasure in this. To revile and be reviled for so long, then suddenly to have a small measure of status, albeit weird status.

"Cool." The football player had an all-ready sheet of notebook paper with an address and time. He gave a sardonic salute and walked away. The agent slid out of the woodwork and held the piece of paper up to the light.

"Not important," she said. They'd developed a kind of verbal shorthand, like a married couple with a diamond anniversary on the horizon.

"It's all important," the agent said, folding the scrap and handing it back to her.

"You expecting to go?"

The agent puckered his lips. "Of course. Your uncle."

"Sure," she seethed, forgetting her code. "My uncle wouldn't approve, and this is an interesting development for the case. Because I'm going to the heart of what I hate."

The bell rang; bodies poured out of musty classrooms like paint thinner from a can. Shelby and the agent were two minor obstacles in the body traffic.

"I'll log this in my report." He made the last word sound like *rapport*. "Are you ready for your physics quiz?"

She sighed but had to acknowledge that the agent made an excellent study partner. Even her parents noticed her improving grades. "Somewhat."

"There's no excuses," he said.

"No." She was tingling, in spite of herself, thinking of the invitation from what her uncle would have called *the devil's brood*. She wasn't sure whose brood they belonged to, but she was fine about putting that eternal question aside for at least a few days.

Her parents were pleased. This was a "breakthrough." They splurged to buy her a black dress, perfect with her black hair and almost gray eyes. Cinderella in reverse. By now, they suspected that she had a male "companion" but had no idea as to his nature. They assumed he was a beau. They gave approving nods for the sharp dresser at the door and were too giddy to speak. The agent had offered to drive, and the black Cutlass Sierra waited at the end of the trailer park. The interior of the car was cool. She touched the soft leather seats. The agent didn't say a word as the car wound up to the hills of Threnody Terraces, the most exclusive gated community in the entire school district.

"What would you do if I left?" she blurted out.

"Shoot myself," he said with his usual monotone. Then his face cracked into a smile. His first smile. She laughed. "I would follow you. Your uncle's not safe for you."

"But what if I thought that he was safe?" She crossed her legs, unused to fancy dresses, trying not to flash the agent. "How would you resolve the situation?"

"I'd try to persuade you otherwise, and then I'd find means to take you back." A bead of sweat formed on his temple.

Means. She turned to the window. Statues of Cupid and Athena were on every block, between hedgerows. A man walked a sullen, expensive-looking golden retriever. She wondered whether this pedestrian could see better in the dark, whether he was telepathically communicating with his wife about the boring dinner they would have in ten minutes by bouncing his thoughts off sunspots—

She rattled her head, and then they arrived. A sloping white-walled mansion with a turnaround. A valet in a red uniform—whom she recognized from a class below her, from her trailer park—offered to drive the car. He had freckles and he glowered at her. *Here,* she half wanted to say, *you can take my spot.* But she didn't.

Whoops from behind the house. Everything that she expected was there—ice sculptures (swans, elves, half-melted snowman), swimming pool, platters with shrimp as large as her two thumbs held together.

"Shelby," her host called out, bowing. Shelby gave a curt nod and appraised the scene. Most of her classmates were in various stages of undress, huddled around several kegs. The agent straightened his tie and put his hand next to his sunglasses. Perhaps receiving a secret message. "Ah, have a drink," the host said, handing her a stein. She didn't know his name. Names didn't matter. The October day was unseasonably humid. She could feel the air envelop her.

A few peered at her, and some managed tentative smiles. She would take tentative smiles any day of the week. *I have no friends.* The words, which she'd never thought in that way before, sounded like absence itself.

She'd had a drink before, but it was always a chug of Jack Daniels in the woods when her parents were away to the drag races. Drinking *socially* seemed like an altogether healthy thing for her to do. Insinuating herself in a circle of girls talking about which hair color they would prefer for the Christmas dance, and which nail polish would match x dress or y dress, she could withstand it. This, she reasoned, must be adult life. It wasn't as bad as her worst nightmares.

The agent kept close by, arms crossed. Young men kept putting beers into her hand. The agent seemed to want to say something, but she stuck her tongue out at him. Playfully. *Let me be, just this once.* Their telepathy of cues.

After the fourth beer, she saw several pockets of girls giving fellatio in the swimming pool. She had to step back quickly after a pack of boys leaped into the pool. Her feet evaded vomit. The boys began taking off their shirts. Wet from the pool, they looked like seals who happened to have legs.

The punter with red hair grabbed her arm and led her into the house. Different tunnels of nonintersecting light. The agent wasn't anywhere to be found; he wasn't in that particular tunnel of light, but maybe some other tunnel. Waves occurred on her feet. The house was much cooler, and she shivered. She slid to the floor. The punter left her there to go to the bathroom, where a few other boys were, with mirrors and razors. She was in the vestibule, a waiting room. Another girl was there, with a blond ponytail, who bent down to Shelby, stroking her cheek. Shelby relented. The blond girl had a cigarette.

"You look awful," the blond girl said. "It's a shame."

"What's shame?" Shelby said, trying to blink the world back in place.

"You're drunk." There was nurselike concern—although slightly sallow—in the girl's voice.

The chandelier had a hundred real candles.

"My name's Star. Where's your date?"

"He's, he's not my date. He's my fury and my holy avenger." The words were slurring, but there was no helping that.

"I think I read a comic book about that once." Star had her belly button pierced and possessed a smooth tan. "People have wondered about you. But I don't think you're a monster at all."

"They say that?"

Star blushed and opened her mouth to rectify and spin; she'd said too much. But then a few of the football players drifted out of the bathroom, including the one who'd taken Shelby's hand. The punter. There was spittle on his cheeks.

One of the tight ends grabbed Star by the wrist. "Swimming," he said, in a high-pitched voice. With his other hand he wiped his nose with vigor. Swimming could mean many things. Star finally relented, the boy's arm around her bare neck. *Call me,* she mouthed to Shelby, but that gesture was in a haze separate from Shelby. Tunnels of light. The punter assisted Shelby to her feet, a millisecond of courtesy.

"Where's my avenger?" she said, trying to decipher the water-colored painting of windmills across from her, trying to decide if it was composed by famous hands.

"Right here, baby," the punter said. "The Silver Surfer." He put an arm around her waist, but this arm gave her no sensation. It was like a strap for a roller coaster; not very comfortable, but necessary for what could happen. He took her up a spiral staircase with a jet black banister. She tried to lean on it but he hoisted her away.

The punter had a tall neck, she noted.

Her uncle would have hated her relinquishment with a giraffe. The agent.

She said, "Where is he?"

"I'm right here." The punter kept one arm to her body, hand starting to burrow into the folds of her dress, and the other hand fumbling for the jeans zipper.

Guffawing down the stairs, a jumble of the punter's friends gave thumbs-up signs. "Fuck the creep!" one of them shouted.

Her breathing slowed and her eyes focused long enough to view the punter's pants at his feet, his blue boxers, his erection. His giraffe smile.

"What are you doing?" she said.

He barked a laugh, and mimicked chewing gum, even though he didn't have any.

"We know about your uncle," he said. "We know he's a freak and you are too. And that *guy* who keeps tagging around. I bet you feel safe around him."

She opened her mouth but he put an open fist in front of it. "He's gone. Bailed. He didn't want to deal with you anymore. Bye."

His tongue lunged toward her mouth. Worse than a bullet shot through both cheeks. The stink of saliva, the clench of his hand along the small of her back.

"No," she shouted. A quiet shout, one that Star didn't hear as she relented and opened her legs inside the pool, the boilerplate boys wading around her; or her uncle, deep in the woods, turning around to reason with his assembled family; or the agent, looking up from a basement window at the moon anchoring the light left in twilight.

She waited for another second until the boy's tongue was in her mouth, and she bit down. Blood in her mouth. The punter kicked away, striking back, but Shelby was already recoiling toward the stairs. Trying to stumble down them without breaking limbs. The spiral vertigoed her.

Her agent had abandoned her.

She spit out blood on the marble floor. It was red, not ocher. Either her uncle was wrong with his theories or the punter didn't have a million dollars to his name.

Shelby quietly cut through the crowds too drunk or high to notice her, or pay attention to the boy wailing after her, trying to form words. But the only language in his mouth was blood.

When she was clear of the bodies and the blowjobs in the pool, she dashed around the side of the house. The alcohol began to sharpen into nausea. The punter didn't chase her; cool disdain was better in the presence of teammates. They would assuage his wounds with hoots and punches on the arm, and he would play off the blood, lie about banging the creep, and then skulk when the others ignored him again. The punter would try to force his wounds, the legion of them, to seal. But it was high school, and nobody had that kind of acumen.

As Shelby lunged into the black sedan (wondering in her daze why the car was still there if the agent had left), the punter held a beer to his cheek and heard the whirl of helicopters. Three of them, black, looming larger and swooping toward the house. The punter dropped the beer. Shelby, too, was slackjawed as she drove onto the main, dead thoroughfare of Threnody Terraces. One of the helicopters darted toward her, shining a beacon briefly on the car hood, but then moved to hold a pattern over the vast house. Blinking, she nearly drove into a statue of Cupid but managed to only clip a hedgerow. Torn white roses, sheared from her back tires, followed in her wake.

One of the helicopters began to lower onto the front lawn. She vomited onto the passenger seat, trying to keep her eyes on the road, and headed to the county highway.

"Jalen," she said.

Outside the Hilltop Diner, she left a message with Jalen on his machine, telling him to pick her up tonight; she was ready. The shabby, nearly deserted restaurant was actually at the bottom of a dip in the highway; she didn't understand the name. She didn't understand anything, especially the caliber of people she just associated with. Was this person a .22? .38? Buckshot?

Every bullet was deadly. It was only a matter of degrees.

Seasick, she leaned inside the phone booth after she made her call. She didn't intend to cry, and she didn't. Instead, she threw up near the dumpster. Heaving, empty, she went straight to the bathroom, where she splashed cold water on her face and neck and washed the puke and punter blood out of her mouth.

The trucker and waitress stared at her, and the waitress had a cup of coffee waiting for her at a stool at the end of the Formica bar. There was another full pot beginning to brew. Shelby mumbled a thank you and started to reach for the creams. The trucker put a hand on her shoulder. She flinched, biting her lip.

"It's best not to dilute it," he said. He had a pastor's face behind the beard. "In your state."

She nodded. Her new state would be arriving any hour. The sky finished its darkening. She had no compunction to call her parents, or wonder where the agent went or what the helicopters were doing over Threnody Terraces.

She would have a new family, better protectors.

Oddly, the only person she thought of was Star, how the sweat escaped her skin, how she stroked Shelby's coarse hair. How her eyes had flickered as she decided to surrender to the boy at the last instant.

Shelby had rifle arms, and armor eyes, or at least she prayed that in her hour of darkness (which could be the very next hour, or the one after that) it would be so.

The trucker left at midnight. Shelby's long siege lengthened. Waiting for reinforcement. The thought of crawling back home left her in horror. The waitress, for hours at a time, would lean forward at the counter, her head sunk down. After a spell, Shelby imitated her, because it was the only posture in which to survive the graveyard shift.

Jalen's not coming, she thought after her fourth cup of coffee, one of the few coherent thoughts of her waiting. *Even they don't want me.*

She raised her head as the thrumming of birdsong began again, and light peppered the darkness. The paperboy, a balding middle-aged man in flannel, left a bundle of the county's newspaper outside the door and scurried away to his pickup, as if abandoning a baby.

The first customer of the new day entered. The waitress yawned, getting a clean rag from under the counter. "I need help," she said to herself, the first words Shelby had heard her say.

Someone sat down next to her. Wary, Shelby turned. It was the agent. He looked haggard, and his breath, when he muttered a hello, smelled like clove cigarettes and beer stains.

"I finally found you," he finally said, motioning for a cup of coffee from the waitress. "I'm sorry."

"Sorry for what? You're the one who ditched me." Her voice cracked from exhaustion.

"Ditched you?" He shook his head and sipped the coffee. "I'm sorry, ma'am, but I got waylaid by some of those football players. They knocked me out and locked me in the basement."

She looked at his face. There was mud along his forehead, which looked like paprika. If she had been holding something, she would have dropped it. Then and there. "They told me you left me." She was nervous, not knowing whether the FBI had traced her call and message to Jalen, whether the agent tracked her down to turn her in.

"No, I would have never left. I had to have other agents free me. I told them to let you go."

"I'm glad you found me," she said, taking his hand. "Look at us. We're both messes."

"Yes. Disasters." There was something else underneath his face, straining to come out.

"What is it?" she asked. Feeling like she'd failed a test, she wasn't ready to tell him that Jalen had ignored her. It wasn't clear to her what kind of test it had been. Then she reasoned, waiting for the agent to speak, people make bad choices every day.

Instead of saying something, he got off his stool and retrieved one of the papers. With a funeral face, he said, "I know you called your uncle. But here." He tossed the paper in front of Shelby. She read the headline and the first story that followed, bending closer to the smudged print.

CULT EXTINGUISHED IN MASS SUICIDE

In an apparent murder of its leader along with the suicide of all of its six members, Jalen McPhail and six others were found dead in a remote compound of cabins in the Allegheny National Forest, about ten miles northeast of Sheffield, PA. Mr. McPhail was found apart from the others, hurriedly buried, with multiple gunshot wounds through the head. The six others...

Names followed that Shelby didn't recognize. Her hands began turning white. Six dead. Her uncle had said forty-five were in his "family."

had all died of a lethal, airborne chemical. North Central

Poison Control is examining the materials and autopsies will take place tomorrow.

It is unclear what precipitated the deaths. The Church of the Fourth Marxist Path was a group under investigation by the FBI in the recent death of lumber magnate…

Details of that case, along with the more crackpot of Jalen's theories, followed. She put her head down on the paper. Her tears blurred the newsprint.

"This," he said, "was what I wanted to protect you from."

"Don't you see?" she said, propping her head up with both hands. "I have nothing left. From both sides. Caught between the shits at that party and my uncle's loons, which I was all too happy to join. Both sides."

"Do you know how they died? What happened? Jalen was careless and left some of his financial data out in the open in his cabin."

Shelby stopped crying. The waitress brought a couple of napkins, and the truckers streaming in left space for her and the agent. "Financial data?"

"Shelby, it was all a crock of shit." The agent's forehead became red, an open display of his belief system, which he believed in greatly. "Jalen was quietly investing his donations to the 'cause.' After ten years, he had 2.1 million in assets. Why do you think he sent you postcards from such exotic locales?"

"I just thought…he collected postcards."

The agent kept his eyes steady on her. "Compassion isn't my strongest suit. But he lied to you. He lied to everyone. We're only now piecing together what he did with the others in his compound." The agent trailed off. "But that's not important to you now, is it? What is important to you?"

She sighed and leaned her palms on the countertop, afraid of not being afraid, of foolish courage. There would a funeral to attend, a few agonizing days of black-clothed relatives, but past that, there would still be Shelby. And inside the body-Shelby, there would be mind-Shelby and heart-Shelby, not exactly friends. Jalen was alienated from her, interred. He had "confused" matters, confused reality with his feelings, tricked others around him to feel the same way as he did. Was that her blood?

The agent's eyes were steady, somehow unjudging and unapocalyptic. Unagented.

"I'll have to pass that Western Civ midterm," she said at last.

He reached into his vest to give her the careful, almost tender notes he had taken on that subject.

The agent has sent Shelby a postcard of a gray government building. Other cases, other states. Star asks many questions about him. The forest winterizes. "He was a great man to me, and yet very small and far away," Shelby says. They walk along a fence running through the woods and pied fields. Star says she believes she understands. After a few months, Shelby no longer hates her high school. It is merely a low, squat building crammed with students who would rather be someplace else, and only that. Wealth can no longer kill her. Walking beside Star, Shelby holds her pistol, her .38 caliber. Goldilocks caliber, not too big, not too little, but just right. They're taking a walk to find the perfect place to bury the gun. Half a continent away, the agent surveys a decrepit hotel room with a single light bulb. It is dry, hot, and dim outside. He's holding scores of postcards in his hands, from every corner of the globe: Fresno, Montevideo, Vladivostok, Brisbane. There is no friendly greeting on them, although each one is scribbled with Shelby's name and address. With great care, the agent begins arranging the postcards in the room, according to geographic position, as if the hotel room is a map. When he has the entire world of colorful pictures arrayed around him—Jalen's world, Shelby's world, his world—he moves a chair to the center of the room and stands on it. He keeps thinking of Shelby's face when, after he gave her the Western Civ notes in the diner, she broke and clutched his shoulders—not a full embrace, but close enough—as if

ALAN DENIRO

he wasn't an agent at all, but just a person; a friend who'd covered for her absence in class because of a difficult death in the family. He keeps thinking of her trembling, small shoulders; his wide, shaking shoulders. In the hotel room, he begins unscrewing the light bulb, very slowly, until night falls over the postcards.

THE EXCAVATION

The day my wife left me, I found her in the middle of our living room, digging. Her trim archaeological tools were by her side—a trowel, a sieve, a plumb. The floor looked like a moat for a sand castle without the sand. She'd made two piles, one of rug, one of piping. The first looked like rainbow sheep clippings. The second looked like a tangled robot that had collapsed.

I shuffled forward.

"Make a pot of coffee, will you?" she asked. Her tawny hair was speckled with white. I could still see only her back, not her face. Her T-shirt shone with sweat. She came up with a hunk of cracked concrete from the hole and tossed it to the side.

"Sure, coffee," I said, sullen without knowing why.

I moved to the kitchen and poured the grounds into a filter. The grounds were only slightly less grainy than the dirt my wife sifted through.

None of the houses in our subdivision had basements. Architects never built basements any more, except maybe in Kansas, where you needed cheap insurance for a tornado. If they'd built a basement in our house, I imagined that I wouldn't have had this problem of my wife ruining things.

A quarter pot of coffee bubbled to life, and I took it off the burner, letting the Folgers drip and sizzle down. I opened our freezer door, got a tray of ice cubes, and dumped them into the coffee. I left the kitchen with the pot still dripping, sounding like a urinating hellhound. My wife submerged her head in the hole she built. She came up, panting for air, with something in her hands.

She held out a baby's smock.

"There's no reason to bring up the issue of children again," I said, crouching next to her.

Her eyes flushed. "This isn't a ruse. I *found* this."

I handed her the pot of coffee. She wrapped the baby-blue smock around the rim, to prevent her hands from burning, and took a deep drink. The ice cubes had already melted.

"I was just hoping to sort things out," she said, setting the pot down. "Plumbing the depths."

I grew impatient with her. I'd settled this dilemma years ago.

"That's the reason we retired from archaeology. How many dollars will it take to repair this?" I pointed at the floor.

She shook her head. "It's not that. I'm sick of repairing. I feel like time's speeding up for me. It's not too long after you bury something that you have to dig it up again."

"You're the one doing the digging," I reminded her.

She threw her trowel in the hole, which was getting deeper. "I have to play the game. Let me."

"Dig?"

She nodded. "Anyway, it's not like we love each other anymore."

That much was true. So I sat on the ottoman and watched TV. *The Cosby Show.* My wife, after an hour, was immersed, rising to pull up buckets of bric-a-brac only occasionally. Nothing of importance, it seemed. In another hour, I couldn't even hear the clink-clink of her shovel. Twilight came and I fell asleep, the TV blaring quietly. I couldn't help but sleep; at my age, sleep was a thief who stole my waking hours from under me. When I woke again it was completely night, and my wife sat on the other edge of the couch from me.

"I've gone deep," she said, and then she held out something. In the dim moonlight I thought it was maybe a teddy bear or rag doll. I reached out to touch it and felt cold, clammy flesh.

"A baby," I said.

"A fetus." I could barely see my wife in the darkness. "Just sprouting there, on the edge of the tunnel. I wiped the dirt off." Her arms sagged and retreated to her lap. "It's the baby we never had. I'm a lodestone for pain."

"I know," I said. "That's why I was drawn to you."

She stroked the baby's forehead. "Do you remember college, when you first proposed to me? Fifty years ago. The college by the sea, the California coast. I had no idea what would happen—we were dating only a couple of months. You took me to the sea cliffs and promised me everything."

"Everything?"

She shrugged in the darkness. "Well, a lot. A comfortable life. A life where I could have independence, yet completeness. Where we could both do our archaeology."

"Sure. I was three for three, wasn't I?"

She ignored me. "I didn't know how much of me is dying, until now. A spoonful a day."

I sighed. My stomach felt upset. "Is the adventure over?"

"No." She stood up. "And screw you. I'm an archaeologist, just like you. I'm supposed to dig up bones, scientifically. But I'm finding these bones are my own." She pointed to her gut with a free finger. "I've wanted to make this," she said. She clutched the baby—was it our baby?—tighter and moved to the hole, crawling inside.

"Your digging form is horrible," I called out after her. "Very messy."

We were both trained to dig. I thought of the bog men, our apprenticeship excavation forty-five years ago. Ritual murders. The remains were in Denmark, preserved in the peat bogs for centuries. Each victim suffered, but all my wife and I had to discover was dead tissue, dried blood, ornamental stone axes. Nothing breathed.

We participated in our own rituals, from an untold distance across time. We tried making love in our camp once, mosquitoes swarming around our tent. I couldn't come, though she wanted me to. The whole experience was a disaster. Bones in careful boxes were stacked at the edge of our sleeping bags.

I preferred the calmness of the graves themselves, where you didn't have to touch anyone really alive.

What did my wife see in me, then?

Wanting to think of these things no longer, I fell back to sleep.

Morning came quickly. My wife was nowhere to be seen or heard. I had no hunger, though I was thirsty. On a self-imposed dare, I peeked in the pit.

I couldn't see the bottom, but there was dim light, and a rope ladder that led down. I took a deep breath and decided to go. I lowered myself onto the ladder. As I moved down, the cold and brightness increased. After ten minutes or so (my body remembering again the physical exertion of a dig, long after I'd retired) I reached the end of the ladder. I stepped onto a platform, and I realized it was a set of stairs, with an oak banister.

I walked down the stairs. I was in my own house, exactly as above, except there was no hole in the center of the living room. Beyond the windows was only packed dirt. The light came from a wooden structure near the opposite wall. I squinted and realized it was a crib.

Moving toward it, looking down, I saw the baby curled up there, bright as flash fire. The baby was still dead, but unharmed.

"Jan?" I called out. No answer. I didn't expect one. Maybe she was already above me, closing the front door behind her with all our money, ready to start over again, even at her—our—age. I moved to the top of the stairs. The hole I had crawled from was gone. Just the ceiling of our house, though it was not our house. It had become my house, deep underground, me and the dead, bright baby. I tried the front door, but it was locked; it didn't even rattle.

I didn't weep. Justice wasn't always just.

In the kitchen, everything was in order—plenty of food, maybe for months. I checked the TV. It still worked but only picked up one station. It showed one moving image, more or less repeating. A woman and a small child—maybe five or six years old, with dazzling blond hair—playing in a field of red poppies. They laughed, tumbling. They played. No impediment or shame separated them. There was shame in me, somewhere, but shame needed two: a box to put the bones, a pit to dig to keep the body. Even then, silence usually won in the end. The bog men couldn't express shame to me or my wife when we excavated them, no matter how much they suffered, or wanted to share that suffering.

I kept the TV on, though I recognized neither the mother nor child. I checked on the baby. It was unmoved.

I moved to the kitchen to make coffee, for one.

Some day they'll find us.

A KEEPER

Tonight the woman who always calls, calls. This time she asks me how to divide a beggar and an arctangent. What could I have possibly said to her? I think she is a keeper. "Stop trying to mix the humanities and the sciences. And go to bed." I nod to the phone and the phone clicks off. Outside, a noise sounds like thunder, though it could be a stray dog tipping over a garbage can for shelter. I turn off my flickering bedside light (brownouts, again, all over central Brazil) and tell the clock, "Wake me at six a.m.," attempting to sleep. I sleep.

An hour later she calls back. "But I can't sleep. I can't stand the fact that all across the Americas windows are opening and closing, opening, and I'm not *looking* out of them, all of them, all at once." I have the vague feeling I ought to know her well; I can't remember a thing about her.

I imagine her panting and wearing a white tie and a black suit and a round opal bracelet that monitors her position at all times when she takes lunches away from the sanatorium.

Hey, that's cruel, I think.

I hang up again and move to close the window. I open the storm window again, I look out, and the sky just hangs there, like it's balanced on the top of the plum tree. Or rather, the re-creation of a plum tree, in quartz. The sagging plums used to be a strong violet, but vandals scraped the color alloys off and sold them a while ago. Long before I reached this tenement as a passing stranger.

I'm rooted now.

⚘

ALAN DENIRO

Brasilia is a nice place to visit, but I wouldn't want to live there.
But wait, I do live there. I mean, here. My job feeds the bills. I am a
painter in the King Juan Juan Center for the Arts. My body of work,
like every other painter's at the center, consists entirely of portraits
of King Juan Juan, which tend to adorn every third block of Brasilia,
half the billboards, and most private and shared huts.

Because of the methane corrosion, I can say it is steady work.

That next morning, I don't concern myself about the call. When
I was afflicted, I did much of the same. The keepers are another pet
project of our king. It's a virus that makes slavish pets out of people,
makes people want to babble sex and make sex babble. After time, it
passes; side effects include utter amnesia. It's what passes for mating
in Brazil since Juan Juan's reign began. To most, all other forms of
sex appear boring. Everyone needs a keeper; I've had about four or
five. Including, allegedly, the one who calls me and asks questions
that can't be answered.

Courtship is not easy cake to eat.

As I get ready, letting the kitchen sink brush my teeth, I see Clown
Man at the tenement across the street, framed in the window. I don't
know his real name, of course. Here, as on many occasions, he's
painting his face in front of the window, peering into an invisible
mirror. He could stare right at me, but he never does. His eyes are
glass, corneas surrounded by red and green chalky paint. Then he
nods to himself and leaves the window, his ritual complete, off to
entertain or hustle or kill someone, or all three. In Brasilia, it would
not be out of the question.

The Center for the Arts used to be a mosque. My studio is usually
in the northeast minaret (They liked keeping the painters in them.
Virtual imprisonment in the towers?), but architects repaint every
room every six weeks by royal decree, and today's my painting day. I
work temporarily in the main wing.

All my airbrushes have been primed by an apprentice, and the
canvases are warm, as well. Light gleams from an open square in

94

the roof, and I can barely hear the triple-decker buses and the carriages streaming through the thoroughfare, past the locked gates of Brasilia's Yale campus.

The piece I have been working on is a potential masterpiece. It depicts King Juan Juan, darkly tanned, shirtless, wearing only swimsuit and socks, peering off-canvas on a rocky outcrop. Beside the rocky outcrop, two courtesans sex themselves, the man's head buried between the woman's legs. The woman, actually, gazes longingly at Juan Juan on the outcrop. The gaze will take a long time to perfect, but I'm already pleased by preliminary results.

I fire up the airbrushes and am about to paint when Paula walks into the studio. She's my boss, and used to be my wife, but a wife from a long, long time ago. How much I am attracted to her I can't say. She silently moves toward the tightly stretched canvas and nods in satisfaction.

"The king would be pleased," she finally says. Her hair is soft and fuzzy, like a platypus. "Are you ready?"

"I guess so."

I spray out the lasered mist of paint, and she kneels down next to me, slips my pants to my ankles, and begins to service me. After about a minute, painting, I ask her to stop.

She looks up. "Why?"

"It's beginning to hurt."

"I'll be gentler."

"No, I mean, it hurts from the inside. *Burning.*"

Twenty minutes later I'm in a doctor's office, on afternoon leave. My name chimes. I go in and the doctor looks calm, like he could easily be a cricket instructor.

"What seems to be the problem?"

I describe to him the exact situation.

"Hm. Drop your pants."

I do, although for some reason I am entirely more fearful than when Paula did it.

"Hm." he repeats. "How did you find this out?"

95

"My boss serviced me."

He raises an eyebrow. "Your boss?"

"Well, I was painting a sexing, and a lot of curators have been heavily influenced by Carlonian lately, who says that the erotic must be heightened in the painter as much as the painting. But this is probably boring you."

Instead he says, "I'm afraid that you have a curse."

"A curse?"

"Yes, a curse in your member."

I have no idea what he means but am frightened anyway. "How? What's going to happen to me?"

"Left untreated, you will probably feel mild irritation, then dementia, until you die. It's a virus—"

"I thought you said this was a curse. And besides, there are no such things as curses."

He gives that patient, patient I'm-a-doctor smile. "Well, our new manuals have a new ergonomics toward disease disclosure for doctors—I mean, shamen. We are urged to prescribe the most superstitious names and causes possible. It's supposed to quell tension."

I'm not quelled. "What do I have to do then?"

He looks at me, as if not sure how to phrase a delicate question. "Have you been sexed with your employer before?"

"No, I mean, yes. But not for a long time." At least I thought.

"Anyone else? Have you been with a keeper?"

I look at my veined bare feet. I am prone. "Maybe. Wait," and I remember the woman who has been calling me lately, "yes, it's very possible. So what do I do?"

He gives another smile, this time with a tinge of pity. "First of all, pull up your pants and put on your socks. Second, you need to find her. Only she can remove the curse, give the password to heal you."

"In other words, I have to find out why she gave me the virus, and get a blood sample from her so that you can remove the virus from my cell system without killing me."

He puts his stethoscope in a drawer. "If you want to put it that way," he mutters.

I walk out to pay.

"Be careful; she may be a witch," I hear the doctor calling out after me.

I call in to take the rest of the afternoon off, and I sit in a cafeteria on the west end (but Brasilia has no center, really), trying to envision a plan of action. But nothing envisions itself, chewing slowly on a piece of American apple pie.

Anyway, she calls before I can take another bite. "Where are you, she asks?" she says. Someone laughs behind her.

"I'm in the, um, Dresden. Where are you? I need to talk to you."

A pause. "You are talking to me."

"I mean, face to face."

"The cheery cherry trees. It's the cool fire of the month."

"Listen—"

"No, *you* listen. Did you open the windows of the Americas like I asked you to?"

This time, I'm the one who pauses. "No, but—"

She tones off. A shapely man comes in selling flowers, and I buy nine dozen peonies.

"OK, OK," Paula says. "It's fine to take a couple of days off if it's a medical condition." Evening time, and I find my way to Paula's office in the Center for the Arts. Her office is in the third basement and smaller than those of most of her subordinates. King Juan Juan, of course, hovers behind her in paint. I think Jesse did that one. The king is giving his constituents a thumbs-up.

"Though, of course," I say, wondering if Paula is snickering inside her head, "I have no idea where to begin."

"Begin what?"

"I have to find a keeper."

She begins to laugh through her nose and stretches back on her recliner. "Now I see what the problem is. How long has she been like this?" Paula was a keeper too, before she took up her lover and married. From what she told me (and she was never shy about these matters), she'd been more passive than the ones I'd seen on television.

"I don't know. I guess I stayed with her once, maybe two weeks ago? It's hard to say. But she diseased me."

She hmms. "Why don't you try the dog market?"

"I was afraid you'd say that."

The next morning, smoggy, I am in the dog market. I really hate the dog market, and hate dogs, in fact. Luckily, the name is deceiving—there are more than just dogs here. It's situated halfway between old Brasilia and what I like to call Brasilia Brasilia, or Brasilia squared, the Guyanese/English section that I call home and work. The dog market is in a wide alleyway since it is, technically, illegal to traffic in smart animals. But no one enforces. The policia, I'm sure, are always looking for good dogs, too.

So I put my credit card (light amber, which isn't too bad, I guess) lightly against my belt, on the right side. The sigil of a serious buyer. I meander through the cages, many of them brown with rust, and sift through the animals and their sellers with about a dozen other buyers. A dachshund catches my eye because it has three. The seller peers at me, his entire forearm winking in aquamarine, less excited than his dog. I move on.

"Psst. Hey." A woman about half my height motions toward me. She is in a sari but her skin is whiter than mine. "Yeah, you." Talking isn't really allowed, by house rules, but furtive whispering usually doesn't bring imprisonment. I look over to her, nod, hoping that will do the trick.

She motions me with a crooked finger to peek underneath a curtain covering a shape on the table. She pulls it up. Shapes, rather. Goldfish bowls.

With goldfish inside.

I almost, almost, laugh, which would have gotten me thrown

out at least. I stifle the chuckle and look at the seller with a grimace meant to show bewilderment. She gives an I-know-what-you're-thinking look and offers me a chip, which I reluctantly swallow. She pulls a wand from underneath her sari and touches the rim of one of the bowls. The goldfish inside squiggles up to the top, sinks down, and spins its tail a little.

Yeah, I'm talking to you. The augmentation, it seems, has finally trickled down to carnival fish. *So are you going to buy me or what?* At first, the goldfish all look exactly the same (well, gold), but upon second glance this one looks a little healthier, the scales a little brighter. The seller's prize fish, then.

Well, are you? Impatient fish.

I'll need you to find a keeper. In days.

The fish makes a blooping noise, which—I guess—is a laugh. *You expect a problem? I'm the best. Let me show you. Come on. Keepers are goddamn trancy-dancy shifty whatevers anyways.*

I meander back in the Dresden, with a coffee and cherry pie and a goldfish bowl on the lacquered table. I come here often enough, and tip well enough, that the cashier doesn't ask about the pet, which is probably a health violation. I am a health violator.

Incredulous, here, with a goldfish worth two week's pay.

"All right," I whisper out loud. Even though I don't have to speak, it is bizarrely reassuring to speak. "What do you need from me at this point? How are you going to find her?"

No problem at all. You infected from her? I nod. I'm not sure if it can pick up human body language but it does. *Ouch. She must be needing you real bad, then.*

"Then why did she ignore me the last time I called?" I hiss, a little louder than I wanted. A family of three in a booth across the restaurant look up at me from their pancakes, in unison.

She's playing a game. It's all a game. That's why she infected you. To make sure you come back. But she wants you to work at it too. There is no pleasure without pain.

"How long does someone stay a keeper?"

Who can say? It's hard to tell. The goldfish—whose name I don't even ask for, it would be ridiculous—swims in a tiny circle in the bowl. *Usually after they've mated, at which time they go normal.* I think of Paula, cold in my flat's bed and babbling. *But not always. Never exactly works out the way people want. I don't know. Are you ready then? I'll find her, don't worry.*

"I guess," I mutter. "What do you need from me?"

First, I need a sample of her virus, the little bit of titanium that's itching your member. So, if you will...

"What?"

You know... The goldfish possesses subtleties unknown in the fish world.

I sigh, a little embarrassed despite myself; I get a little cup from the water dispenser and enter the bathroom. The family, probably enjoying a day off from work rationing, stare at me. I don't blame them.

The servicing hurts—hurts worse than the first time, a burning like a little dwarf star—but I finish it in the cup and walk out to my table. The family, blessedly, has left.

All right now. Good. Now dump it in.

I hesitate.

Go on! You have to do it if you're going to ever get better.

I sigh and tip the cup into the bowl. The water gets milky and the goldfish swims around faster, even frenzied. After a half minute, when the water settles, he sploshes up, nearly out of the bowl. Can a goldfish be in ecstasy?

Great. I got the scent. So to speak. I don't know whether to be relieved or frightened.

"So do I carry you around, while you...trace her?"

No, no, no. It's going to be a lot easier for you. For me, it'll be a bitch, but hey, it's my job. It pauses. *I want you to throw me into the toilet.*

"What?"

That's the only way. The fastest. I swear, I'll find her. All you need to do is sit pretty and wait. Then I'll give the signal.

"Look, I mean, this is too weird—"

Do you want to help yourself or not? The fish sounds angry, even a little disappointed, in me. *I'll be jacking into the network at the same time, which runs parallel with the plumbing lines. Believe it or not. They're like roads. I'm not going to force you, but...* It trails off.

I breathe deep, pick up the goldfish bowl, and head toward the bathroom. The cashier is doing her best to ignore me, and I know I can't enter the Dresden again for another year or two.

The toilet is dingy, small, and brown on the inside.

All rightey. Dump me in.

I slowly pour, and the goldfish whirls out, almost spinning.

Now flush. And like I said, I'll give you the signal. Just wait.

Dutifully, I flush. I almost hear the goldfish laughing as it spirals down the pipes and disappears, but then I realize it's the cashier.

So what do I do, when I find my life confused beyond description? I paint. Off the street, just in front of the gated Yale commons, I peel off a newspaper from the back of a vendor boy. I lay out the snake-skin foil in my studio and dash off four quick Juan Juan portraits, the head only, all nearly exactly alike. I am my own forgery. The airbrushes have good pressure, and the paint flows well from the tubes. A very productive morning. I look down at the newspaper, which I didn't buy to read, just to cover the ground. *Queen Abierta Mysteriously Sick—or Detained? Analysts Are Confused.* A flickering image of her, her lashes long as butterflies. *Three Guerillas Hanged in São Paulo. Government Accuses Bolivia of Sanctioning Terrorism.* I weld the paint onto the canvas all morning. Paula drifts in and out occasionally, grunting, but agreeing to leave my member alone, at least for a while. Twice, though, I have to escape to the toilet room, doubled over in pain. *A Dozen Keepers Killed in Illegal Black Mass,* another column says. *Court Geneticists Still Hope to Retrieve Keeper Fluid for Reuse.*

I don't go home that night; I order out a gyro, eat at my canvas, curl asleep there, counting goldfish leaping over a fence instead of sheep.

The night passes slowly, like an argument. I wonder whether Clown Man has returned home. Most likely. I foggily realize that, most likely, I will die by the end of the week.

I wake up at about six. Peering at the painting, I notice something that wasn't there when I finished the painting and drifted off.

King Juan Juan's face is rubbed out, scumbled. There are enough lines of flesh to let the viewer know that it was a *deliberate* act. I must have arisen in the middle of my sleep and done this, somnambulant terrorism against the state. If nothing else, this would finish me quick. King Juan Juan is a punisher. He funds the keepers.

Hey.

I start, turn around; I'm suddenly heaving for air, as if my lungs are wounded by breath. "What?" I say.

No, look, it's me. I found her. I found your keeper.

I pause, on all fours. "Where are you?"

You'll never believe me.

"Where? Where?" I don't need a goldfish playing games with me.

The palace of the king! Can you believe it?

"No. I can't. There's no way I'll get in."

Now, keep your pants on. Let's say you get three wishes from me, overall. Let's pretend. The first was, of course, finding the queen—

"What did you say?"

Let's say you get three wishes from me—

"You said the queen. Oh no." I get up and begin pacing the studio.

Look, stop your whining. It's covered. Covered. Just follow my directions and I'll get you to her.

"You?" It stops talking—thinking—for about thirty seconds, and I think, perhaps he has gone away.

Are you done complaining? it says at last. *Are you?*

"Fine," I sigh.

Good. I've jacked into the royal schedule. There's a way to intercept her.

"Inside the palace?"

No, not really. She goes to the Oleanders. Pack up. Bring a knife.

Three kilometers squared, gardens that never close, public bowling greens, hedge mazes, ice sculptures, kitty corners. The pleasure-servicing park the king has given to Brasilia on the west end of town, where I can see the edges of the Rainforest Preserve, and the dull orange of cooking fires beyond that. I have taken the rail to the gate of the Oleanders. No vehicles inside, so I begin walking. Very early in the morning, so there are few strollers, revelers. A jogger or two and a couple stragglers from the night before, splayed in each other's arms, trying to hide from passersby but not really hidden.

So I stroll.

Aside from the trash here and there, the park sparkles clean, like teeth. The sidewalks point in many directions, so I take the western one. Walk. The trees, upon further inspection, are glazed. *Just keep walking west,* a tiny voice says inside of me. *That's it.*

The moon is so large I feel it can bend down and lick my face. Of course, at this point, I might be becoming delirious from the illness. I see someone ahead of me on the serpentine path, ambling slowly. In a tattered but somehow jewelled cloak. The words of the doctor flash into me. That this is, perhaps, a sensible fairy tale. I rush up to her and spin her around. She doesn't resist or run. Merely puzzled. A grotto of United States elms circle to the left and suddenly remind me of home. A pond within the ring of trees.

Her lips flush. Yes, the same as the pictures I have always, always seen of her. Her image is second to that of the king, and in fact on many state occasions when she can not attend, Juan Juan carries an animated panel of her, attendant by his side, sometimes worn around his neck.

I suppose he loves her. Her roan eyes look at me.

"Hi, it's you," she says. As if I'm meeting her for a wine and I'm five minutes late.

"Yes, and I don't remember—"

"You don't really understand, do you? I mean, the world is too wordy. People take up too many words to talk about the most trivial things."

"What should I say then?"

She shuffles her feet and kisses me.

"Yes, but," I say, trying to calm myself. "That has gotten me into trouble."

The queen laughs. She must be twenty years older than me and must be trained not to show it. "That's the trouble with trouble. Once you feel you've got it licked, it goes off and jigs off with another. And you miss it." It occurs to me that Juan Juan must have given her the keeper codes, the titanium injections, as a game, to see what might occur, how she would react, whom she could snare.

"Look, I've something important to ask you," I say, trying to soothe, soothe myself most of all. "I can't remember you from before. I can't. What happened?"

"What happened," she says, trailing off. "I met your painting, remember? You painted dearie one. I'm sure you had his look. I met you here." She points to the pool and the grotto. "There." She takes my hands and I'm trembling. "Then I cast you so you fell asleep and don't remember a thing. And now you've found me again."

"I'm sick," I say in a low voice. "Something inside of you has made me sick."

"You *are* sick," she says.

I consider biting her and drawing the blood I need. How long do keepers usually last? Most times they resume normal life within weeks. Some, years, and some, never.

"Look," I say, feeling desperate, "*I'm* the cross between a beggar and an arctangent. I am a parallel line about to intersect with a point which has no height, width, or depth."

And the thing is, I believe it. I do. I never listened to keepers until now. Maybe the scrambling words and the sexing isn't such a curse to listen to.

She looks at me, understanding somehow, with a glint in her face, even though I do not completely understand.

"I will see you again," she says.

My queen offers her arm.

The guards, I'm sure, are looking for me, combing out from the Center for the Arts. Not as much for the escapades with the queen, as for the defacing of the painting. I have left the queen to think and bandage her arm in the grotto, where she will return, I suppose, and eventually dekeep herself. What she will say to the king at that point? Who can say?

At this point, though, I'm running, hard, toward the West Gates.

Hey, wow. I wonder if the goldfish's body is dead, if it is just a presence now. *You did well.*

"Well, I have to find a doctor and hope I don't die." I don't know if it catches the double meaning, but it kind of laughs to itself and thinks to me, *No worries. One is meeting you at the gate.*

"Come again?" A unicyclist careens down the opposite way and nearly kills me, which, I suppose, wouldn't have been ironic, only moronic.

I'm saying, a doctor is there to take your blood sample, and there'll be some other people, too. To protect you, give you a new job.

I nearly stop, just then and there, from both exhaustion and disbelief. "Why? How is a goldfish arranging all of this? I don't know—"

At this point, it may be used to, or sick of commenting on, my complaining. *All right, think. You go to the dog market to find an animal to find a keeper. I have been bred and engineered specifically for that purpose. Do you think we grow on trees like oranges?* I can see the gate, vaguely, ahead of me, meandering closer. *There are those who would like to make all the keepers return to normal, every one of them. People—who you don't need to know—who want to exile the king.*

These are the people at the gate. Ah. Who are seeing you now. Do you see them now?

"I see them," I say, and nearly lean and collapse against the hull of an armored truck, just past the open gate. A hand touches my shoulder, lightly. A man about half my height with darting eyes, leaning from the insides of the truck. "Get in," he says, in a voice slightly deeper than that of the goldfish. I am ushered into the dark hull. It takes a few seconds for my eyes to adjust to the light; there are several others besides me. I am not too much surprised to find the woman in the sari, from the dog market. On her lap is a wide, ceramic bowl with about a dozen goldfish, flailing in the shallow water, the shallow space of water.

"All right," the short man says, leaning over me, as the truck chortles into life and begins to move west. "We'll get you fixed right up." I only realize at that moment that I have been broken all along. I mean, from more than just a keeper virus. More broadly broken.

Juggling took a long time to learn, even with the skill injections, but I'm getting better at it. I can keep four objects in the air now—and they don't have to be plain round balls, either. Sometimes one or two knives, although not four. I don't want too much with knifes anymore. One time a child gave me three gravity balls, and they veered and veered when I threw them up. But I caught them and cycled them into the air. The boy was maybe awed, in a six-year-old kind of way.

The makeup and costume make my skin itch, but that just means I have to take cold baths in the morning and evening. And I get to stay in the city—the goldfish people make sure of that. Granted, I work on the opposite end of town from the King Juan Juan Center for the Arts, but maybe it's better that way. The queen, despite her promise, has never come to check up on me, though she probably would have a hard time finding me.

"Pass the cup, goodfolk, pass the cup." I have a minor circle around me. I have them enthralled. But probably not for long. They will go home, forget about me, the juggler. They will suffer amnesia and live their lives, never knowing about my secret history or my identity. Which, in the end, isn't so much of an affliction.

A man passes by me, with a briefcase, dressed in nearly identical costume to mine (though with a clown's nose, and a strange pointed hat that I wouldn't care to wear). As I juggle, feeling my heart taut with all the secrets kept inside there, the Clown Man pauses for a moment and nods at me.

I have no idea whether he recognizes me.

Then he sets up shop on the other side of the block. From his briefcase, he pulls out a few tiny objects—which I can't make out, from this distance—and swallows them. Ten seconds later he tips his head back and breathes fire, wide into the air in a fan. The Clown Man stops and bows, and already the crowd starts throwing hard-earned coins at him.

FUMING WOMAN

Under the trapeze, there is always a secret trap door that allows the circus's employees to escape a mob. It is written on the door in white stenciling: Enter in case of a mob. And people do. The gnomes, customarily, dig a tunnel from the door to a safe place "some distance away" before a circus takes root on a city block, usually on an abandoned car lot.

The mob usually occurs when a drunk tries to steal a fermented beverage from one already incapacitated from the beverage. Children never attend circuses anymore because of this, and I tell you that is a shame.

It is a nice night for a circus. The mosquitoes have burrowed holes in the big-top canvas. An elephant is reciting Tennyson, punctuated by Dumbo's Mom–like cries of empathy. This moves the crowd. This is probably the highlight—the old male elephant pretending he's female and becoming a compassion vacuum. No one's dead yet. The ants have begun their motorcycle escapades. The ringmaster holds up an iconoscope, which transmits a projection of the ants on their ant-sized motorcycles. They are doing wheelies. Most colorful for the audience are the Taco Bell logos pigmented on the ants' safety jackets.

And the trapeze woman—and here she is, the story, really—is limbering, for she's on next. Her family emigrated from an imaginary country when she was still in the womb. A snap of her ankle could snap a neck. And has. There is that power; do not think this is amusing or that I'm being a fuddy-duddy.

The ants finish, putter off; the ringmaster's smile is coked out and incredibly genuine—he misses the children—and the fight in the crowd, over alcohol, begins. The whiskey bottles drop, and gnomes deep underground quiver because they know what's next.

The woman climbs the ladder. She's blocked out from her mind the two men—bankers both, still in their funerary suits—stepping around the downed man with a whiskey bottle still in his hands. Suddenly he leaps up and surprises the bankers. Fisticuffs ensue. How are we to know what he's thinking? The woman doesn't generally bathe forty-eight hours before a circus, and this is the circus's second day. There is a musk, then. The odor drifts over the crowd, which is trying for the moment to pay attention to the crux of the woman's face and not the drying-machine effect of the fight, making everything hotter.

The ringmaster doesn't give her name. She jumps, catches the bars as one banker breaks a bottle and places it onto the other's face. The other steps on the downed man's stomach. Vomit arises. The woman whips her neck forward and leaps again. She's gained momentum. She catches the higher bar with her teeth. The crowd is despondent—they *want* to like her, but there is so much else competing for their entertainment dollar. She's losing internal performance evaluations—faces she can't see mostly—because she hasn't burst into flames. Or because she isn't naked, or doesn't wear a Taco Bell jumpsuit, like the plucky li'l ants.

Fighting spreads. A husband starts hitting his wife with cotton candy. The two bankers who started the fight are both dead, but their spirits kick and punch at anything in their way, which is a lot.

The trapeze woman twirls to hold herself by the knees and catches the next bar with her belly button.

No one notices except for the ringmaster, who is bawling, because he's never seen her more paradoxical and beautiful, swinging from the high big top by her belly button. If there wasn't about to be a riot, and seventy to-be-dead, the papers would have exclaimed "Woman Holds on to Trapeze with Belly Button!" But her timing, when right, is wrong.

The giant poles begin to sway with the weight of the assemblage pushing against it—the very foundation of the idea of a circus. There has to be a big top, an enclosure, or else the circus would bleed into the weekday, and we wouldn't want those "issues" on our streets.

The woman leaps again and holds on to the second-highest bar with her kidney. The ringmaster isn't watching at this point—he is ushering the performers into the special trapdoor. He is afraid to warn her, afraid that if he distracts her, he will forever combust in hell, like the fuckhead who knocked on Coleridge's door when he was dreaming up "Kubla Khan."

Body kindled in sweat, she strains for the highest bar, plummeting up for dear life. She holds on to it with her slightly ironic, melancholic disposition. Her hold, with this character trait, is tenuous at best. With her free hands, she begins pointing at those destroying the big top, slaying each other and the animals, including the stunt-ants. The mob got the ants. Her fingers are like saucers of hot pitch spilling from space, and rather than burning up in the multilayered atmosphere (a device created by God much like a big circus top made out of oxygen and nitrogen, designed to protect us from the cosmos and perhaps protect the cosmos from us), her attacks land. The rioting stops as each rioter feels the stigmata of the trapeze woman's rebuke on their cheeks. How embarrassing! Many of those still alive hold hands. The woman stops her performance, arcing to a stationary position, much like a child on a swing set who loses the push from her parent(s), parent(s) who wander off to do something more important, like pet a needy dog or put on a tie. The woman hangs there by only her irony and melancholy, thinking of her circus mates inside the escape tunnel, in flight away from her. She half expects someone to reach up with a pole with a vinegar-soaked sponge.

"Shame on us!" the assemblage cries out as one, except for a young man in the cheap seats who discovers for the first time that he can give himself a blowjob. But that's OK; the woman doesn't mind.

Unfortunately, enough of her irony evaporates that its once firm grip on the trapeze bar is loosened! The woman falls, out of control, like a car chase, straight down.

Some jackanapes in the rioting have cut the safety net for later use as a hammock. All those assembled murderers cry, "No, no, we're sorry!" But it's a little too late for mewling, isn't it.

The woman, rather than doing something foolish like hitting the ground, or even splatting her head against the mob trapdoor (*that* would have been ironic!), turns into a kind of vapor. By *a kind*, I mean she aligns her own atoms to pass through the other atoms blocking her way. She keeps falling—not all the way to China, but rather popping out in the ocean about fifty kilometers off the coast of Tasmania.

In the city she leaves: gnomes weep. Ringmasters pull out their dentures. Angry mobs the world over—even at football matches—give ten seconds of silence in her memory.

No, she thinks, I'm right here. I've been rescued by a seafood restaurant. I'm still a vapor. These people are lambs. This is apparently an island full of giant lobsters. Narwhal-sized. People dine on them on the beaches. Chainsaws wielded by strong waiters open the shells. They use me as a spritz on the tails of the lobsters. When I enter the atmosphere, I evaporate and rain again. I'm an ecosystem. There is no such thing as a circus here. All along the beaches, the family dogs breathe my spritz. My vapor. I'm effervescent. People don't expect this. Fumed by me, the dogs start jumping higher than people! Someone from the seafood restaurant calls the papers. The dogs jump over and over, higher each time. What the fuck is happening to our dogs, the tourists say, snapping pictures. They don't realize I'm inside of them, fueling. From this distance, the giant lobsters about to be eaten look sad that they will die, and I will not.

Soon the dogs will have to don masks, because the air gets thin up in the stratosphere. My cosmonauts. Memories become thinner. Voices, too. No one can throw a Frisbee that high. There are only the jumpers. The island of lobsters looks so tiny from the vantage point of a dog. In the flashing second when there is no up and no down, only the absence of motion. That moment of suspension is a tonic to the dog and I. There are no nets, no trapdoors, no cables, no ants, no canvas, no ticketholders. Nothing to hold on to. We begin, again, a fall.

THE FRIENDLY GIANTS

What Better Symbol of the Future Could There Be Than This
Madly Rushing Machine, Turned Loose at Full Speed Between
Two Pasteboard Landscapes, Steered by a Charming Woman?
—Georges Duhamel, *America the Menace*

The giant has a beanie cap on his head and rides a tricycle as
large as my bedroom. The giant is obviously a child, beginning
to lose his baby face. The family of giants is the only one on our well-
trimmed block, and we all feel grateful for the cultural experience.

They seem friendly.

No one's talked to them yet. I have my shy telescope pointed at
their lawn and their massive white Cape Cod. They had to take a
double lot because of the size. Their size needs. The child giant steps
off the tricycle in a tantrum with an unseen parent. But I see it all.
I wonder how many others in this neighborhood have similar telescopes, similar voyeuristic appetites.

Maybe *appetite* is too strong a word. Curiosity. Healthy curiosity.

The giant enters the screen door of his house.

On Saturday, while the housewives of the block have extra time, they
bake identical fruitcakes for the new giant family. They leave them
on the doorstep, piling a diadem of fruitcakes onto the welcome mat,
big enough to make a pup tent.

I spy the cluttering fruitcakes in my telescope and note in my diary: *Did the Welcoming and Steering Committee plan this explosion of fruitcakes? Or was this a spontaneous outburst of congeniality? Will observe.*

By twilight, rains come, water in its crazy falling, turning the gifts into a sludge of batter, slimy candies, dates, and apricots.

It's summer. I imagine that next summer I'll have to get a job, hopefully one that will allow me to read *Sky and Telescope* for large quantities of the day.

I fall asleep at the helm of my bedroom window.

When I wake up, I realize I've overslept. The Charming Woman has already begun her motorized tear through the neighborhood, nearly upon our street. The Charming Woman deserves some explanation. Every Sunday morning, when most of the block prepares for church, she speeds down our street in a car that I have nicknamed Death. It's a convertible. The car is not black. The car is garishly colored in a pink coral.

I know the woman is charming because of her scarves. Someone painted the scarves as starry skies. When she speeds past, the scarf wrapped around her head becomes a miniature pocket of night. Different stars with different coordinates—sometimes a dark blank space in the sky. One is a highlight of Jupiter and the Galilean moons. Another captures a nebula.

I know astronomy. I can speed-read her scarves with help from my camera. Only charming people can hold and be contained by such fabrics.

The Charming Woman never goes to church and never stops, at least not anywhere near us. I don't blame her. She usually wears a raincoat. I am terrified of her and yet I lust after her. Lots.

I notice as the Charming Woman roars past, the family of giants—mother, father, and son—sit on their neatly trimmed and large lawn. The front doorstep is wet. Perhaps the father hosed down the fruitcake sludge.

They aren't going to church, and they don't have lawn chairs. I don't blame them for either misfortune. I don't physically go to church either, but I watch an Eastern Orthodox televangelist every Sunday noon, the only one in our broadcast range. I'm sure our Religion Committee on the block would welcome me or the giants into the fold, if I approached them with such an intent. As the Charming Woman cruises past, I ready my still camera and my timer. Three shots for good measure.

As always, she stares straight ahead. Her age is thirty or forty, and she wears UV blu-blocker sunglasses, somewhat too large for her face. But this, too, is charming. Her UV protection against deadly cosmic rays.

The giant family waves at her, click, in unison.

Click, unbelievably, she waves back still looking straight ahead, click.

Her hand like the neck of a crane.

I develop the photos. The giants' waving makes me sad. The block reveres the Charming Woman but never acknowledges her. Making eye contact with her, I might explode. A wave of her hand could set continents adrift. Or I could die. I didn't nickname her car Death in some willy-nilly fashion.

The giants hate me. The boy on his massive tricycle scurries on the sidewalk, slowly chasing a cricket.

Why are people so cold? I write in my diary. *Oh, wait, I am, too.*

Tues. Wed. Thurs. I cut myself three times, one two three, buckle my shoe. I place the blood in a Ziploc baggie. I'm considering sending my blood to the Smithsonian, for posterity's sake.

But then I realize—it's my astronomical work that will make me live. The sky is for everyone.

The giant father doesn't work, like me. I'm pretty young. I'm no longer mad at them. Perhaps he's a writer. I write too! In a diary. I'm sure there are many giant publications that I could investigate if I have the time. Perhaps I could write away for guidelines.

Friday I develop the picture of the Charming Woman's scarf. Came out just as she waved. Like the commercial told me: I saw what developed. She has a brilliant ring on her ungloved hand. I'm nearly blinded by looking at that photo. A supernova hanging outside the perimeter of a pocket universe.

The constellation in her scarf is Virgo, and I hope she still is.

Sunday is bizarre.

I hear the Charming Woman's Death from a distance, and I ready my telescope and camera. She doesn't speed past as usual. I repeat, like every other known day. Instead, she slows at the giants' house and pulls into their driveway.

The block hushes. Telescopes whirl. She exits her car. Click. Her dress—which I've never seen until now in its entirety—is opal, pure sheen. She rings the doorbell, which has to be as large as her opened palm. Click. After a few seconds she's ushered in, and the door quickly closes. Click.

I'm so flustered and bamboozled that I forget about the Happy Orthodox Hour, a troubling yet calculated choice that leaves the eternal state of my soul in a precarious position.

I mark the time by eating a packet of oyster crackers each hour.

My supply of oyster crackers is nearly endless.

The block returns from church, children play bleak soccer on the AstroTurf lawns, and nothing changes at the giants' house. I barely breathe, much less move my position.

God, I want to crush her into my arms.

The block's mood swings. The frozen pendulum moves and swings. I know that in church, the block prays for the giants' souls, especially the child's. Nature is better experienced—by Nature I mean lawns, picket fences, death cars—from a more innocent perspective. I, too, try to maintain a childlike disposition.

By Monday my window bleeds transparent blood. I know it's blood since I open the window and taste it. Like water, though slightly acidic.

All liquids are blood. Frozen water, caught in the rock of comets, is blood. Blood is everywhere, and when the red giants simmer lots of light years away from us, the hydrogen and helium spewing out of the star's core is just another name for blood, leaking into the vacuum. The same vacuum surrounds us, all of us, even the Charming Woman, still in the giants' house doing godknowswhat.

Death still parked in the giants' driveway. Nothing changes. I'm changing.

The next week, the neighbors commiserate on the sidewalk outside the giants' house. It's not the executive board per se; the meeting is impromptu. The husbands smoke their cigarettes as they come home from work, hands shaking. I think at first that this is a happy unity tide in the block. But no one is happy. The wives bring their prams and talk in hushed tones. I can't read lips, but their lips barely move. I take a few pictures for good measure, but I'm not happy either.

The Charming Woman has made everyone unhappy. I take that back. The giants—although they are still technically newcomers, and gain some amnesty from that—have made everyone unhappy.

All week, the sky is too cloudy for observation, though it doesn't rain.

Next Sunday, it rains.

I burn my TV with kerosene. The fumes don't bother me, not really. The patriarch's face melts on the screen. Rain, rain everywhere. The entire block is morose as they don their raincoats and look funerary during church time.

Death doesn't come speeding down our street. Of course not.

Death's still parked in the giant's driveway.

In the silence below me, I think, Why can't she do anything?

In the diary I write *everyone wants to confess their sins and secrets to her, silently, as she passes by.*

Time to crawl out of the window in the rain. I take my telescope, my camera, twelve packs of oyster crackers. I doubt that I'll be back in my room ever again. The girl in the tower. Who needs it?

This is the first time I've been outside in ages. I wear my black galoshes, my black cape, my black dress, my five mood rings, which are all black. I can't help it if I'm a parody of death. The block Fashion Committee would disapprove, but they are all out of the rain, dry. Praying for the end.

I walk the three blocks, hiss at a stray dog, jump in a few puddles, limber up for what comes next. I do some stretching exercises. Then the friendly giants' house looms in front of me, and Death in front of that. Its coat of peach paint is dull in the grayness and the rain.

The window is unshuttered, though I hear laughing inside. Framed in the window are the giant family and the Charming Woman, playing Monopoly. They all laugh, in unison. The board is supersized. Pails of hot chocolate rest on the four corners of the board. What else did I expect? The Charming Woman's piece, the Dog, is as large as her stomach. The giant boy helps her move the Dog, rolls the dice, moves the Race Car into the jail. The figurine of the Race Car isn't the Hasbro standard piece; it's a perfect replica of Death, down to the peach coloring. Oh no, the Car is in jail. The father rolls snake eyes. He has the Hat but instead of a bowler Hat he has a version of the boy's beanie cap.

Did I mention both the giant wife and the Charming Woman are in silk pajamas? I can see the heavy curve of the Charming Woman's breasts through the translucence.

She is happy. She has abdicated.

Suddenly the giant boy looks at me. His mouth is agape. The mother shakes his shoulders, What's wrong, What's wrong?

Turning away, I open the door of Death. The Charming Woman's purse is on the front seat. I slide onto the sneaksin, I mean, the snakeskin seat. This car and its contents are a part of me. It's always been a part of me. I look through the purse. I find a dildo, a tranquilizer gun, a real gun with real bullets, a packet of Certs.

I look behind me. Many of the neighbors are standing on the sidewalk with no umbrellas or raincoats, staring at me. I'm an awful travesty. But I'm also necessary. *Go on, go on*, they seem to say. *You need to drive, for the Charming Woman secedes.* Though they say nothing and I could be kidding myself.

I'm not surprised the keys were in the car. I start the car. I wave good-bye. Death rumbles below me, my blood burns.

Death drives the car, really. I'm just a passenger with my hands clenched to the wheel. The speed nearly kills me, but doesn't. Speed is fast.

I like the diet of Certs and oyster crackers.

I take many pictures of the circumference of the world. I drive across both oceans, across deserts, rain forests, tundras, prairies, and, yes, suburbs. The world spins around me. I am a celestial object. Is this what the Charming Woman recognized, seeing the giants? Someone that she saw on her way on the *x* axis in the world, who made her nostalgic for a long-lost place? A solace, seeing a giant in such a normal place?

I know, that word *normal*. I don't think that the neighborhood Language Committee would ever use such a word on me.

Maybe she was tired. I get tired but can't sleep, because I'm trying to persevere.

Once a week, I course through the old block, and each time, I wave. Sometimes the husbands and wives wave back, though I don't think they recognize me. I think they mistake me for the Charming Woman. I guess that makes me one.

The giants stay indoors. The Charming Woman could be inside

with them, still playing Monopoly, passing through the square circumference of the game. Maybe she's cashed in her earnings.

A troupe of dwarves has moved onto the other side of the block. Do I have the nerve to introduce myself?

They seem small, and kind.

QUIVER

When Iris was in the Quik-Mart to buy a twenty-ounce of Mountain Dew and a Sunday paper, a man robbed the store with an antique crossbow. At first she thought it was the most idiotic thing she'd ever seen. Yet the stickup had a certain panache, and the robber left with a lot of money, so maybe it wasn't so stupid after all.

The man had viridian eyes, visible through the slits of his gray mask. He wore black jeans and a gray overcoat that was almost a cloak. There was a lot of mud splashed on his clothes, and he smelled to Iris like one of the backwoods kids who came into Wyvern every other Sunday for Sunday school.

And yet he had well-groomed fingernails. Dainty, soft fingertips had he. She didn't think this observation was of any forensic value; it was no crime to have nice hands while committing a crime. Iris noticed this in the split second that it took the robber to take her purse. The crossbow's bolt, cocked and strung, grazed her hair, cut a lock. It fell to the floor like a feather. She imagined him, later in the evening, rifling through her purse, which contained a lot of not much: a credit card about to expire, a credit card overdrawn, her Wal-Mart name badge, some sticks of gum without a pack, an address book with the Y section ripped out, a pepper-spray vial, a stick of crimson glory lipstick, and other uneventful clues to her persona.

Iris didn't shift her feet as the pale, teenaged girl behind the counter gave the robber many twenties, which he stuffed into his pockets. He didn't speak. One hand on the crossbow at all times, very steady. It looked oiled, not dusty at all. When the crossbowman had completed his robbery and dashed out of the store, Iris knelt and picked up her lock of hair, the color of cornsilk. Those five minutes seemed like something that had happened in a fairy tale or a silent movie, one of the two. A story in which the tiniest symbol was connected to larger and more symbolic symbols. She put the hair in her pocket, as the man had placed the money in his.

At last the alarm rang, old-fashioned sounding, as if classes were out in the fifties. The store trapped his musky, mountain smell.

Although Iris no longer had money for the Mountain Dew and the paper, the clerk, who was small boned and in pigtails—Iris could have been her mother if she had been pregnant at the clerk's age—said *take it, just fucking take it*, and Iris did, before the police arrived, who were certain to ask a lot of boring questions that couldn't possibly have had any answers to them.

A few hours later, Iris sat on the front porch of her peach stucco house on the outskirts of Wyvern and wondered where a man with a crossbow could have come from. Didn't grow out of thin air, as far as she could tell. Didn't recognize him, which was a feat in Wyvern.

She thought that her shift in housewares at Wal-Mart would help clear her mind of this wondering. But between moving large quantities of new coffeemakers to their rightful position on the shelves, she spent time on the company phone trying to cancel her credit cards. She was told that they had already been canceled for her, "incredibly overdrawn." She was incredibly overdrawn. Her manager gave her a supervisory stare when she slammed down the phone. The receiver cracked.

"That's twenty dollars from your pay," the manager said, crossing arms. "And you're also missing your name badge. That's another twenty."

Iris put her arms on her hips. Her left arm was slightly longer than her right. No one noticed this except her. Only one man in her life had ever told her this was beautiful (he had to be told of her condition), but her husband was long gone and away.

"I got robbed," Iris said. She stalked back to Housewares, wanting someone in a mask to rob the Wal-Mart. Perhaps a troupe of dragoons.

Michael Youngblood was her husband, but he was off in Ohio. The two weren't speaking. He had once been on the monster truck circuit and made really good money. But Jesus talked to Michael in his sleep one night, sat right down at the foot of his bed, and told him to stop messing around and get an English degree. So he followed the call and went to college. He lived in a dorm.

Iris was thirty-six and wasn't unattractive. But Wyvern was just backwoods Pennsylvania—a place that couldn't place Michael. A few weeks into his tenure at college, he called her to announce that he had a nineteen-year-old girlfriend. "She's a sophomore, an older woman," he tried to joke. She asked him if Jesus had told him to do that, too, to fuck college girls and then boast about it, and then she hung up. Last she'd heard from him.

Iris crunched out the cigarette and sighed.

"Fuck," she said to herself, "I have to *know*."

It was a moony night. There was a pallor in town. Encroached by the green juts of the Alleghenies, fog or haze (depending on the season) often hung around more than in other towns close by. It was a logging town. There weren't a lot of logging companies left, but there were quite a few bars. Iris didn't drink. Her sole addictions were Mountain Dew and antiques (cigarettes, picked up after Michael left, didn't count), and she figured that the latter could come in handy. What could be more antique than a crossbowman?

She walked three blocks through the dark, empty streets to Belle's Attique. Iris was pretty sure "attique" was a made-up word, an affectation. Still, she kind of liked it, like the way she kind of liked Belle. She knocked on the warped door of the tidy shop. Iris knew Belle lived in the shop, and if she had any doubts, they were allayed by

Belle herself, in a nightgown, wielding a flashlight that could have also been a billy club. Iris admired that versatility.

Belle opened the door. "Iris, it's almost one a.m.," she said. Iris was one of Belle's most loyal customers, or at least browsers—she did work in Wal-Mart, after all—but even Iris could sense Belle's patience was being tested. That fine line between browser and loiterer.

"I know," Iris said, "but I wanted to know if you'd heard about the Quik-Mart robbery."

"I'd heard." Belle shuffled her feet. "Someone with a bow and—"

"No. A crossbow. Looked like an oldish crossbow. You didn't sell any crossbows lately, did you?"

Belle raised both eyebrows. "Why does it matter to you, anyway?"

She shrugged. "What else is there to do in Wyvern at night?" Truth was, Iris didn't know why she had this *need* clawing at her to find the robber, as if he were a wounded animal and she his burrow, or as if after he had cut her hair they were now forever locked. Suddenly, though, she guessed that it had something to do with the robber's hands. The puzzle of his soft hands; wondering foolishly if she could unlock their secrets with her own. All foolishness, she knew, but sometimes feelings and impulses were foolish.

"Look, I know this guy who specializes in medieval weaponry who's not too far from here. He's in with the Ren Fest crowd. So if I give you his card will you promise to leave me alone?"

"For twenty-four hours?"

"Forty-eight."

"Thirty-six."

Belle scrunched her face. "Done." She went back inside to retrieve the card.

The only thing Iris was able to afford from Belle's shop was time away from it.

Holden's Armory Shoppe was at the top of Bull Hill, a lonely low mountain about ten miles from the south end of town. Iris had never heard of Holden, but there were a lot of places up in the hills to slip through the seams. Monday was Iris's only day off, so she slept in until 8:30, which felt good to her bones, which she suspected were getting older. Recalcitrant bones they were. As she slept she'd dreamed that a man was in her arms. Not Michael Youngblood, but rather his hare-lipped brother Earl, who wasn't exactly what she had in mind. It wasn't a good augury for the day. She dressed in hiking shorts and a Jethro Tull T-shirt and bounded into her Geo Tracker. The midmorning air was cool yet somehow fetid as well. She closed the windows as she drove through the two stoplights of Wyvern and began the long, winding incline up Bull Hill, gullies to her left and hemlocks and aspens to her right. Not a lot of people lived on Bull Hill; most of those who did were derelicts and loners who resided in shacks or abandoned school buses amid the bears and bobcats.

After a ten-minute, slow climb on the part of her tiny SUV, she turned onto a long driveway. A triangle sign was painted with one word in medieval calligraphy: Holden. The house at the end of the driveway looked like a deer camp converted into a forge. Large cement blocks were strewn on the scraggly lawn. Deeper back, the woods encroached again, as it tended to.

Iris got out of her car and started listening. There was no one, no sound. She picked her way through the ruins; not a touch of habitation for a year or two at least. She felt like an archaeologist, disturbing graves.

"I'll be," she said, having no idea whether Belle was devious or just clueless. Inside the cabin (there was no door, a perfect invitation), patches of roof were failing, letting in tendrils of sun. The one room smelled like gunpowder and camphor. There were a couple of cracked mason jars in the corner.

Stepping outside, she heard hoofclaps coming on the logging trail about a hundred feet behind the house.

A horse, galloping hard. An old hide-and-seek instinct hit her. She ducked behind a cinderblock fireplace, the ashy concrete scraping her knee. The horse whinnied, reared a little, stopped. Sniffed. A man coughed.

She recognized that cough. Her heart, despite her best intentions, was in her throat.

Swallowing hard, she stood up and waved her arms. "Hey," she said.

The man nearly fell off. He was dressed in a loose, mail tunic this time, still grimy but a little bit more dignified. He had a knife strapped to his ankle. Iris wondered for a second if Wal-Mart would ever go for a line of clothes called Chivalry Gear, to help promote the doing of good deeds.

The man couldn't decide, it seemed, shuffling on his quilted saddle, whether to good-deed her or kill her. Iris's arms started getting warm. The horse was a sorrel, eyeing Iris with considerable unease.

When the man didn't say anything, Iris approached by a couple of steps and said, "What's your name?" She was almost tempted to say, "Give me my purse back, you fucking bastard," but the words didn't come out. She also wanted to scruff the robber's hair.

"Look," she said, getting a little exasperated by the silent treatment, "I'm looking for Holden, do you know where Holden is?" She pointed back toward the sign.

His eyes, already large, widened. He raised the crossbow at her, leveled it at her face, and fired.

Iris ducked and dove again, backward, hitting her elbow on that cinderblock again. A whisking sound, like someone diving off a long diving board, falling into shoals.

The crossbow bolt wobbled and thunked into the ground about five feet in front of her. She breathed hard, stared at the man frozen in place on a horse, and realized that he had probably never shot a crossbow at a live human before in his life, and couldn't have shot fish in a barrel if he wanted to. And he probably, most days, didn't want to.

"Fucker," she said, loudly ambling up. She wanted to feel betrayed and then do something about it. "It's over." The man bit his lip.

"You'd better be afraid," she said. Maybe it was her time with Michael that made her so unafraid of this aimless, albeit dreamy faux-man. Michael had once showed her how to strap into a monster truck, and she'd felt for a few minutes what the sounds and smells of a giant truck ripping and searing through a baker's dozen of doomed Impalas must have been like, with the not unlikely chance of a flip ripping the tank, jet fuel and sparks exploding the whole chassis, which the attending customers all probably hoped to see anyway. They paid good money for explosions. Didn't matter if it was scripted; it never mattered.

Man on horse with an unloaded crossbow didn't hold a candle to that.

As he tried to steer the horse around in a circle—the horse really didn't seem inclined to obey—Iris picked up a broken corner of the cinderblock, large as her fist, and hurled it toward him.

The corner smacked against his temple, and with a groan he fell off the horse, one of his ankles still caught in the stirrup. That ankle torqued, snapped. Eyes rolled back. The horse, with great calm, didn't trample the man (and rushing closer to him, inspecting his plum-colored bruise and almost white lock of hair, she saw that he was barely a man, probably in spirit as much as body), much less budge.

She put a hand on the horse's flank and, pulling the knife out of his ankle holster, cut the stirrup. The foot flopped and she winced for him, though he probably didn't deserve a wince.

Free, the horse began to trot away.

"Wait, don't go," Iris said, rising. The horse apparently didn't hear, or pretended not to. The latter was entirely possible. The horse made it back to the logging road and cantered away in the direction it had come from. Iris ran to the road, tempted like all hell to saddle up and arrive wherever the horse needed to go. Wherever that was. The robber's family? Where? How far back in the unimpeachable forest, with the glacial boulders large as frigates and crusted with moonstones that looked like barnacles, the rocks cracked in two as if from a giant's karate chop? Iris didn't like going back there unaccompanied, and she'd certainly been unencumbered by company since Michael left (and further back, since Michael hadn't made love to her a year before he left). Except for the man who took her purse while wielding a crossbow, and who fell so easily when she wanted him to. She almost whispered *poor thing*, almost sheepishly, but then shook her head.

She watched the horse recede until it was nothing. Then she turned back, with reluctance, to the fallen robber.

"Well, Iris," Sheriff Coleman said. They were standing in a hospital room, bleached with anonymity. He picked his teeth. The robber was in the bed, not yet awake but handcuffed by the arm anyway. "You have certainly brought something interesting to the kitchen table."

"You make it sound like we're going to dine on him," she said, resisting the temptation to sit at the robber's bedside, stroke his hair. The sun was setting. Something like moor fog was lying in wait, ready to pounce the town at the first sign of darkness. Iris was sure of this.

"Heh. Maybe so," the sheriff said. He tossed the toothpick away. He and Iris had been in high school together, and he'd been friends with Michael Youngblood for a long time, until they'd had a falling out over a "business investment" into Michael's monster truck, the Spellblighter. Those trucks were expensive; Iris had never understood why Michael wasted such a moronic name on something so expensive. After Michael left for Ohio to read *Red Badge of Courage* and *Middlemarch* on a quad, the sheriff, it seemed to Iris, thought he had vindication about Michael's miscreance. He kept an eye out for her. But now, it seemed possible to her that she was keeping an eye on him.

"What are you going to do with him?" Iris asked. She didn't like the suddenness of this protection, a blanket over her shoulders when cold. Maybe she was cold after all.

"Jesus, I don't know, Iris. He doesn't have any ID. Nothing. Just those loopy little books. I haven't got any idea. We got prints of his from the Quik-Mart, and we're getting those checked out with the database in Harrisburg. But State Police are slow—" He snorted. "At least to get things up to little old Wyvern. A couple of days to see if we have anything."

"And you might not have anything."

"Right, right." He stared down at the robber. "You know, you knocked him out pretty good, Iris."

She shuffled from one foot to the other. "Well, you know, fight or flight. What about Belle and that Holden guy? She's the one who sent me up there."

He put a fraternal hand, as in the Fraternal Order of Police, on her shoulder. "We've got it covered. We're investigating, and we'll seize if we need to. I have no idea what else is up there. Robin Hood boy wonder. Jesus." He removed his hand, and a modest part of her was grateful. "You'd better rest up, Iris," he said. "You've had quite a shock of a day."

"I guess. But what if he wakes up?"

Then the boy woke, trying to sit up but catching on his chain, turning on his side, leaning toward Iris. It was a frowning smile, or a happy snarl. The only certain thing about the face was its bruise, and the penumbra around it.

"Well, look," the sheriff said. A nurse came in with a needle that looked like a tranquilizer gun used to take down elk. "You'd better go now," Coleman said to Iris, even though he kept looking at the boy. The boy started screaming in another language, something almost Russian, with big woodcuts of words, no fine print. Livid and hot. Iris's neck started getting hot. He stared at her, pleading and hating, as she left.

Back in her car, she touched the plastic bag that had been lying in her back seat. She'd stuffed it with badly photocopied pages, smeared and tracked with black marks. But the pages that she'd photocopied at the Quik-Mart quickly from the crossbowman's "loopy books," before she deposited the unconscious man in the hospital and called the police, were legible. Legible enough.

Without exactly knowing why, she craned her arms around the steering wheel and tried to cry, but couldn't.

With darkness, she was calmer, though still feeling like a thief, a betrayer. Worse, a double agent—crossing the authorities by duplicating state evidence, crossing the nameless man by smiting him and delivering him to his no-doubt adversary. Irrational, she thought, washing the dishes at night, so fucking irrational—he took my purse, he cut my hair. But she knew, equally irrationally, that this didn't bother her one bit. She took out the lock of her hair from her pocket, twisted and braided it a little, and set it on the kitchen table. Owls and bats sharked the sky outside. She had her windows open and could hear both species. She wondered if there had ever been a time when they warred the skies, like some old battle of different tribes.

After putting away her dinner (no leftovers, which reminded her that there was a time when a second helping would never have had to be frozen), she collapsed on the couch and started flipping through the man's papers. The lamp she read by was her grandmother's, a river logger's wife; her grandpa took logs all the way down the Allegheny River to Oil City every summer, had a foot crushed after being pinioned between two two-ton logs, and then died from gangrene a few days later. Her grandmother had liked Sir Walter Scott novels that she sent away for. As if she cared that she'd never gone to high school. The lamp Iris sometimes considered her grandmother's ghost. A warm, brass light. It helped her see what she pored over, curled on the couch, the smell of the copy-machine residue like tar, notes and notes about something called "Quiver: A Live-Action Role-Playing Game of Dark Fantasy."

She read. There were also grainy, abstract pictures to scry. The prose was dense, often nonsensical to her ears:

When depicting your character, you must lose your self. Only this way will the mechanics—the simplistic determinism of a

paper and pencil, character-based simulation—fall away. You
must treat your new self unexpectedly.

And:

Psychology of the Crossbow. Esp. if masculine, the metaphysi-
cal properties might be obvious: unlike a bow, the crossbow
stores its potential energy, cocks it. Only in this way can the
fierceness of the warrior reach an energy of activation in less
than an instant, halving one's quiver.

There were rules, although they read more like cantos to a barely
comprehensible poem, or a manifesto on metaphysics.

She'd also photocopied a map she'd found among his possessions, a U.S. Geological Survey—she recognized the contours of the
National Forest—with delicately wrought drawings along the edges.
There were also depictions of landmarks within the forest that Iris
assumed were illusory, fantasy. A keep of a castle named Eldyrwood
(complete with a moat). A dragon, tail curled, blowing smoke along
the edges of the map. Wyvern itself, close to the epicenter of the forest,
seemed an appropriate home for a town in this skewered map. She
knew a wyvern was a kind of dragon or giant worm, or something,
but always assumed the town's name really came from Colonel
Jesphat Wyvern, Mexican-American War veteran who'd founded
the first sawmill on the verdant banks of the Upper Allegheny. She
blinked and tried to will the name of her hometown, the only home
she'd ever known, to something mundane like Potterstown, or
Smithville. Something beyond doubt, a town where no young man
wandered the streets waving crossbows around.

It was stark and quiet outside. She scanned a series of about
twenty Post-it notes, which had inscribed upon them, in the tiniest block letters, a treatise on the "sociological ramifications of an
activist gaming environment." On the back of the last Post-it (she
couldn't bear to read the whole thing), she read something in a

wobbly script, a note-to-self, probably from the crossbowman:

"A thief's purpose is to make people less afraid to be afraid."

There was a soft knock on the door. Iris stood up with a startle, the papers fluttering around her. "Shit," she said. She scooped up as many as she could and blindly stuffed them under the cushions of her musty, lime-colored couch.

"Is that you, sheriff?" she said, moving toward the door. No answer. She looked through the peephole. It was Belle, looking down, arms crossed, tapping her feet. She knew it was dastardly foolish to open that door, to let in what Belle might be mixed up in. But dastardly was becoming her middle name those days. Michael would've clucked at her if she hadn't. She decided he probably would have been right. And she wasn't afraid, at any rate.

"What do you want?" Iris asked, after she had done it. Belle burst inside, closed the door, leaned against it.

"I need to hide a bit," she said, closing her eyes. Her bare arms were dew-moist with sweat. "Catch my breath. If it's OK. Your house is close to mine."

Iris had never given Belle her address. They'd had coffee, once or twice, but always in town at Wyvern's lone diner, to talk antiques. Iris shrugged and said, "What are you hiding from? And why did you send me to that abandoned place up on Bull Hill? And do you want tea?"

"What the fuck do you think I'm hiding from?" Belle said, almost growling. "Police. Tea would be nice, yeah."

Iris moved to the kitchen. "You didn't answer my question. Who's Holden?" The mole feeling continued—aiding and abetting the enemy—but a double agent working for whom? Certainly not herself.

"It's a complicated question. You ask too many of those." The brass teapot started.

"Of what?"

"The complicated kinds."

"That's in my nature," Iris said. "It's not like I can help it."

"Maybe not." Belle sank down on the couch. "Holden's just...an old friend of mine. More of a drug dealer than an antiquer. He uses my shop as a safe house."

"What kinds of drugs?" Drugs and drug production were everywhere in tiny, undetectable shacks in the forest.

"The usual." Belle sighed. "Look, I just wanted to send you up there as a red ruse. I didn't expect you to kick that boy's ass."

The teapot started hissing, and Iris wanted to start hissing too.

"Jesus, Iris, talk to me."

Iris moved back to the living room, where Belle suddenly sprang up from the couch, and twirled like a dodgy ballerina, and pulled a knife out that had been holstered to her torso, holding it a couple of lashes from Iris's neck. The blade was serpentine, had a tourmaline handle. It was, a disembodied part of Iris's mind thought, a really pretty knife.

"I think it's time to get moving," Belle said. "Before the police arrive. You know, Iris, if you don't mind my saying, you were always a better loiterer than customer anyway."

On the drive up to Bull Hill in the tar-pitch black—taking Iris's car, Iris drove—Belle told a couple of stories. Some of them might have even been true. Iris tried not to be shaken by her kidnapping. She hoped that through small talk she would be able to remind Belle that they were, in fact, friends. Or at least not enemies.

"So who are 'they' in exact terms?" Iris asked. Belle had indeed relaxed a little, as if they were going out to the woods to go deer spotting. Belle had a briefcase—kind of incongruous—that she'd stuffed in Iris's hedgerow, and she'd forced Iris to gather up the photocopied papers.

"'They' have no exact terms at all. They have no particular place to live in the forest, no ideology or anything. They don't even have a leader."

"That can't be true. They need a leader."

Belle turned her head and stared at Iris in the dark. "Fine, then. Holden. Holden's their leader."

"You're in love with him, aren't you?"

"Stop asking so many questions!" Belle said. But in saying this she made it obvious that she did love Holden—whoever the hell he was. And it sounded like something from a movie as well. Like she was on the verge of chaining Iris to the rim of an active volcano or something.

Iris paused for a few minutes before speaking again. "OK. Then inexact terms. Is all this part of the game? Their game?"

Belle laughed. "No, you've been reading too much of that shit. Even if it was a game in the past, it's not a game now and won't be in the time to come."

Time to come. Iris wondered if she'd live to see the time to come. It wasn't as if she were "mortally afraid," not really, but the last twenty-four hours were perplexing, not because she didn't understand the events swirling around her (and she didn't, either), but because she was beginning to figure out that she didn't understand herself, and hadn't, for a long time. And that was the real tragedy—to get her head lopped off by a pretty serpentine knife before she could make heads or tails of anything inside her. The around-her parts would sort out, she was kind of sure of that.

A couple of times Iris nearly veered off the road into the guardrail. The inclined roads were nearly inscrutable in the best of conditions.

"So if it's not a game, what the hell is it?" Iris whispered.

"Well, I'm not going to... well, all right." Belle took a deep breath. "They're time travelers."

Iris nearly slammed on the brakes then and there. "Time travelers."

"Well, that does explain a lot now, doesn't it, Iris? The funky clothes and accents. They are a mercenary troop, after all—their weapons are old fashioned but in great condition. That's how I found out about them in the first place, those beautiful weapons. They hide under the cover of Ren Fests and campus SCA meetings. Wandering jousters, if you will. They think that role-playing game manual is a sacred text—" Belle's voice started to get more insistent, high-pitched. "They're just trying to find a way to get home, Iris, you have to believe me!"

"Stop shitting me." They reached Holden's "studio." Belle didn't even need to say where they were going. "If they're skilled mercenaries, then why did that guy go down so easily? His aim sucked."

Belle kept silent as the SUV bumped over a rocky stretch of tattered field, then hit the logging trail. The darkness was nearly complete. Stubborn clouds were coming in; that, and the canopy of trees, and the new moon all conspired to let no starlight pass. The car rattled. After a minute of silence, Belle turned and said, "All right, you got me. They're not time travelers. They're aliens."

"What do they want with me?" Iris was trying to divert the flow of conspiracies by not acknowledging its existence. Wasn't working very well.

"Well, they'll probably probe you and decide whether you're fertile enough to be their sex slave. Like me. They like the antiques—they're cunning and running a cultural simulation from the role-playing game, but taking it far too seriously." Belle leaned her head back. "I'm getting too old for this." It was as if she didn't even believe what she was saying, and had no compunction to hide it.

"Old for what?" Iris said.

"Running into the woods when things don't go right."

The car choked and then coasted until it came to a halt. The languid sheen was off of Belle in a hurry. "What happened?" she asked, pointing the knife closer to Iris's skull.

"Um, you're not going to like this," Iris said. Hell, she didn't like it. They were a few miles away from Holden's abandoned house, encroached on all sides by the thickest forest in Pennsylvania, and she had a knife to her face. But she had still planned this to happen, this gambit. "We're out of gas."

"What? Why didn't you get some more?"

Iris tried not to laugh, to keep her shrug slight. "You didn't ask."

Belle opened the door. "I should slit your throat right now. But I won't, yet. Come on, we're walking in."

"In where?"

"You'll find out."

Slowly, with a creak, Iris opened her door all the way. Shaking her head, Belle went around the front. Belle, for the first time, looked old, like a crone. It wasn't a bad look for her, Iris thought, drifting back for a second to the cinnamon-dust smells of her antique store, the pale lift of light sinking through the windows. A moment of peace. A moment of quelling before Iris closed the door again, almost all the way, and while Belle shouted and ran toward it, Iris turned in her seat and kicked the door out. Glass spider-webbed and smashed against Belle's forehead. Hauling coffeemakers and fifty-pound bulk packages of Kool-Aid at Wal-Mart, twenty-pound weights of Goosebumps books, and cartons of plastic swords and light-up laser guns a hundred at a time had given Iris strength. Belle fell backward. Iris slid out of the car. The air was cool; it almost felt like crystals melting against her skin.

"God," she said, "you people are shitty hijackers." She kicked Belle in the ribs to make sure that Belle wasn't strong anymore. She scooped up the serpentine knife, which glinted in the diamond headlights.

Still. She tried to keep still. She turned off the headlights, loaded Belle uneasily into the car, and started walking.

Not home. In further. She started trembling in the hill-cool. She knew she was close to whatever she didn't want to find.

Iris followed the trail for what seemed like hours. It could have been hours. She disembodied herself. The woods started bleeding into her, and she started beating it out again. Convection. She couldn't see her face or hands. In a way, it didn't seem like a journey at all, as much as a different way to stand still. A more novel method.

After this inordinate collection of endless instants bundled together, she saw light's noise. To her right, an orange crackle of fire, and a voice, loud as a jet in the midst of all that stillness—

"You! Are you Iris?"

Sheepishly, she froze.

"Don't freeze," the voice said, almost—almost—jocular. "I can see you pretty well." Iris thought that should have been inversed. "Come closer to the fire. I won't kill you."

She noticed, clinically, that the man didn't say anything about maiming her, or calling her a bad person. A giant, glacial boulder loomed as her eyes adjusted. The rock was moored on a slope and was carpeted with millions of dead leaves.

Well, she thought. It was too late to start walking back to town.

A man came from the darkness and held out his hand after she moved closer to the light. She blinked her eyes. "I'm Holden," he said. He could have been an ex-hippie businessman: ponytail, jean jacket, turquoise rings. "Let me show you around."

He didn't ask about Belle. Maybe that enduring love was another lie from her, akin to the time traveling and the aliens. All that Holden seemed to care about was that Iris was there.

There was a bustle, two dozen men, women, and children in torch-light. They were rolling up bedrolls, clasping a mismatch of armored plates to their bodies—even the children—scooping swords from a center pile and sheathing them, not really paying that much attention to Iris, her approach.

The area down the slope had torchlight and pitch, a rocky clearing surrounded on three sides by bramble, torn trees rearranged into a kind of hedgerow compound. Horses trembled on the edge of her sight. A young girl in a calico dress and bonnet was plucking marijuana buds from the inclined corner, putting them in a Colombian Coffee sack. She was about nine and smoking something. There was a pile of weapons on a tarp in the center, quiet weapons for the moment—scimitars, cat-o'-nine-tails, daggers, darts, falchions, pikes, katanas, maces with spikes for piercing, and maces without spikes for bludgeoning. It was a gluttony and embarrassment of armament, with no guns in sight. Iris blinked and tried to figure out why they wanted her. No reasons sprang to mind. There were other piles in the process of collection into bags by children: cellphones in one heap, credit cards in another, Walkmans in yet another, the black headphone cords twisting around each other like the medusa's hair in a fight.

None of them bothered her as she wandered around, in a daze. Holden must have told them something.

"Ah, that's all junk," a girl explained, with great wisdom and patience, like a don from Little Italy. "The stuff that we don't have batteries for. What we need has to be portable and valuable."

Children needed to be tucked at this hour, she thought. "Where…where are all of you going?"

The girl smiled and wandered off. This frightened Iris more than if they had been brusque. Holden stayed close by. Dogs brayed. One man put a spike through each horse's neck, one by one. A horse cried. The night trees managed to swallow even that sound up.

"The horses will slow us down," Holden said from behind.

"Why are you so calm? Don't you know that the police and Forest Service will be all over you?"

"They won't find us until it's too late. We'll be attacking the hospital, after all. To rescue my son, Dominick."

"Your what?" she said, stopping and turning around. She didn't see the resemblance. Maybe "son" was a loose metaphor in Holden's world for fondness.

"Belle told me you felled him pretty good. But we're honorable. You bested him in a duel, and he'll be appropriately handled by us because of his failure. It's part of the rules. He needs to make a saving throw."

Another horse went down. Dogs surrounded the fallen beast. A few women, one in a crazy-quilt dress, the other in a Styx T-shirt and black jeans, started pouring metal containers of liquid onto the brambles surrounding the "compound."

"What are you going to do, kill your own son?" Iris said.

Holden raised both eyebrows, and paused, and then said, "Oh wait, here he comes."

"Who?" Dominick?

"Someone to see you." Holden pointed. A silhouette emerged

out of the woods, and at first Iris truly thought it was a ghost, even though it was a visage of someone not yet dead. A brown tunic, but underneath, a stained white jersey with iron-on patches of various automotive and malt liquor logos.

He carried a lance on his shoulder. Iris almost collapsed. The great test, the one she dreamed about, was nearly upon her—and she'd had no time to prepare. The adversary who, until now, had kept his distance.

"Hello, wife," Michael Youngblood said, approaching her.

Iris clenched her fists and didn't say anything.

"Iris," he said. It was almost a question. He was grimy but jaunty, not at all fazed by her presence.

"So, the English degree was a crock of shit," she said.

Holden and Michael both laughed. "What?" Michael scratched his head. "You thought I'd actually go to school? I mean, what the fuck can anyone do with an English degree? Come on, you thought I was in Ohio all that time?"

Iris had had no way of knowing otherwise, but she didn't tell him this. He'd kept silent, though he must have been close to Wyvern all this time. So close. She wasn't sure whether she wanted him close anymore. She was about to shout something, but Holden put a hand on Michael's shoulder. "It's time," he said. All of the horses were at last dead. Most of the dogs had red mouths. The women pulled out the torches from their holsters and started lighting the canopies and tents, the brambled walls, the tarps. They lit quick. Everyone started walking away, as if after a sporting event.

"Good-bye, Eldyrwood!" Holden called out, sylvan, running and fading, as if Iris didn't exist.

Iris started to run after Michael. "Why?" she said. "Please just tell me why."

Michael shrugged, tugged away. "It didn't seem like a stretch from the monster truck circuit. It's all fantasy, isn't it? Holden used to come to all of my shows around here. He recruited me. Besides, I could never be grounded by someone like you." He ran up the slope toward the logging road with the others.

Iris was surprised they hadn't killed her, thrown her into the encroaching blaze, knocked her out, anything; in a way, she would have welcomed that. But the band of quiverers filed out. She could have followed. She could have lived with them or tried to stop them.

Instead she turned toward the blaze, which was suddenly around her on three sides and growing. They'd made a clearing of about fifty feet, which would slow but not stop fire throughout the entire forest. The boulder started popping like a bottle rocket as the fire licked its crevices.

Iris did her best to block the afterimage of her husband in her mind and crouched next to the cairn of cellphones. Smoke burned her eyes. The plastic was hot. Her hands trembled as she tried the on/send button of each. Nothing, nothing, until the twentieth, when she got a weak pulse. Its battery wasn't quite dead, didn't quite acknowledge itself as a corpse despite being surrounded by corpses. Iris punched in 911 as the flames rose, as in a disaster movie. She moved to the boulder, tried to find footholds, hoped the dead leaves on the top wouldn't go poof.

"Hello?" she said, when someone answered. Her own voice was hoarse like a troll's, or a tree's, suddenly finding speech and needing to do something quick about it. She told the operator where they were. The phone then died.

She watched the blaze from the pinnacle of the boulder, watching a red sea from the mast of an immovable ship. She tried to clear out the leaves—pure kindle—but as she ran across the boulder's slanted surface, looking for a way down that didn't involve a plunge back into fire or breaking her ankles, she tripped in a deep, brisk puddle. The edge of a pool carved naturally into the rocktop. Shaking herself, she crouched and pressed her arms into the brisk water, the depression in the rock. She put her arm in and didn't feel the bottom, just water.

She slid in, hoped that hypothermia wouldn't come from the spring. She drank it, dousing herself from the smoke, kept inside as the air turned orange. Treading water in the impossible pool, she wished more than anything that someone could have reshuffled the deck of days. "Michael," she said, wondering for the first time whether he had actually been there. The woods invited apparitions—could Holden have had one of his men impersonate Michael? And in her confused state, would she have accepted it as fact?

Either way, within the smoke and cold, it didn't matter. She exhaled and tried her damnedest to let him at last go.

As the flames rose, she decided it was high time someone invented a time machine to satiate those desires she couldn't quell, to cure the sensation of being "out of step" with Wyvern, and the country around her. Doubtless, in the fifteenth century there had been people with callings to be firefighters, and damned good ones, who really would have known how to use hooks and ladders, but who'd had their talent squandered by accidentally being born in an era before advanced extinguishing techniques had been developed. These men and women had probably tried to douse fires, but with no large water wagons or hydraulic hoses, their efforts were wasted, leaving only burnt hands and cindered hearts.

Ten acres of Bull Hill burned. Thousands could have easily ashed out in a flash scorch if not for the Forest Service and Wyvern Local 3 arriving when they did. Iris supposed she should have felt honored and heroic, but she was barely relieved. Maybe thousands of years in the future, the glaciers would come again, erase everything in ice again—the forest, the river, the tiny and lonely towns, connected to each other with the most tenuous of tendrils—erasing any memory of the quiverers.

She was surprised, but not too surprised, to find, once Sheriff Coleman took her home, that Holden's band hadn't raided the town's hospital. No sign or sigil of them. Iris would become less surprised by this with each passing day.

Once home, she didn't sleep. Her teakettle had all the water boiled out. The metal was beginning to smolder. Belle was in custody; Iris didn't feel bad about that, since that woman hadn't even taken the tea she'd asked for. Iris made some more, for herself, in the microwave. Dawn was faint but unmistakable through her eastern bay window. It was a good house, her grandmother's house. Everyone, she decided, needed a grandmother's house, something old and reliable and larger than a human body.

Maybe that was what Dominick wanted.

The next day, doubtless, there would be questionings. She had an intense urge to flee, all of a sudden—not with her husband, but maybe to Erie or Buffalo. Leave the past past her. Maybe she would. She would talk to Dominick tomorrow, too, if Coleman let her, and she would touch the wound she'd made with the rock, and kiss it, kiss his hair, kiss his lips, not like she was his mother at all. Because she wasn't. Because no one who loved him was ever coming back. Because everyone deserved, at least once in a while, company.

CHILD ASSASSIN

No one knew what to call him, which suited him perfectly well, because he liked to kill babies, and it was better not to have a name attached to such acts. Most of the babies he killed were the sons and daughters of high-level bureaucrats from around the world. He liked to strangle and not cut; in fact, he was quite afraid of knives and never had a barber shave him. Only his mother had shaved him. She had worked for thirty years at a turnpike toll booth, grimly dispensing change on a bridge that led from one state to another. An overpass had collapsed on her, and since then his beard reached to his chest and knotted in the worst possible tangles. The collapse was considered an accident, though he knew it wasn't true.

He also liked orange juice, but it was harder to make a living by simply liking orange juice, than it was liking to kill babies. The market for such services was quite lucrative, though "below the table," as was to be expected. Despite the proliferation of kindness that television brought upon the world, it didn't change the fact that somewhere in the world, at any given time, someone wanted a baby killed. And that was where he came in.

It was hard to know where he lived, since he was always in motion, never staying in one place for too long. Passersbys suspected him without probable cause; alcoholics dreamed about him and then recounted those dreams to therapists, who became strangely tempted to report those dreams to the police, and sometimes did.

The sale of security products to orphanages spiked dramatically whenever he drifted through a town. He knew this and himself dreamed about being caught and eaten by high-level bureaucrats. So he didn't sleep under a bridge for too many nights in a row. In daylight, or when the moon was full, he hunkered down in all-night juice bars. That, or porn kiosks, which were usually more readily available. Sex didn't interest him. He wasn't into his profession for kinks. When he killed a baby he ended up crying a lot. He liked to wear muscle shirts that were a few sizes too large.

He knew that a couple of people had taken to following him, but he wasn't sure who. He wasn't blind to sociopolitical trends and realized that people, in general, were against killing babies, and so he tried to always be careful. For example, he made sure that he received his assignments through bewildering means, primarily through classified ads in "Bargain Shopper" newspaper foldouts. It wasn't an easy skill to read these for the correct clues, but the papers were free and widely available on many street corners. After completing a task, ads would then tell him—in an altogether different code—where to pick up the payment, usually in garbage cans. He read with great fervor; not only classifieds but also encyclopedias. No one read bound encyclopedias any more, and thus they were widely discarded, unwanted. He collected volumes from different sets and buried them under his favorite bridges, for when he returned to a city. After many years, he was only missing V and half of the Rs, and he was quite proud of this. However, reading the Supersaver classifieds was hard work and not at all pleasurable. In between the ads for vases, mattresses, and RVs were desperate cries for help that required his immediate attention. He had no innate gift for cryptography. Only through strain was he able to decipher a message.

On one such occasion, he was parsing a message disguised as an ad for handcrafted quilts. He sat alone in a juice bar at 3 a.m. with an empty smoothie and a magic marker. It was a twinge in his gut that tried to speak to him, in the patterns that only he and his contacts knew. After crossing out the required letters, he came up with:

FATHER FATHER why have you abandoned your only daughter I am waiting under the awning of the best Lebanese deli in town please come quick because I don't know what to kill

He said the word daughter a couple of times. It was clear that he was agitated. Who wouldn't be, after a sudden revelation of secret paternity? He finished the smoothie and folded the newspaper six or seven times, until it was the size of a wallet, thick enough to stop a bullet. Heading to the deli, he had no idea what to expect. The night was cold. Not that it bothered him, but he still noticed. Always vigilant. People steered clear of him, crossed the street before he arrived anywhere near them. Except for the girl standing in front of the best Lebanese deli in town, arms crossed. She resembled him, kind of, but had a softer face, a more wiry body.

She smiled and hugged him and said something like, Dad it's great to see you finally, after all these years.

He tried not to show anything too, well, strange, and asked her who her mother was, because he was curious.

She then told some story about mom drugging him at a juice bar and then artificially inseminating herself while he was out cold. The mother had her reasons at the time, most of them reckless, but that was the spirit of the age, after all. Even she knew that she had to sequester her daughter and never speak to him again. For the obvious reasons. And so, the girl continued, she lived her early childhood in an abandoned farmhouse out in the country with her mother. They grew apples. At this point his attention began to wane, since he liked oranges much more than apples. But then she mentioned that she would like to learn the family trade, so to speak, and gain the skills necessary to kill babies. She crossed her arms, suddenly embarrassed. She was only thirteen or fourteen, and he asked her whether tomorrow she had school, and she replied that she was homeschooled, so no, her mother gave her an extended weekend.

He moved a lock of stringy black hair out of her eyes. She laughed. Garbage was all around them, swirling in the threshold of the deli, the window dark with fat fig leaves.

He told her that it would be fine to train her, when there was more work to be done, but she put a hand on his shoulder, standing on her tiptoes, and asked him to check the Supersaver shopper again. He raised both eyebrows and asked her how she knew about his method of communication in the first place. Perhaps his secrets were not so secret. She promised that she'd found him because she had this bond with him and just knew how to write the ad. Then she laughed again, too deep throated for her throat.

This was clearly a test of faith in his parenting, and he was sure that passing it didn't involve asking too many questions, or questioning the bond between father and daughter, which would never be severed between them, no matter how awful it might have seemed to those with more stable home lives.

He unfolded the newspaper and by lamplight deciphered more ads, beginning with home furnishings. She offered the use of her back as a kind of easel, and so he placed the paper onto her as she was hunched over. For this he was grateful. She smoked a cigarette as he struck letters with his marker. He considered dispensing fatherly advice, such as, That's a filthy habit, you ought to stop, but he decided against it. She was adult enough to want to kill babies and could decide to quit when the time was right.

After a few minutes, he paused because he'd found a task within an ad for handmade cribs:

QUINTUPLETS

An uptown address followed.

When he told her this, the daughter straightened her back. He gave a stiff smile. Already his mind was racing inside itself, to those secret places where the baby-killing desires were kept until needed. He always had those desires, but unleashing them on an unsuspecting household required the courage to wait.

He tried to explain this to her as they walked north, block after quiet block, but it didn't seem like she understood. It could have been his stammering delivery. She kept talking for miles about how she'd had little direction in her life, and how the few friends she had all wanted to be optometrists when they grew up. It was an unsettling state of affairs. She asked him what his strangest assignment ever was. Without hesitation, he thought of his time in Nepal, tracking down a famous novelist, who'd tried to hide at the South Base Camp of K-2 with her baby. The windswept precipice was no place for a novelist. He had to pretend to be a mountain climber, lost and frostbitten, stumbling into her tent. He killed the baby by throwing it off the nearest ledge. Her subsequent blows didn't hurt him, really. The pages fluttered in the darkness, like snow crystals blown up and flattened. When the novelist was done screaming, she took a few deep breaths. It was quiet, except for the wind and the nearby red tent, where they were playing cards and laughing. The novelist looked at him, nodded a few times, and then without warning—or maybe there was ample warning—she jumped over the cliff to follow her manuscript.

Beforehand, in the tent, he'd skimmed a few pages, but couldn't tell what it was about.

He told his daughter this, and she swallowed hard and stopped walking. She said she didn't exactly follow what he said. Then he tried to explain a common misperception in his chosen field, that a baby had to be a baby. Everyone had a baby. Many times it was a baby, but he had also killed cars, books, toys, grandmothers, yachts, dogs, an eighteenth-century Prussian writing desk, parakeets, anacondas, Winchester rifles, stuffed polar bears, ice-cream trucks, oboes, a ten-acre field of marijuana, and so on.

She cocked her head and said that she hadn't considered that before, and this baby-killing business was more complicated than she'd originally thought, but in this instance it was babies, five of them, was it not? He nodded. This satisfied her, and they walked again. He began to say something about refraining from bloodthirst whenever possible, but then they were at the house. Dawn was coming with the faintest of eastern light. The house was three stories high, resplendent, with replica Greek statues and also a Buddha or two in the midst of a herb garden. Little spices. He breathed on the latch of the gate and after opening it, they moved to the front door. He kneeled and breathed on the front knob, rubbed it for good luck, and it opened too.

He had a knack for doors and told her that maybe she could try the door to the babies' room, to see if she had it as well. She shrugged. They crept inside. The house smelled like clean quilts and ten-dollar candles. He pointed upstairs and then skulked there. The house slept. The stairs had no creaks. He motioned toward the doorknob, anxious to test her skills, but she crossed her arms. After a few seconds, because he was tired of waiting, he knelt in front of the door. He pointed to the empty guest room, across the short hallway from a small white door. He whispered that she should grab a pillow or two.

She hesitated. Sweat was on the corner of her eyes. He told her to go on, this was what she wanted, wasn't it. He was getting a little angry with his suddenly stubborn daughter. He wondered if he would have to admonish her. But then she relented and went to the guest room.

He kneeled and breathed on the brass doorknob, the hardest of them all to crack. He shined it with his hand—far too large to fit the knob comfortably. When he heard his daughter approach, he turned around, reaching for the pillow he thought she was about to give her.

And then it was all different. Her knife, long and silver, sliced at his outstretched hand, cutting tendons, sending red everywhere on the egg-white walls. He screamed, not nearly as much from the physical pain as the betrayal. For the snarling young woman lunging at him wasn't his daughter at all. This was clear now, when she loosened the fair gaze of daughterhood that she had assumed. The babies started crying on the other side of the door. Her knife missed its second jab, and he grabbed her head with his one good hand. A wig of stringy, greasy hair flopped off when he pushed it, revealing blond, bobbed, soft hair. Not at all like his. He pushed her away. People were running up the stairs, shouting. He hated knives and she must have known. She muttered something, spitting it out, something about killing her little sister and now he was going to pay. He kept trying to ask her when, when, putting a name to a face, but she had recovered and stabbed him again. He opened the door behind him and scuttled backward like a crab. He didn't want any of this to happen. She slowed, taking her time, as if he were a wine. His chest was cold and wet. He pushed into the cribs, five of them, three blue and two pink. Leaning on the closest for support, he saw that they didn't have babies in them at all, but rather life-like plastic dolls. He hoisted himself up. The girl paused for a few seconds, to let this seep in, to make him realize fully the errors of his trust. Or maybe time itself had slowed; it was hard to tell. He tried not to cry, lifting one of the dolls. The porcelain boy had those glass eyes that opened and closed, depending on the tilt of the body. The eyelids raised with a click as he turned the doll over. Printed on the back like a newspaper headline were the words: Property of the International Legion of Child Assassins.

He set the doll back in its crib, tucked it in with the blanket, and turned around. His almost-daughter was clenched tight. Her face had no remorse, showed no sense that this scene was touching or would move her to mercy. He wanted to show her that he had faults and foibles, it was true, but on better days he called them quirks and went on living without having to look inside his conscience every other minute to see how wrong he was. He leaned forward to make this point when she shouted, and from the closet a half-dozen children, none older than the girl and many much younger, burst out. Each had a long knife. They made use of these. He tried to make a run for the window, but he only made a few steps in that direction, and the window was barred anyway.

Hours later, the children dumped his hacked body on a garbage barge and sent it off to whereabouts unknown, but presumably far away. Barges like that helped people forget about what they discarded, sending it across a body of water to sleepy, quiet places. This provided closure.

He opened his eyes. Dawn had come in full force, sparkling the coastline. He couldn't see it but could hear the gulls. Squawking, landing, taking off again. Pressed on top of him were about two dozen flattened cars. Below him and to all sides were all sorts of refuse—mangled and distilled into abstract, elemental shapes, all generally taking a brown cast. He wondered how distilled he had become, after meeting the child assassins. He knew this wasn't the same as being unhurt, but he didn't feel much of anything. It wasn't a matter of will; he simply didn't know how to unlock the nooks inside him where he kept the pain. Still, it was hard not to remember the times when he had gone wrong. Although the incidents were small, like little gusts sending a toy boat this way and that in a bathtub, there were many of them.

Below him, he heard a grunting whine. He thought at first that perhaps the International Legion of Child Assassins had sent a liaison to keep an eye on him. But then, recognition. It was his mother. She was further below in the compacted trash. He kept trying to say things, and she did, too. The tremors of their voices were on the furthest edge of comprehension, resembling the speech of minor earthquakes or lichen cellular growth. But all the same they talked, and it was clear from just a few moments that he regretted very much that he wasn't able to introduce a granddaughter to her. But she made it clear that children were hard to come by for their baby-killing kin, for all the obvious reasons, and that it didn't do any good to worry about what didn't come to pass. She also said that they would have a lot of time to kill, to recount and reckon what had happened, to imagine the future of their nonexistent generations.

And they did have the time. He found out, as she had in the last several years, that there were few places in the world that really wanted a stray garbage barge. Year after year, port after port, the barge would dock, wait, and then be forced to launch again. Though they sensed little of it, he knew that they sailed around the world, in every direction, several times over, searching for some kind of harbor. No one wanted other people's trash, no matter how emulsified. No one could muster enthusiasm, or even a halfhearted gesture, to welcome what was unwelcomable.

He listened hard for the scavenger birds. It didn't matter what species they were in a particular part of the world. A ragged flock would skitter and land. He heard them pick through the uneven surface of the debris, but it was clear they found precious little among the rusted slag and molten plastic. They would take off again. He liked to think that they were trying to feed the young back home. He imagined the tiny newborns, bald faces poking out of a nest, desperate for nourishment, beaks shrieking. The parents wanted to stop the screaming. This was natural, admirable. He liked to think that.

The Exchanges

Two men met on the top floor of a parking ramp. It was snowing. There were no cars; the ramp had closed for the night. One of the men had a gun and the other didn't. One of the men had a bag full of money and the other didn't. The man exchanged the gun for the other's bag of money. Then they left. They took the stairs and the man who had the gun held doors open for the man with the money. When they reached street level they went in opposite directions—one toward his hotel downtown, the other toward the university along the river. It was very cold. Something they didn't notice before but which they shared as they departed. Someone had just salted the sidewalks, so their footing was good, sure.

They had only gone their separate ways for twenty seconds, maybe thirty, when the man with the money started a conversation with another man who had a knife. The man with the knife convinced the man with the money to exchange the knife for the money. After the bag and knife exchanged hands, the man with the gun came rushing down the street. He had heard pieces of the conversation. When he was close, he shot the man who used to have the gun and the money, but who at that moment had the knife. The man with the bag of money looked at the dead man, and then the man with the gun. The sound of the bullet entering the man's skull hit them at the same time, and they both recoiled. The man with the gun gave the man with the money his gun, and the man in turn exchanged the bag of money for the gun. The bag of money was beginning to sag and distend from the cold. The man who now had the money exchanged it with the dead man's knife.

Why did you do that? the man with the gun said.

I like knives, the man with the knife said. He leaned down and straightened the bag of money on the man's chest.

No, I mean, why did you *shoot* him.

I thought he was you.

The man with the gun paused at this. I saw you two on the parking garage, he said. What were you doing up there?

Exchanging, the man with the knife said. He looked at the knife, turned it around in his hand. A car sped by. The man with the gun shot the man with the knife, who fell parallel to the man with the bag of money on his chest. The man with the gun then took the money back and the knife back and started walking toward the university and the river. His apartment was on the other side of the river. His wife was sleeping in the apartment. The night was quiet and the snow landed in his hair. The gun had an orange-green glow from the streetlights.

He skirted around the edge of campus and reached the bridge crossing the river. It was an old bridge that only permitted foot traffic. In the middle of the bridge he saw his wife. A cop was standing next to his wife. They were kissing. The cop also had a gun, and a badge. The man with the gun, knife, and bag of money froze for a few seconds. He then turned around and tried to walk back, toward the city and the bodies.

What are you doing here? his wife said to him.

I found some things, he said to the cop, ignoring his wife. Some evidence.

The cop approached the man, blocking view of the man's wife. Has there been some sort of crime? he asked.

Maybe, the man said. It's hard to say.

Stop being coy, the man's wife said. Either there was a crime or there wasn't.

I think you're trying to change the subject, he said to his wife, looking back and forth between her and the cop.

The cop moved closer to the man and snatched the bag of money out of his hand.

I need something in exchange, the man said, thinking of the two people he had killed.

No fucking way, the cop said. I have it all. I have your wife.

The cop was about to launch into a lecture, but the man leaned forward and cut open the bag of money with the knife. The bills flitted out and swirled around the bridge and over the side, with the falling snow. The wife started chasing stray bills on her hands and knees.

You've tampered with evidence, the cop said, pulling out his gun. The man did as well, at around the same time.

After about a minute of standing off, the cop said, I propose an exchange.

The man laughed. He looked at his wife, who had stopped stuffing money into her coat. She looked upset that this was happening and gave a look to both men, both tender and remorseful. The man nodded to her. It's okay, he said. Then, to the cop, he said, What do you propose?

Your wife for your life, the cop said.

Don't be stupid, the wife said to the cop. That's not much of an exchange.

How about, the man said, my wife for your badge.

You can't be serious, the cop said.

I'll throw in the knife, the man said.

The cop, both corrupt and confused, turned to the wife for guidance.

It's a good deal, she said. If you love me, you'll take it.

What about the guns? the cop asked.

We'll trade them, the man said. Mine is worth a lot more than yours. It was worth all that bag of money.

Eventually the cop assented. The exchanges were made. The cop, who was no longer a cop, pinned the badge on the coat of the man who was now a cop. The cop then gave the knife to the man. The wife moved to stand by the side of the man, and waved good-bye to the cop. After they traded guns, the man said, You're right. This *is* a nice gun.

The cop tipped his hat and they all departed, each the way they came. The man and woman went back to their apartment, and the cop went back toward the downtown, to a crime scene that he had encountered earlier. The gun was cheap, but he didn't care. The badge gleamed green-orange in the city's late lights.

When he returned to the place where the crime had occurred, there were no bodies to be found. Their silhouettes were becoming indistinct from the new snow. The cop saw some footprints, two sets of them, close to where the bodies were. He decided to follow. The snowy footprints led to the base of a parking ramp. He went inside one of the stairwells. The steps were wet. He climbed them until he reached the top floor, which was outdoors. There were two men on the other end of the ramp, speaking to each other in low tones. The cop slowly approached. He could not hear what they were saying. The two men shook hands and then, hands still clasped, looked at the cop.

Are we in trouble? they said at the same time. The cop thought about this for a few seconds. Then he thought about what he used to know, what life he used to possess.

The cop said, What are you doing? Then I can tell you if you're in trouble.

Exchanging, they said. They released their right hands and then shook with their left hands.

But we thought you'd know that already, one of them added.

The cop said, What would you give me for the badge?

It's a nice badge, one said, releasing his hand and moving closer. I'd give you nothing for it, he said.

And the gun? the cop said to the other.

Nothing, said the other.

Well, the cop said. I'd be willing to entertain that offer.

The two men conferred briefly, and then agreed. The cop gave his badge to one man for nothing, and then the gun to the other man for nothing.

Thanks, the man said to the cops, brushing the snow out of his hair.

Our pleasure, one of the cops said. The other cop gave the man a quizzical look and then said, But you have nothing to exchange now.

That's right, the man said.

I see, the other cop said, though he didn't. Giving advice, which was his role, he said, This part of town, it's not safe. You'd better get home.

I will, the man said. He looked at the city, a good view from the top of the ramp. The first orange-in-plum light was beginning to creep into the east. He nodded at the cops, who ignored him. They bent low toward each other, to discuss policing strategies, no doubt.

The man bounded down the stairs. He felt warm, not chilled at all. He had no idea why. The first commuters of the day, and the first delivery trucks, were beginning to seep into the streets. He walked around the edge of the university. The buildings were like monoliths from a country that borrowed its styles—here dusty brick, there gray plastic. He reached the bridge. The river was half-frozen and the ice shelves groaned as they coursed around the rocks. He started running across the bridge, hoping he wouldn't slip. Even though he was soon out of breath, he pushed himself to keep running. They would not be expecting him.

Salting the Map

M<small>r.</small> Goud dropped the massive stack of index sheaths on Casey's tiny desk. Both Casey and the desk groaned.

"It's only your second week at Originpoint, Casey," Mr. Goud said, wiping his thick brow, wet from exertion. "You don't really have a place to complain."

Casey leaned back in his chair, trying not to sigh. His job as an editorial assistant, so far, was extremely boring. Of course, right out of college, he hadn't expected much with a quasi-useless degree in English. Originpoint had seemed the most promising of his potential jobs because of vintage cartography, a field he didn't know much about but which had at least sounded exotic. That hint of excitement had been quickly squashed by the sheer volume and relatively arbitrary nature of the paperwork: bills, client databases, purchase orders. Most of his fellow office workers were twice his age, and aloof. The air conditioning barely worked, which wasn't a strong point in D.C. in late August.

The bone-crushing reams that his boss deposited on his desk, however, seemed the coup de grâce. Casey, reluctantly, nodded.

"That's the spirit," Goud said. Goud looked like a cross between a Renaissance bursar and a turn-of-the-century prizefighter. His tie was velvety, his teeth were crooked, and he wore four to six ruby rings at any given time.

"Look, I don't know if you're ready for this yet. But it's time for you to salt the index."

A few coworkers looked up from their computers at Casey and quickly looked away.

"Salting the index?" Casey loosened his tie a bit.

"Or salting the map. Same thing. You see, Casey…" Goud began to enter into his already familiar Corporate Lecture Mode. "Originpoint is the leader in vintage cartography. Our atlases are second to none in historical accuracy, geophysical skill, and artistic elegance." Nearly verbatim from the company propaganda, Casey realized. "Therefore, we have to make sure that our competitors don't steal our ideas, particularly through our indexes. It's been known to happen before that fly-by-night competitors scan a few uncopyrighted maps from Victorian travelogues and photocopy our indexes, only recoding the coordinates. And then they sell the product to Wal-Mart."

"Wal-Mart?"

"Or wherever. The point is, that if we salt the map with cities that don't exist, we can cross-check our enemies—I mean, competitors—" Goud cleared his throat. "—to ensure that no one's stealing from us."

Casey didn't like the sound of this. "So I have to…?"

"Sow this. About every other page, I want you to make up some place names. Just sprinkle them here and there."

"What if they're from a place in Germany? I don't know German."

Goud gave a toothy grin. "Just make them up. Use your imagination. It can't do any harm; the atlas is so big that a few grains of salt won't destroy the field."

Casey nodded again. "All right. I'll see what I can do."

"By tomorrow morning."

Casey couldn't help laughing. "What?"

"Tomorrow morning. If you can't get it done here, you'll have to take it home with you."

Restraining a groaning sigh, Casey flipped through the thick ream. "I'm on my way."

Someone in the office snickered, but Casey couldn't tell from which cubicle the noise came. The ceiling fan droned on, pushing the sweltering air from one end of the office to the other, which didn't do a lick of good.

Casey stared at the motes of dust caught in the beams of window light (though the windows themselves, arched with gray stone, were high and small) before turning to the first few pages, the A's. His red correction pen hovered over page three. His hand shook a little and his whole body was tense, as if he were about to jump off a high-dive platform. Casey had never been good at artistic license; his papers in English classes were steady and methodical. "Silly me," he muttered to himself, before lowering the pen onto the page. ABTACAS, he wrote, pg. 455, C3.

Not a bad start. He flipped through a few more pages.

ARGH, pg. 59, F9. A town name that summarized his state of frustration. He was definitely a full-time resident in the town of Argh.

Goud passed by with a cup of coffee in one hand, a cornucopia of donuts in the other. "Don't forget to put the population figures down."

"What?" Casey's heart, which was already ground-level, sunk into the basement. "But that's not in the atlas itself." Casey didn't even know the name of it; all he knew was that it was—allegedly—their "big project," soon to be released.

"You're right. But we have a separate database where the population figures DO enter into the equation. For our CD-ROM. Sorry I forgot to mention that. Get to it." Goud stuffed a donut into his mouth and kept walking.

"Shit," Casey said to himself. He flipped back to the first few pages.

ABTACAS, population 4122. He wet his fingers on his tongue and found the listing for ARGH. Population 310,210 he scribbled.

He decided Argh needed a lot of inhabitants.

After Brogen (pg. 75, E5, pop. 12560), he went to the coffee machine for a desperately needed midmorning fix. A woman whom he'd seen before only vaguely, and only from a distance, slammed her fist against the side of the coffee maker. The machine spewed black blood through the filter and into her rainbow-colored cup.

She wore thin, wire-rimmed glasses perched delicately on her nose. She looked twenty-five or so, slightly older than Casey, wearing two silver bracelets, a carefully smoothed green dress, and a scrunchie in her strawberry blond hair.

"Sorry for the ruckus," she said with a sheepish grin.

"Don't worry about it," Casey said, running his hand over his face. "Once I get some caffeine in my blood, I'll be more cogent."

She laughed. "I like that word, *cogent.*" They exchanged names. Vanessa. "You're the new guy, aren't you?"

"Isn't it obvious?" he said, taking a scalding sip of coffee. It burned his tongue.

"More than you know," Vanessa said. He asked how long she'd worked at Originpoint.

"Ages and ages." She looked away briefly, but her edginess was smoothed out after a few seconds. "What are they having you do? Follow the elephants in the parade to clean their shit?"

This time he laughed. She didn't look like the kind of person who would use the word "shit," and he appreciated that he was actually having a conversation with someone from the office. A few coworkers in camel-colored suits passed by in a caravan, speaking in hushed tones, as if there were a funeral in the break room and can you please be quiet? Casey did his best to ignore them. "A lovely task called 'salting the map.'"

She looked pleased. "Ahhh...I imagine they're getting close to finishing the project, then."

"That's what they're saying at least. So if you're not working on this atlas, which are you working on?"

"Oh, I work in Room A."

A silence followed. Should he have known about Room A? He looked into her eyes and figured, no, I don't care if I look stupid. "What's Room A?"

She stepped away and leaned against a filing cabinet, looking dashing without really trying. She raised her chin. "It's a special project. Kind of hard to…explain. So I'll see you, OK?"

"OK, Vanessa." His brain was a mash of imagined place names—Kipling, Gessepy, Dandyolio, Barktempest.

The smell of her hair (lilacs, maybe) kept with him as he slumped back to his deck, barely out of the Gs.

By closing time, he'd only reached the Rs. Goud gave him a sour grimace as he left but thankfully didn't provide another corporate pep talk.

Casey gathered his bundle of remaining index pages together and left the building, which on a rainy day could have been mistaken for a mausoleum. The entrance was a heavy stone arch, built on a larger scale than the windows, set with glass doors. A chilly breeze hit him as passed through. No motions or sounds on quiet M Street just a few blocks from DuPont Circle; for an instant, all was silent. Casey blinked. Then the sounds and motion of pedestrians, cabs, and boom boxes leaked into the block. He walked the dozen blocks to his flat in Adams Morgan, where the streets were already beginning to swell with the early evening dinner crowds, yuppies from Maryland mixing with the Salvadorian vendors selling roses and baseball caps.

Once at his apartment, he arranged the atlas pages on his orange sofa. The musty couch—if it could even deserve that name—simmered against the wall like a melted horse carriage.

Cooking some ramen noodles, he started the Rs. Retinal, pg. 670, A1, pop. 344.

Hmmming, he added two zeros to the end of 344.

The phone rang. An old friend from George Mason had been supposed to call two days ago, to go drinking. Instead, there was a raspy voice on the other line.

"Is Casey Van Houssen there?"

"Um, speaking." Listening to a telemarketer with a voice from the grave was not on his list of priorities.

"Casey, you have the spelling wrong on your last entry. It's supposed to be Retinul, not Retinal. With a *u*." The man gave a spewing cough that lasted for a few seconds.

"Is this Mr. Goud?" The only quasi-conceivable explanation.

"I'll make you eat your tongue, boy, if you say that again. Now get it right. Retinul. And the population is 344, not some crazy thirty-four thousand. Get your factuals straight, would you?" The person hung up.

Casey sat there in dead silence, holding the receiver on his lap until it started beeping. Not knowing how to process the last conversation, he did the only thing that made sense to him. He added the *u* to the village name and erased the extra zeros with white-out. He finished at 3 a.m. and dropped asleep on the couch, reggae music blaring from the street outside. He dreamed of being a saddlebag doctor and visiting each place he had invented.

What surprised him when he woke up was that he had remembered, in the dream, each place name in the dream, as he planned his long itinerary for his visits of the sick.

When Casey was ten or eleven and socially inept, his Dungeons & Dragons playing had often led to imaginary-world building, scribbling maps on the backs of his father's abandoned inventory logs from the teddy-bear factory. Most of the maps had never been used in the adventures he'd had with his usual cadre of introverted friends. Growing up in Vienna, Virginia—the farthest ring of suburban hell away from D.C.—hadn't always been easy. Casey had retreated from his own life; coping with a hobgoblin in a dank dungeon had always been easier to deal with than getting a swirlie from a seventh grader much larger than him.

The names of continents, rivers, mountain ranges, and cities would had rolled off his No. 2 pencil in a cavalcade of mediocrity: Mountains of Tears, Teal Ocean, Forest of Elves, Gehenred River. Geographies with no correspondence to the real world. How could there be a rain forest adjacent to a desert? How could this city of half a million souls exist, with no roads, in the middle of the mountains?

He knew that, in the end, he shouldn't have been so hard on himself. When his parents called him "precocious" at dinner parties they hosted, he had taken it as a compliment. Only years later, when he bothered to look it up in a dictionary, did he understand his parents' slightly disparaging use of the word. But by then, all of his Dungeons & Dragons stuff had been sold at garage sales. That part of his personality withered away, as it did in most of his friends. Casey's life took on real qualities, and although he wasn't the most successful of his friends in acclimating to "real life," the goals in his high-school existence became more concrete than the ones of middle school: losing his virginity, smoking pot, and reading Dylan Thomas.

The world of invention could hold no surprises for him. In college, books had clear beginnings and endings, and the etymology of words was cast in soldered iron. He'd wanted, eventually, to go to law school, to delve into the hard-edged nuances of justice. He was certain of what he believed—until he salted the map.

After lugging and depositing the now salted index on Mr. Goud's desk which was strewn with miniature tablets and smooth orange stones that Casey assumed were souvenirs from trips to Crete or Micronesia, he went to the receptionist, a bone-thin old man who tended to scowl at Casey when he entered for the day.

"Is there a map for the building?" Casey asked.

The receptionist, balancing a stubby pencil on his thumb and index finger, squinted at Casey. "Why?"

"I want to know where the fire exits are. You know, if the whole place goes up in smoke. Poof." He made a David Copperfield-esque wave of his hands.

The old man, who smelled like beet juice, rattled his head. "What's your security clearance?"

Was this in his employee handbook? Something that he'd forgotten to commit to memory?

Casey paused. But the receptionist cut off his pause. "Evidently it's not high enough to secure the map." The man turned back to his tattered copy of *Archaeology* magazine.

"All rightey," Casey said, going back to his desk. Thank God his medical and dental coverage was good. On the back of a Chinese menu that he'd found in his desk—the place must have closed ages ago, for he had never heard of or seen this place, even though it was supposed to be across the street from Originpoint—he sketched a large island in the shape of an ibis. Along the island-continent's neck, he devised a series of coastal city-states, seven of them, each with names from a secret alphabet that couldn't be written in anything but invisible ink. This exchange between pen, paper, and hand left Casey breathless.

"Casey, can you see me?" Goud said on the fizzy intercom. Reluctantly, Casey set his pencil down and went over to Goud's desk. The color of Goud's tie was dolphin gray. Casey, trying to cut the verbal horses off at the pass, said, "So what's in Room A?"

Goud let out a long, bellowing laugh that was pretty unpleasant. "Consider that your Antarctica. Your terra incognito."

"Don't you mean *incognita*?"

"If you say so, Casey. If you say so." Goud sank lower into his chair. "Anyway, I'll be reviewing the salting tonight. We're going to get you back to tasks more up to your speed."

"But—"

"There's a disk of a client database on your desk, Casey, as we speak. You know the drill."

Casey was twenty-two, and too old to whine or simper, but it was damn tempting.

After two hours spent cranking out letters to clients, lunch break nearing, he got up from his desk to go to the bathroom, with its olive ceramic urinal. When he sat back down at his desk, his continent doodle was missing. He scoured his entire desk but couldn't find it. "What the hell?" he muttered. He knew he hadn't misplaced it; someone had snitched it. His coworkers wouldn't meet his eyes.

Goud would meet his eyes, but usually it would be to add effect to a sneer.

Vanessa would have met his eyes, but she was nowhere to be found as he left the building for the day. On K Street that night, still bitter that his map had been stolen, he stopped at a stationery store and purchased a sheaf of onionskin paper and a thin, elegant ballpoint pen. Back at home, the entire apartment building eerily quiet, Casey rolled out the onionskin on the coffee table that was branded with burn circles from the mugs of previous owners. He took off the cap of the pen; he could almost hear the ink swish, like tree branches in a steady breeze. "Fuck off, Goud," he muttered, and he began to draw the building he worked in, drew the map that he was denied. He drew the straight lines freehand. Some of the rooms he knew from memory, but many he had to improvise. "Hello, Room A," he said, and he devised it—a narrow room with vast windows facing east, letting in actual, usable sunlight, a utopia compared to what the building actually was. Long tables for mapmaking, of course, and lots of globes of the earth and moon. An hourglass, large as a giraffe, which he placed in the corner. His marks were swift and precise and right. Casey knew it.

Finally, he was careful to put the proper amount of fire exits throughout the building.

The next day, fire trucks barricaded the Originpoint building.

Casey stopped with his mouth open in front of the stone arch doorway. There was a faint smell of ozone in the air. The fire trucks didn't have D.C. insignia; they were painted red and only red. The drivers of the fire trucks waited, blank eyed, tapping their fingers on the steering wheels.

As Casey entered, he heard a hustle and bustle that he'd never encountered before at Originpoint. People, to put it in the vernacular, were freaking out. His anonymous coworkers, calm and cold on every other occasion, gossiped rapidly and ran from cluster to cluster, up and down the spiral staircase along the opposite wall. Casey clutched the onionskin map he held in his sweating hands.

Goud, or Vanessa, for that matter, was nowhere to be seen. Some of his coworkers gave passing glances at him, but rather than seeming disdainful of Casey, they seemed almost afraid to meet his eyes.

A hush came as four firemen, in gray uniforms and gray plastic hats, came down the stairs with grim faces, shoulder to shoulder. They pointed at him in silence.

"Casey!" Goud's voice boomed from across the room. Casey walked to Goud's desk, and silence followed in his wake.

"Sit down," Goud growled. His face was purple, and a vein stuck out on his forehead.

Casey looked around, afraid of what Goud had to say. "But there isn't a chair."

"Do you think I care? Sit down."

After a second pause, with the glare of Goud's eyes like prison searchlights, he sank to the floor and sat cross-legged. He could barely see the tip of Goud's nose from his vantage point. The floor was caked in a fine layer of dust that was almost like silt.

"I've looked at your work salting the map, Casey, and I have to say that I'm extremely disappointed." His voice quivered, and Casey couldn't tell where the quivering came from.

"What did I do wrong? I followed your instructions to the T." The firefighters reached the bottom of the stairs, gave a curt wave to Goud, and left through the arch. A smell of camphor and burning fuse boxes followed in their wake.

"No," Goud said, "you followed them to a Q. Q as in *questionable*. You didn't get close to the T."

"What are you talking about?"

Goud cracked his knuckles. "It's quite simple. You copied down places that actually exist and put them into your salting, instead of imaginary, fanciful ones. What index did you crib the names from?" Goud leaned over the desk. "Did you think that would save some time, Casey? Cutting some corners? Did you?"

Casey tried to look as dignified as possible but realized that was impossible sitting in front of his boss's desk, covered in rich dust. "That's impossible. All those names I made up, I swear." The jumble of them, like unruly horses, ran through his head. "What about Barktempest?"

"A lovely village on the northern coast of New Zealand, founded in 1863 by the inventor of the collapsible kennel."

"OK, um, what about Argh?"

"A city on the fringes of the Talamakan Desert. Known for its prayer rugs and the grave of a Czar's son who abdicated his position, became a missionary, and died in Argh in 1707. Funny, but you got the population figure right exactly. Funny how that happened."

Casey put his hands on his forehead. "No, that's impossible."

"It was very possible, and very easy, since you cheated. What you did violated the integrity of our entire profession."

"What's with the firefighters?" Casey hoped this question would be a good distraction, but it only made Goud angrier.

"That's none of your concern. I'm putting you on probation. I've talked to other members of the board, and you're lucky you aren't fired. Until you're deemed fit to do more than utterly menial tasks, you'll be doing utterly menial tasks. Just be warned…" Goud trailed off. "Where are you?"

Humiliated, his head pounding, Casey said, "On the floor, sir. Where you told me to sit."

"Well, stand up where I can see you."

Grimacing, Casey wobbled to his feet. His left foot had fallen asleep, so it took all his concentration to stand upright and not be embarrassed again by falling. He only heard bits and pieces of Goud's soliloquy on values, cartography, and the worth of an honest dollar. "Is this clear?" Goud said at last.

Casey, nearly at the point of tears, weakly nodded.

"Here, then." Goud handed him a quiver of blunt pencils. "Sharpen these. The only sharpener in the building is in the basement—" Goud caught himself, and stammered, his composure lost for an instant. "I mean, it got moved, to the end of the hallway at the top of the stairs."

Casey took the pencils and wondered what kind of business had only one pencil sharpener. But Casey knew the answer immediately: a fucked-up business. He also knew something hadn't been right in that last exchange, but he couldn't put his finger on what. The best he could do was to slink away.

Moving up the stairs, he beat the dozen eraserheads against his palm. "It isn't fair," he muttered, grinding his teeth. None of it was fair. Originpoint was the problem, not him. At the top of the stairs, the smell of ozone assailed him, and he decided what he would do. What he needed to do. He would drop the sharpened pencils on Goud's desk and quit.

The light from the high windows was diffuse and milky. He saw the pencil sharpener, silver and looming on a black pedestal, at the other end of the hall. Then he stopped and took the map he made the night before out of his back pocket. Uncreasing it and tracing his finger along his sketch of the second floor, he froze.

He had sketched the pencil sharpener on the map to appear at the end of the hall. His head swam. He looked at the doors of the rooms; their labels were hastily scratched over with a magic marker. "Storage." "Shipping." And "Room A." Each corresponded exactly to what was on his map. He couldn't read what was under the chicken-scratch. A weird warmth crept inside Casey. He didn't consider it possible to predict the order and location of things. But there was evidence, and Casey needed to cling to evidence, no matter how implausible. Perhaps Goud felt threatened by him; perhaps Goud was crazy. Casey couldn't be sure.

He paused in front of Room A and listened, feeling like a spy in the house of malaise.

Nothing much. The scraping of pencils, a murmuring of inter-mixed voices like continual static feedback. A cough here and there.

A man piped up from behind the door, more loudly. "What do you think of this place? Arctangent City?" A rustling of paper.

"Definitely falsified. Who wrote that?" A woman said this, in a thick accent that sounded Greek.

"Calculus teacher from Boston, 1911. He killed himself in '35 but theorized the distances of imaginary cities based on algorithms and the distance from the sun to Uranus. What do you suppose Arctangent City looks like this time of year?"

"I see it now," the woman said. "Serpentine streets. Their king has a scimitar for a left arm." They both laughed, but it wasn't sarcastic, more the remembrance of a pleasant vacation.

"So what do you think of our new quarters."

"They're OK. I don't know why we moved. The big hourglass is a nice addition, though."

Casey almost let out a surprised cry at the mention of the hourglass, his hourglass.

The "Shipping" door opened and Casey's back stiffened. Lame excuses ran like greyhounds through his head.

It was Vanessa, wearing khaki slacks and a blue shirt.

"Hey!" she said, cheery enough. "What are you doing up here?"

Casey tapped his feet. "Um, sharpening pencils." He paused, took a deep breath, and in a halting voice, described what Goud had told him. "I mean," he said in a whisper, "it's bullshit. I didn't falsify those cities, Vanessa."

She put her hand on his shoulder. His shoulder tingled. "I know. I'm on the board. Goud wanted to fire you, but I persuaded him to keep you on."

"You did? What the hell is going on?"

"Internal struggles. Paradigm shifts. The usual corporate bullshit."

Casey sighed. "I'm going to go down there and quit. I can't take any more of this."

Vanessa bit her lip. "It's your choice, Casey. I'm not going to tell you how to think or act. But I wouldn't quit. I want to explain more of this to you, but not right now."

"How about over dinner?" The words blurted out of his mouth, seemingly of their own accord. Casey didn't mind that they had.

"Are you asking me out?" Vanessa laughed, somehow making a giggle dignified, and even sexy.

"I guess I am."

"All right. Yes, Casey, I'll go out with you." They decided on an Ethiopian restaurant, and, walking on air, Casey went to sharpen his pencils. The pencils that, after much temptation, he later didn't jam into Goud's throat but merely placed on his desk.

Everyone at their desks stared and scowled at Casey, but Casey beamed at each and every one of them.

Kill them with kindness.

Casey walked to the DuPont Metro stop with the wide maw of the down-slanting tunnel and the slowly moving escalator. He took the Metro to the Mall. The Ethiopian restaurant skirted the edge of the Capitol district, on Connecticut; Casey wanted to walk the extra few blocks, watch the tourists and Vietnam vets mingle in the summer twilight. The Smithsonian museums, the Washington Monument in the distance, the Capitol itself—the D.C. that existed in everyone's mind, even when that D.C. was only a snippet of the story, and a fanciful one at that.

Vanessa waited outside the restaurant in a sleeveless, white sundress, a pearl pendant dangling below her neckline. Her body had the color and curves of an alabaster vase. Casey put his hands in the pockets of his gray dress slacks and straightened his tie. His shirt was ecru. The three best items he owned.

They sat on low wicker stools and drank beers, waiting for their lamb. "You know," she said, "it kind of surprised me when you asked me out."

"It kind of surprised me, too, actually."

She smirked, but it wasn't an unkind smirk. "You were eavesdropping on Room A?"

He paused, trying to read her expression.

"Don't worry," she said. "It's natural to be curious. Besides, you were probably reeling from your hornlocking with Goud." She took his hand. Her skin was cool.

He laughed and kept his hand interlocked in hers. "I wouldn't say we locked horns. It was more like an angry bull running through a drunken bullfighter."

"Goud has his good points," she said. "But I have to admit that they weren't exactly in full force that day. He's going through a lot, with the company."

"That might be true, but—"

Their lamb came. Casey loved Ethiopian food, and he rarely got a chance to eat it with such good company as Vanessa. He tried to push away the myriad questions, at least for a few minutes.

"The Ibexians cooked like this," she said, her mouth full, eyes closed, savoring. "Only their bowls were ten times this size. You had to climb into the dough, and eat your way out. It's been a while."

Casey paused in midchew. "Isn't an ibex a type of goat?"

"Yeah, but that's where the ibex comes from. Ibexia."

"Where is Ibexia? The name sounds vaguely familiar, but…" His toe tingled, a sign, since his childhood, that his brain and body were getting nervous in tandem.

Vanessa gave another laugh. It sounded more like a defense mechanism than actual mirth. "South of Basque Country, east of France, I guess. Somewhere in the Pyrenees. I went there on vacation when I was a kid." She shrugged. "Are you going to have that pepper?"

Casey relinquished the pepper. He decided, if he didn't tell her now, then perhaps he'd never find the nerve to tell her.

"You look beautiful," he said.

She leaned back, about to return a similar compliment.

"There's something I have to ask you," Casey said, cramming his words in edgewise. He told her about the man who had called in the middle of the night, who had corrected the spelling of his imaginary town. He scooted his stool forward and said in a low voice, "And I have to let you know that Ibexia is one of the names of the towns

I made up yesterday when I salted the map. Population 2,500." He folded his hands together, scrying her face for any clues. But her face was of stone, the non-Rosetta variety.

All she said was, quietly, "Oh dear. It's true."

"What's true?" he said.

Vanessa wiped her hands in four swift strokes with a purple napkin. She scrunched her eyebrows at Casey. "Curiouser and curiouser, huh?"

"I guess. Please tell me why Goud hates me and accused me of screwing up. And why I shouldn't quit."

"It's like this, Casey. I've debated ever since you salted the map whether I should tell you. Some at the company want secrecy under the penalty of death, but…I like you. A lot."

"Is there a penalty of death?" Casey said, momentarily distracted.

"Well, some at Originpoint would like one, to tell you the truth. What is important is to have you think about maps differently. They're not static representations of geophysical space."

"Um, OK," Casey said, wanting a shot of tequila. Instead, he paid the bill.

She pressed his hand against the table, hard. "I'm serious, Casey. For the cartographers at Originpoint, maps are much more complicated. They don't represent the landscape. They define the landscape. That's the best place to start. I'll leave the political bitching for last. By the way, do you want to go?"

"Yeah, sure. Let's go."

They walked out into the busy street. Vendors gave the names of their roses in low whispers around them. Casey waited for Vanessa to continue, but she remained quiet and pensive as they walked slowly toward the Capitol. "Where are you at?" Casey said. "I can walk you home."

"I took the Metro. I'll take it your way. Past DuPont. I can get home by myself after your stop."

"Do you live in Maryland, then?"

"Not exactly." She kept her speech clipped.

Casey decided to let her sort it out—whatever *it* was—in her own head before he blundered and said something stupid.

On the red line, heading north, there was no one else in their car. Only three stops to DuPont; Casey wanted to hear what she had to say, but he didn't want to rush her either. He gave his *I'm curious* look, his slightly raised eyebrow.

Vanessa sighed and leaned her head on his shoulder. "I don't know, Casey…this is all so difficult. I'm not supposed to talk about this."

"Will this affect my employee evaluation?" he said, trying to make a joke of it. "I'm already in deep shit." But Vanessa puckered her lips. Apparently she hadn't heard him.

"It's like this," she said. "Throughout time people have made erroneous maps. People don't know the lay of the land, and yet they decide to draw it anyway. Kings, academies of mapmakers, the Phoenicians, the Hittites…just because you can travel to a place doesn't mean you can know it. And some people falsified maps, just as larks. Do you know what I'm talking about?"

"Not yet. But go on," Casey said. He began stroking her fine hair, and she didn't pull away.

"What if there were people, though, who had to live in those places? The places drawn erroneously? Or even imaginary utopias or dystopias?"

"Do you mean the bad maps were accurate? In their way?"

"Yes, in their way. The sea serpents and krakens dotting the Atlantic Ocean—before it was called the Atlantic Ocean—were real for us. We had to confront them. The Auroras and the north winds, huffing and puffing, blew our houses down. We had to learn the customs of these countries, but we didn't understand them."

"Who's 'we'?"

"Let me finish. We didn't know why the imaginary maps affected us. But, recently, we've found that with Geosats and computers doing most of the work, there's been no room for error. We thought we'd be happy, but it's been killing us. We lived so long in terra incognita that its imaginary contours began to affect us, and we couldn't quite place ourselves in terra firma. God knows we've been looking for terra firma, and one day maybe we'll find it."

Casey stood up. He was beginning to get frustrated. "Vanessa! Would you please tell me who you're talking about?" His stop would come in another three or four minutes. He clenched the pole. The subway rollicked through its tunnel all around him, like a worm racing through a burrow.

"Originpoint," Vanessa said finally, "isn't just a company. It's…a tribe. We found ourselves accidentally in one of Ptolemy's maps 2,600 years ago, after getting lost in Asia Minor on a hunt. There was a stone archway. We entered it. We found the world to be divided in four quadrants. Which was fine, except the rivers flooded the perfectly flat plains, having no seas to empty into, and the sun stayed in the same place all the time."

She began to breathe heavily. "We didn't die. Goud, the other workers, none of us have ever died. We found another stone arch—"

"I get the picture," Casey said, not completely understanding. "Look, let me come with you to your place."

"You can't." She stood up and looked behind her to the metro map set on the compartment wall. She traced a finger along the representation of the orange route, north into Maryland, and continued pressing her finger against the map's plastic case. A beige trail followed, as if her finger were a crayon or magic marker. Casey stood there with his mouth open. Her finger continued its brownish trail past the map; she stood up on the hard cushion of the subway and traced the continuation of the Metro line to the car's ceiling, where she stopped with her arm outstretched. Her belly button showed.

"That's where I live," she said. "On the ecru line." She smiled. "To match your shirt."

A smattering of comprehension came to Casey. "So when I salted the index, it wasn't that I happened to be lucky in finding place names that happened to be real, or could even prognosticate them…"

"That's right," she said, with her arm still extended. "You created more fodder for us. But we need that. Imaginary maps are our lifelines. That's why we do vintage cartography. We always need new places to add to the mix, to call our own. The maps are our subconscious. Silly, huh?"

"Silly isn't the word for it. So what happened when I made the map of the office building—" He thought of the stone archways of the doors and windows, and what that must have signified.

"Casey, you rearranged the entire building to fit what you drew in the map. There shouldn't have been a way for you to do that. Most of the people in the tribe are afraid to talk to you, to tell you the truth." Casey didn't know what to say or expect next. It wouldn't have surprised him if the entire subway car melted or broke out of its tunnel and flew across the Potomac.

"So all those imaginary and misnamed places, Originpoint has been to all of them? Even Barktempest and Argh?"

She touched his cheek with her palm. "Yes. And the guy who called you in the middle of the night was probably the mayor of Retinul, who wanted a smaller village rather than a large one. So, yes. Originpoint has been to all those places. Goud is afraid of you, but I'll try to work on him." She paused and looked down.

"Is this where the bitchy politics part comes in?"

Vanessa tapped his stomach playfully. "Hey, you're bright. The tribe has really been in a bind. Divided. Goud and a lot of the older people in the tribe don't want to solicit the help of 'outsiders.' They think it's too dangerous, that someone could easily turn on them and ruin them. But there are those of us who want to open things up. We had no idea when you got hired, and salted the map, that you would be able to change things like you did. But now, we need you, Casey."

"I want to help."

"I know you do, I know." She kissed his forehead. "So after I've spilled the beans like this, do you still want to quit?"

Casey took a deep breath. "I'm pretty sure I don't. But tell me this—will you get angry if I go up to Goud and tell him everything that I know? And demand an apology?"

Vanessa whistled. "I don't know, Casey. Goud's a tough nut to crack. But you're right—he's not being honest with you about why he put you on probation. It's better to bring this thing to a head."

"Tomorrow, then. I'll be back tomorrow."

The train came to a sudden halt. DuPont Circle Station. The concrete and chrome outside the subway windows mixed like ice and black ice. Vanessa lost her balance and collapsed, somehow artfully, into Casey's arms. Her body folded into his, like a letter into an envelope, and before he blinked he was kissing her. Kissing her neck and eyelashes and finally her mouth, as her hands clung to his shoulders. She returned the kisses with grace. Casey realized that this was what she had wanted all along, but now they were both surprised that he actually had the nerve to put himself in this position.

The door to his compartment slid open.

"Thank you," she said, "for a wonderful evening." She leaned her head against his and looked up, briefly, at the map of the Ecru Line on the ceiling.

Straddling between the hard concrete of the station and the thin carpeting of the subway car, holding the door open between the two…worlds? No, he decided. It might have been accurate but also too pretentious. He turned around. "I don't understand, though, why you have to worry about imaginary places. You're here. In the real world."

Vanessa grasped the pole and gave a sly smile. "It's interesting you're sure of that."

He stepped away, the door swung closed, and Vanessa sat in her seat, facing away from the station. The subway swung into the tunnel and Casey waited until even the noise of its departure died away.

Footsteps echoed in the station. Businessmen scurried down the stairs to get home after second shift, trios of men and women scrambled up the escalators to loll around DuPont Circle, to people-watch and saunter in the last remnants of the summer.

Casey loosened his tie and made for the stairs. Winding up a level, he walked a hundred more feet and stepped onto the escalator, which would lead him from the subterranean to the terranean. He leaned against the guardrail and peered up as he moved on the escalator. The DuPont station was the farthest underground in D.C. He'd always imagined himself arising from a pit mine or, better, soaring from ground level to the celestial sphere, a motorized Jacob's ladder.

Vanessa's scent stuck to his clothes and skin. He mulled over their conversation and their kiss. He had no idea if Goud, when confronted, would bite off his head. But Casey had facts and maps on his side. He would find out. He wanted to find out how much Vanessa wanted him in the tribe, and her life.

The full, bulging moon showed its face from behind a frieze of clouds, then ducked away again, the Sea of Tranquility obscured by the condensation of water in Earth's upper atmosphere...Casey rattled his head and blinked hard. Five minutes could have passed, or fifteen. He was still on the escalator, still going up, and the surface appeared a long way off. The moon cast its gloss into the diagonal escalator tunnel. Looking down where he came from, the Farepass vending machines and brightly lit maps of cross-wired subway routes appeared like the landscape beneath a plane immediately after takeoff, when the fast cars and big houses still had normal perspective, still held some measure of the significance the owners of those cars and houses had in their own eyes.

"I am my own Geosat," he whispered. Perspective leaked out of Casey. The moon was like a scientist, craning its face to stare down the barrel of a microscope at the well-dressed creature rising out of the depths.

A fan kicked in above Casey with a gargantuan hum. The escalator tunnel could have lengthened and contracted. After that night, Casey wouldn't have doubted it. His place on the escalator finally broke the threshold between the enclosed space and open air. He could see the end: the vendors' carts piled away, the children screaming at each other in Spanish and skipping toward the Circle. Casey closed his eyes. The contours of the bewildering city didn't need a map. The city mapped him, etched his steps into the interplay of everyone else's steps. Each person was a map, he decided, as his feet hit sidewalk, the ground zero of moving bodies. Everyone was equal parts flesh and imagination, bound together like sodium and chloride, like the salt of the earth.

HOME OF THE

1.

Cleo was completely happy and devoid of hope. At night she dreamed of photocopiers left on in an office building overnight. On Sunday she walked to her church and prayed outside of it, for those not inside. Bullet trains passed by. She always waved. They didn't stop. She contemplated what steps she would have to take to make the trains stop. By the time Erie's churches let out, she was back home, watching the minister on TV. No one called on her. Her house was red stucco, painted blue. Which defeated the purpose of stucco. Her mother had painted the house blue in her late middle ages. Her mother bequeathed the house to Cleo. Cleo relented. She was penitent without exactly knowing why. The house was on a cul de sac on the East Side, Dunn Boulevard, between Saint Anne's and the bay. Behind Cleo's lot was a cemetery, and across the street from her lot was the black cat factory. Of the two, the cemetery was by far the most interesting. For starters, Cleo had been conceived there, in the groundskeeper's shed, which didn't exist anymore. Her mother had had an affair with the groundskeeper, who was from western Kansas. Nearly all care had abandoned the cemetery and the headstones inside. There were a few Revolutionary War veterans buried there. Cleo would have loved to celebrate this. Few people left flowers or wreaths. Obelisks tilted. People in general were leaving Erie at a fast clip. There were fewer dying people left. Faithful people often were left behind. The church, which had fed the cemetery for a century, had burned to the ground a decade before. The congregation didn't reconvene, for lack of funds and municipal edicts. No one caught the arsonists. The members joined other churches, more theocratic churches, or turned their faces from God entirely and took up drag races on Saturday nights and hunting on Sunday mornings. Or they died, which didn't have anything to do with church. Even in winter, Cleo would visit the foundations, the ash square set in the ground jutting against the railroad tracks. There were no deer to hunt anymore, and few small mammals and birds. Generally there were only people left.

She was the only one left alive on her block, aside from the cats and the foreman, who didn't count. Her hair was black with a few gray strands. She resisted dyes. She resisted many things, including the need to smile or laugh at comedic movies at the theater. Movies were small hearted and easy to coast through, like fog puffs. Movies ended with a public service announcement from a tribunal. Of some sort. A tribunal was a collection of citizens on the lookout for citizens' interests. They declared these interests, which usually involved enemies. Everybody always left right after the shiny heads stopped talking—cameras in the projection room watched the viewing—and right before the credits rolled. People were tired. But Cleo liked to stay and watch the references to gaffer, puppet master, and key grip. She thought that befriending a key grip might have been interesting fodder. She would take the bus to the failure mall downtown. She knew her worth. The bus had issues. Groaning escalators leading to empty shop fronts on the second floor. Abandoned kiosks with Scotch tape half-torn off the counters. Huffer cans in the corners. The only open establishments, besides the dollar theater, were the adult bookstore, the tobacconist, and the store that sold nothing but pewter figurines. The store was called Pewter There. That last store made her sad. No one ever entered. Cleo was like the train passing by a strange woman making waving motions. The proprietor wore a white, tight-fitting mask and fretted with his hands. As noted previously, she didn't stop to inquire. She wasn't in the mood for small, pewter figurines of dragons and unicorns. Miniatures were not powerful. The house wouldn't have approved. The house was mindful and resisted paraphernalia. Knickknacks that Cleo bought would disappear shortly after acquisition. Paintings of burning barns she purchased from starving artists' sales, a smiley-face clock she resuscitated from the break room, all gone. So she gave up. She didn't like giving up. She took the bus back. Its hood usually smoked.

On rain days, which came often in the summer, spring, and autumn, she liked to walk the East Side. Umbrellas could conceal cylindrical bombs and were thus frowned upon. Tribunals warned against bomblike people, who required eagle eyes at all times. Evil truly was wicked and could quiver to life after any misstep. That was what her betters said. The dealers on the corner of Buffalo and Downing didn't bother Cleo, nor the gyrovagues parading on Tenth and Parade. She knew the hoarse ghosts of those boulevards were more terrifying than sixteen-year-olds with post-heroin and .44s. Most sidewalks resembled narrow gravel roads from the despair. She wore beautiful galoshes. They were black with small fleur-de-Frenches along the upper trim. Her mother gave her the boots before she died. Before her mother died, not Cleo. After Cleo tried them on, her mother noted that she pulled them off a dead woman, a homeless woman with no hair in the bus station. Before Cleo could recoil, her mother said, no, sorry, I was only joking. It was a good story, though, wasn't it? Cleo liked the boots anyway. They made her look taller. The litter and wind would collaborate on sculptures along chain-link fences. Some of the plastic litter was positively antique. Rivulets roared into drains underneath. The drains emptied into sewer tunnels, which coursed toward the bay. The water carried delirium. Mercury could also be called quicksilver. Stray cats died underground. In chain-link fields, cranes built to hoist up rusted cars with magnetic forces rusted. Art was everywhere. It wasn't good art. The city was a nonmuseum. These were not stories in their entirety, but rather stories that a person might be reading out loud to friends in a bar, and then the bartender would tap the reader's shoulder and say, Your house is on fire. Your mother's dead. No one loves you, not really. One of those types of responses. No one read anymore, out loud or silently. Heliotropes flew overhead, shouting bulletins (all points) to precinct commandantes who might have been listening. Hand signals projected onto the cloud banks. Heliotropes lived in milder climes. Cleo covered her ears. Once there was a boy who had loved her, her age, but he fought in California and she never heard from him again. He had delicate fingers and ankles. He was an apostate, though neither of them really *felt* what that meant. She imagined him in prison—a converted gymnasium holding thousands of bunks, snipers in every nook, spies and assassins enforcing second amendment zones, itching to penknife livers. Cleo wondered if it was better to hope he was alive, or dead. His emails were in a banker's box somewhere in the cellar, amid a tangle of potato roots. She'd often wondered what his penmanship was like but had never had the chance to ask. She was thirty-five years of age in the thirteenth year of our Lord.

When it was sunny and she didn't have to wear her containment mask (red, like the stucco underneath her blue house), she worked at Wal-Mart. There was one five blocks from her. People shopped indoors when it was sunny. This, too, was encouraged. Retractable roofs, unless they were broken. Nearly everyone who worked worked in a Wal-Mart. Her Wal-Mart was a bowling alley. The greeter always snarled at her, even though they were on the same team. He'd lost his heart in one of the wars. Because her bowling alley was a Wal-Mart, it was a nonfailure establishment. She cleaned the robots that cleaned the lanes and stocked the shoes. Her blue smock smelled like burnt hot dogs. Nearly everyone bowled in solitary fashion. Bowling in duos or trios wasn't banned, per se, but it was certainly frowned upon, and there was an extra tariff per head. The robots usually didn't complain, but they belched silicates. They were already oldish. She loved them, in her fashion, even though she couldn't tell them apart. That happened a lot. They were both blond. The TVs in the snack bar fixated on victories, which were hard to tell apart from failures. The greeter would tap his plastic chest, where his bonobo heart beat. Personalities tended to be unfortunate, even on sunny days. She worked hard. Her smock had one yellow smiling face and one red, white, and blue smiling face. The robots didn't like the buttons. It sounded crazy, even to her, but she could just sense this. Every month the regional heresiarch would visit and play a frame or two. The lanes had to be calibrated to ensure he bowled at least a 250. But he didn't want a 300 either, for that would have been hubris. Her mother hated bowling because the sport could not exist solely in one's mind. Those visits were horrible for Cleo. She would have nightmares in the days leading up to the inspection, involving her robots defecating on the well-oiled lanes, prompting her quick termination. After the heresiarch's frames, there was usually Bible study. Cleo would sit quietly through Corinthians, sipping lukewarm tea. Revelations scared her. After shaking everyone's hand too firmly, the heresiarch would depart for the damask domes of Cambridge Springs, where the wife would just be returning from the market with their children, Abercrombie and Fitch, and she would offer a towel to her demonstrative, balding husband, a God-shepherd, and he would wash his hands of the helots' stench. That was how Cleo thought, at least. Once when he bowled a 248 he shook everyone's hand except Cleo's. She cried all that night, though she did not want to. On her ten-minute lunch breaks, the sun would play on her face in the break room and the ether from above would settle on the vending machines in a fine film. The break room was a tent outside the bowling alley. She had to be alert to the possibility of white phosphorus falling, in which case there was a plastic tarp for extra protection. Enemy manna. Her shoulders didn't sag. No one would talk to her ever. She wanted to be an action gardener, garden in one of the sky fortresses. Peonies on the battlements. She heard about that job when watching the Sky Fortress Channel. There was one gardener for the entire fortress system. Let luck work! the public service announcements told her. On occasion she contemplated emigrating to India. She couldn't afford passage. She also wanted to keep an eye on the house and cemetery, and she didn't like traveling too far too often. Once in high school her class took a trip to Antarctica. At the South Pole, they didn't stray out of the Super 8 much, except to go to the penguin wax museum. The vending machines down their hall had a brand of Burmese cola they'd never seen before. That kind of local color excited her classmates. The South Pole bored her, except for their flight away from it, when she saw two service workers make out behind the McDonald's on the Ross Ice Shelf—what was left of it—their mouths frozen to each other. She could see what the attraction was. Their fiber-optic mittens touched, and no doubt they sent love mail to each other. No doubt. Cleo's plane kept flying, over glaciers, over floes. The lovers kept getting smaller. The plane flew over the greenhouses larger than Rhode Island, where workers harvested kelp and krill inside. When Cleo was home again she wanted nothing more than a kiss like that. A year later her mother died. Her graduation ceremony came in a box. College was out of the question. Her grades were Erie good but not actually good. Her few girlfriends saw marriage and conversion as a proper and just path. Her guidance counselor wanted her to become a Baptist. The complexes on upper Peach had excellent career placement networks. She declined. The guidance counselor never communicated with her again. The mayor was assistant pastor at Church of Christworld. He complied.

She wondered sometimes if the world was flammable. She tried to think of her father's face. He had loved crocuses and jumbo puzzle variety books. Invisible ink puzzles. Her face was thin, like pictures of him. No one was perfect. He left for the moon with the furries when he found out about her mother's affair with the gardener. He won the lottery. How lucky was that. Cleo hid underneath the garbage disposal to hear his teary farewell. It smelled like disposed garbage. She remembered her mother's burgundy silence. Her mother was a failed chess champion and didn't like to talk about it. Her father milled around the house to say good-bye to Cleo, looking without really looking. He gave up after five minutes or so. She didn't want to reveal her hiding place. He was wearing his fluffy skunk costume. Her parents had met when her mother dialed the wrong number. Cleo imagined life in space. She would land on the station. She was in the deep for six months, orbiting Triton. She needed supplies or else!

What do you want, the general store manager on the station would ask her. He wore an old-time bowler hat.

A view of Earth, a great view of Earth, she said. The greatest demand she could think of.

You have it! Look portside! She looked portside, and it was there. She could see America underneath cumulus. She knew it was just a hologram of Earth, but she wasn't going to spoil her own illusions.

What else, the proprietor would ask.

Carrots, raisins straight from the vine, pumpkins.

We have those!

Great, said Cleo, lay them on me!

The fruits floated to her.

Eat these.

Okay, Cleo said. Wow, these are great!

They give superhuman strength and fertility.

Why do you think I need fertility. And where are you hiding my father.

Then she awoke from waking, a can of wrench spray in her hand. It was time to go home. The clock told her this. The clock worked; it smiled; it had a job. The robots brayed as they were shepherded into their pens. They, too, could see the futile machinations of the clock. To keep time. Clocks had agendas all right. On her way home the sun obscured itself. Winds began to stir from Presque Isle Bay, carrying danders and debris. The wind held her still for a few seconds in front of the black cat factory. The foreman steeped his tea in the tower office, as he tended to. He waved. He didn't live there. Cleo didn't wave back. The man turned back to his tea and shook his head. The wind let her go. She ran away from the manufacturing unit, as fast as she could. The sky turned teak. She passed the laughter inside the factory, the bullhorns far away. Everything was far away. In her book, the less thought about the foreman, the better.

She entered the house and locked the door, to prevent October from entering. From the kitchen window she saw an entire copse of trees sway. A few of them were sick, but she didn't trust tree doctors. Talk about agendas. No one was hanging around or hanging there. On the To Do notepad on her Frigidaire she had written: *I am proofing the book of the living against the book of the dead. They are concurrent, for the most part. Sort of. A few typos.* Cleo used a permanent marker. The paper had butterflies. She hadn't seen a butterfly in thirteen years. The ukulele fixed to the wall fell down. Her mother had won the ukulele in a tournament. Her mother's admonition: never touch the ukulele under any circumstances. She left it where it fell. In fact she really didn't want to look at it. Sirens and klaxons rose a few blocks away. Which didn't really mean anything.

She then drew a bath. She slept in the tub. She heard the cats opening their books across the street, though that couldn't be. She dreamed this time of the photocopier display reading: TONE LOW. A red light blinked, illuminating the entire copy room with emergency. Cleo cried and then floated through the rest of the dream without complications nor reproductions. The absences were pleasurable. She awoke at dawn in a cold sweat, still in the tub. There was a knock on the door. Cleo had no idea who she could be.

2.

Erie was founded in 1697 by French Cathars. Religious persecution was rampant at the time. Seven canoes launched from Quebec City in September, when water was most tumultuous. Lake Erie was the shallowest of the Great Lakes and the one most likely to storm. The boats were the Asphodel, the Asphaedel, the Asfodel, the Aesphadel, the Asfaedel, the Aesfodel, and the Asfaedel. They were named as such to confuse the shipwrights and dockmasters of New France. No one really noticed their departure; if anyone did, they probably would have been pleased. They landed on what would later become Beach 11, the swimmer killer. Sleeping under constellations, the twenty-one colonists all wondered what fateful wind had brought them to those finely sanded beaches. There were no breakwalls to prevent beach erosion at that time. Clearly, their kingdom was at hand.

Yvain led them, but he was quiet for a long time. His wife, Nicollette, was also quiet. On the first morning when the Cathars woke, they sacrificed a goat specifically brought for this purpose. They broke fast over organs. Gulls fought over the red sand. When they moved inland, to construct their city of black brass—the city that some of them, at least, wanted to construct—they found themselves at another body of water, a bay. They reasoned that a city either could be found or founded. Their landing place was actually part of a peninsula, an almost island, jutting out from the mainland like an ichor finger. They walked the *presque isle,* discovered several deadened marshes and ponds, tidepools, hardwood forests. A little of everything. On the peninsula, the world was a pocket-sized encyclopedia; every step was a catalogue. They felt bountiful. They slew butterflies and foxes. They looked for caves in which to consecrate themselves to God. To become perfect. Finding none, they decided to move inland and utilize the bay as the natural harbor for a city. If there were no grottoes or caves, they would have to be built. They brought their boats through the channel and landed on what would later become the foot of East Avenue. They missed State Street, which was the center of the American town for many decades, by a good mile or two. They built huts using thatch and smooth antler-shaped driftwood. They dug sandy holes that filled with water after a few feet. So much for the caves. To pass the time, they wrote long letters to their compatriots around the globe: France, of course, and also England, Paraguay, Belgium, Guinea. There was no means of delivery, but few would have answered anyway. The letters were hard-to-read exhortations. They dreamed of panthers and leopards, which didn't make sense.

After fall's leaves dying, their first winter came. Snow so cold it felt hot against the skin. They caught rabbits. Some they kept as pets. They prayed, not only for food, but also that the French would not find them. Particularly the Jesuits and Dominicans. The Cathars remembered what had happened to their spiritual ancestors. In the first year a few children were born. None were sacrificed. Lost bears wandered to the lake shores, onto Presque Isle, wandered back. Frostbite clarified thought. In spring, construction began on a temple. French voyageurs were killed. The women lured them, hoisting high their dresses on the shores. The canoes slowed. The women had muskets tucked in their sleeves. They were not against eating human flesh, as a matter of principle, but they didn't feel that the times called for it. They realized cannibalism was against Cathar edicts, but then again all flesh was abject, unworthy of long contemplation and self-entreaty. The women were skilled with guns. The Iroquois, who had exterminated the Eriez Indians a few decades before, left the colony alone for the most part. The Cathars cared not. Hearing what had happened to their brethren, a few trappers asked to join in the first summer. These trappers later were revealed to be a troupe of Russian jugglers who had lost favor with the czarina. They were initiated and received perfection. A few in their ranks were born many times over. The Eriez were also known as the Cat People. For them, the cat was a skunk. Three hundred years before, eight thousand Cathars had been slaughtered in one day by one of their former protectors. They actually didn't call themselves Cathars to begin with, which was a name designed by a mad German prince. Many Christians thought the Cathar initiation ceremony involved kissing a cat's ass. The branding and identity campaign against the Cathars, as evidenced by their near-extermination, was a well-received success.

Berries came in summer, in thickets. They built a lookout tower on the tip of Presque Isle, where the Coast Guard station would later appear. Lashing logs together. They wanted to build a giant chain across the channel into the bay, as was done in Constantinople. That had protected the Byzantines for a time. They didn't have the funds or the smelting proficiency for such a project. They had a master woodworker and bone lather in their company. Babies ate magnanimous berries. Streets were laid, sloping up from the shore. Straight lines and grids. What was once a morass of bodies, indistinguishable from each other, began to take on hierarchy. For a few months they felt they didn't have to have any single person deciding anything for the rest. That it lasted so long was remarkable. Yvain, before his expulsion from the University of Paris, had taken a class in classical geometry. He plumbed sight lines. He began courting allies. His wife, Nicollette, wasn't content with discretion and quietude. Everything they were taught in school turned out to be true: Yvain ended up leading because he financed the colony. Still, France seemed a long way away. The surf had no conch shells, no naiad bones. Zebra mussels would not be introduced into the ecosystem for almost three hundred years. They all except for Yvain came from the yeomanry. They were adrift from the small villages of their birth, always among wolves. They wanted to stumble to their own village, as one would from a tavern toward home late at night. The night was late in their minds. The wolves were at the door. Don't open the door! No court, nor *mare liberum,* could weave heraldics close enough to ensnare. Griffin, bull, bulldogs, kings—all mythologies, glad tidings on bloody ears. The summer wheat was not successful. Waterspouts touched down on the lake, and they prayed to be spared. The berries turned black in soups and cremes. Yvain wanted to build a cathedral, of sorts, on Presque Isle, inside the dead marshes. A contemplative building made of local stone. At times, he really did seem peaceful. This in addition to the temple on the mainland. More converts came, this time from Saint Augustine. The irony was lost on no one. Yvain wanted the second temple in the marshes to demonstrate a mind as wide as thought. Nicollette disagreed. She was a kleptomaniac, which was a hard compulsion to honor on the edge of God's world. She played chess. She always beat Yvain. She always played white and Yvain black. Yvain took a few builders to the swamps in the center of Presque Isle and started to cut down cottonwood trees. To clear a space. Then he changed his mind and decided that the marsh wasn't an ideal location. They painted the stumps black. The bog didn't help. The temple's foundation kept sinking.

Actually Nicollette was quite beautiful. She had long black hair.

She excelled at writing sestinas. No training or schooling could account for this. End words to the lines came to her with succinct ease. Most of the time they rhymed. She would rarely show her compositions to her husband. Paper was precious. She took to carving sestinas on trees. Yvain didn't approve of poetry or lending his knife. The summer heat came. The eldest colonist swore he saw, while scything hay, a giant panther charging from the south. The panther had six eyes! And a tongue like a cat-o'-nine-tails! And had constellation markings on its fur! And spoke Basque! This was corroborated by others, although the language was debated. Fissures crept into the colony. Centipede-slow spoilings of their bread stores occurred. They were hungry but not thirsty. They prayed together less. An English caravel wandered close to their lookout. The English were only in transit. The Union Jack shone. The Cathars wished they had cannons. Two weeks later, a French caravel landed on the point of the peninsula closest to the mainland. The thinnest land. Two Jesuits, several marines. The Cathars lost three. Five were wounded. Yvain lost a pinky. But they gained many supplies and weapons. They dropped the weighted soldiers into the moors. The priests they kept with the rabbits. Nicollette slept with a sixteen-year-old boy. No one remembered his name, not even Nicollette.

Yvain had a dream about this involving those pesky panthers. The panthers had some worthwhile pillow talk. They dragged him by the collar to their cave with their teeth. But they also had hands with opposable thumbs. Yvain was not afraid. Inside the cave was a glass box, human-sized, with a star inside it. The star was too bright to look at; he asked them to cover it, and remarkably, they covered the box with a purple cloth. They told him everything. From inside the box—Yvain covered his eyes—the cats pulled out paintings of his wife's transgressions, in glades. They told him that God's work would emanate from him long after he died. When he woke, he didn't know how long he could keep up his façade, his scaffolding. It turned out to be approximately three days, and then he killed the boy, Nicollette's lover. He used his favorite knife and took the corpse, along with the captured priests and ten colonists, to the peninsula. A splinter. Two colonies, two architectures. Nicollette wondered how the quickness happened so quickly. How she came to this. She reasoned that she was sacrificing the great for the greater good. Or maybe it was the good for the greater great. It was hard to tell. Yvain began plans for a lighter-than-air craft as August and its skies came upon them. Skies arrived on the tips of Nicollette's fingers. She started drinking coffee, stolen from the French soldiers. Most, including all of the Russians, stayed close to her. They guarded her sleep. In fact, Yvain and his cohorts did eat the sixteen-year-old boy and saved his bones. Yvain had realized at a young age that he was named after a famous epic, one important to French natural identity. The unit of French poetry is not the accent but the syllable. Yvain and the settlers weren't able to get the balloon off the ground, but they certainly tried. They tried the fumes of quicksilver, the smoke of burning foxes. They didn't possess profound amounts of scientific acumen. Except for geometry. And theology, which was considered a science in those days. As it would later be.

With Yvain on the peninsula, the city planning on the mainland floundered. Little huts became the norm again. Dreams died, thrown against the rocks and burned in fire pits. The peninsula temple was completed as the fall colors turned. Nicollette didn't grieve. Yvain's temple was consecrated with a lacquer made of blackberries and Jesuit blood. One of the Russians, of his own accord, secreted to Presque Isle and humbly asked for a little of that blood. Just a dollop for the mainland village. Yvain told him that it didn't work like that. The Russian was allowed to return. These sudden kindnesses made Nicollette angry. She wasn't sure why she had slept with the boy after all. Maybe it was a sense of sorrow. Love stories lay around in the furs next to the campfire. Belief that the world was ephemera necessitated a belief in God's permanence and justice, kind of. Most of the Cathars really didn't see it that way. However, the two hundred French soldiers who pushed toward the settlement from the newly founded Fort LeBoeuf did see it that way. Fort LeBoeuf was about twenty miles south. It was on French Creek, which flowed into the Allegheny, which flowed into the Ohio, which flowed into the Mississippi. A road from LeBoeuf to Lake Erie would allow for powerful movements. The soldiers came across Nicollette bathing outside. The Cathars didn't expect trouble from the thicketed south. Nicollette regularly bathed with the other colonists. They were all naked. The wind was Indian summer. Yvain called his temple *Usine de Chat Noirs*. Nicollette and the others had a few minutes to flee. Everyone was rather startled. The Cathars crammed into boats. A few were killed. The dead were pushed overboard. The French horses buckled. The Jesuit in the soldiers' party forbade them from pursuit until the temple was destroyed and the ground reconsecrated. They did so. The smoke alerted an English sloop docking along the shore about ten miles away. Yvain didn't welcome Nicollette and the others with open arms, exactly. But close enough. They gathered on the lookout tower and the temple roof with their arquebuses and muskets. They waited. The soldiers didn't come until vespers. The French had engaged in a tough firefight with the English sloop. The Jesuit was killed. The Jesuits couldn't seem to get any luck. The sloop burned, eventually. Bayonets blazed. The hotter-than-air balloon wasn't invented until one hundred fifty years later.

The Cathars watched and prayed. They had kept quiet for centuries in Toulouse and its highlands, becoming perfect in secret. They saw the New World as their tabula rasa. Waiting, they played chess and cards. Yvain held Nicollette's hand. The French battalion came toward the temple slowly. They looked for traps, blinds, snipers, and feints. There were none. When they came upon the temple, arquebuses recoiled. The Cathars, with a sense of déjà vu, pounced, rapt in dark curtains of gunfire.

When reinforcements came in the spring, there were no signs of a previous human settlement. The French were confused, to say the least, but nevertheless began establishment of a fort at the tip of Presque Isle. Garrison commanders over time assumed that reports of a previous colony were fabricated. The year was 1699. Skunks found egg nests. Deer ate crops. There were absolutely no panther sightings. Cathars would not come to Erie for another two hundred years. In a way they weren't even really Cathars. No one important ever came from Erie for the most part. Rain clouds were not considered people by most people. The peninsula shifted eastward every year by a few inches. At a few points in its history, the land bridge flooded, making it an actual island and not an almost island. Burnt firmaments settled but did not rest. Before dawn, Yvain dug a hole in the sandy loam and placed the chess pieces in a moleskin bag. He filled the hole and smoothed it over. He hurried back to his tiny black temple, which was only wood painted black and mostly a dream. He could hear the French soldiers braying, approaching the heretics. No one could have pinpointed the exact moment when things started getting out of hand and small. It was better, Yvain reasoned, not to even try. Seeing him return, Nicollette thought: words about this ought to be put down, like strays.

3.

Then one day, the woman who always gawked and dawdled at his storefront came in. She wore a red mask and carried a burlap bag. She cradled it like someone else's child. At first she stayed near the vestibule, eyeing the crystal unicorns in their dusty case. Business could have used some work. The lease was rising. Some of his most loyal customers were in custody. Their collections were deemed terrorist threats. Mostly they collected books, with the occasional purchase of figurines "tied in" to those books. The woman had smooth, pale hands and wore tall black galoshes that neither fit nor become her, in his opinion. But then again it was raining. She could have just thrown them on. She was agitated. The failure mall—he hated the term, which was written into his lien—was built on the site of the old Union Station. Once, he had cracked open the plasterboard covering a door in the back of his establishment, revealing most of the station intact, albeit unused. He had fallen asleep in the old waiting room, on a hard bench. It reminded him of childhood.

When he woke up he hadn't known where he was. The next week the plasterboard had been sealed again. An inside job. He never figured out how.

Can I help you? he asked the woman.

She was sheepish. She didn't acknowledge that he had said anything at first, but instead fingered a synthetic jade Buddha on a shelf in the middle of the store. On the bottom of the Buddha was a disclaimer from the mayor's office: the statuette should not be used or construed as an actual deity. Federal compliance. He waited with his arms behind his back. He was hungry. The nearest non–Wal-Mart restaurant was two miles away. He had a hot plate behind the counter that was currently cold. Suddenly she approached the counter and took off her mask. Her eyes were blue and empirical.

Yes, she said, coming to, I'm wondering if you make purchases of collections.

It depends on the collection, he said. While he was thinking: I am wasting my time and dishonoring my lack of cash by even speaking to her. Is there a reason for this? Aside from the fact that she is the first person I've talked to today? Why are her eyes like that.

Well, I'll show you what I have, then, she said. She set the burlap bag on the counter. Dust rabbits arose. She opened the bag and with care she took out a chess board. And then each piece, the white pieces first.

The black queen is missing, she said. I apologize for that. I never had it. I inherited this from my mother. I'm sure the lack of a valuable piece will depreciate the entire ensemble.

Shocked, he wanted to sit down. Instead he said, Let me look at this more closely.

Do you play, the woman said.

The man shook his head. Once, but... She was clearly disappointed. He swallowed and opened a combination safe behind the counter and took out a magnifying glass, one he had used for his insect collection, before entomology had become obsolete. He took the white queen in his hand and peered at her. The queen's features were iconic but nuanced. A little pouty and come-hither. The piece was heavy, even though the material suggested lightness.

May I ask why you're selling this? he asked.

It's that—

She coughed.

The factory near my house is expanding operations. Claiming the rest of my block in a seizure. I need something for a bribe.

He knew she meant the black cat factory. No other factory was experiencing a boom. He had visited it once as a teenager, when looking for a summer job, but didn't remember much about it. He fell into seeing the pieces. Sight made real things seem less realistic. The pieces were made of bone. The white pieces were a natural off-white. The black pieces were lacquered with a deep red stain. It might as well have been black. She raised her eyebrows at him when he didn't say anything for a long time. He hadn't played chess in years. Decades. Do you play, he asked her.

She shook her head. I never learned how. Other people learned around me. Her fingers twitched.

What's your name, he asked her.

Pepin, she said. He startled without exactly knowing why.

Well, Pepin, considering the craftsmanship, and the age of the pieces, I'm thinking that not only would this set make a handsome bribe, it might very well allow you to *buy* a factory.

She was breathless and said, Oh, I had hoped and hoped that this was the case!

However, I can't buy it myself.

She was crestfallen. Why not?

It's worth more than the entire store, Pepin. I can try to find a buyer for you. Out of the city, most likely.

She shuffled her feet. How do you know how old it is? And how old is it?

Early eighteenth century, late seventeenth. The pieces are in the French regency style. The flumes with the stylized heads at the top. They often used this style with ceramic. It was rare that someone could lathe and carve bone in such fine detail.

It must have been quite rare, Pepin said, folding her hands and pursing her lips. She was offended so easily!

He took one of the pawns and squinted at it. He didn't want to fetishize dead bone. The pawns had tiny child heads. Their eyes were wide.

And there's the fact, he added, pressing his word luck, that all of these faces look so *angry.*

Anger's an emotion, Pepin said. Her face grew red.

The man held out his hands. It was no criticism. I swear.

Pepin's shoulders sagged. I apologize, she said. Of course. If you could find a buyer... She trailed off.

I can certainly try, he said, setting the pawn down. He had forgotten many of his favorite openings. Not the moves themselves, which were easy enough to memorize, but their temperaments. I'd like to borrow the set overnight, he said. To take photographs for potential buyers. It's standard.

Her eyes grew dim. Out of the question, she said. Pepin scooped the pieces back into the bag. She left the board. They both knew it was probably worthless.

Call on me if you find anyone. She gave her number and turned away. He was too stunned by her departure to say anything, except, If you want a truer sale, then try to find the black queen. She didn't appear to hear him. The black queen might have been irretrievable. He locked the front door and retreated to the cot in the back room. He lay there for a few hours, saying Pepin, Pepin. He imagined her hovering over him. He couldn't make himself come all the same. Erotic satisfaction could not be achieved by looking at a blurry photocopy of a photograph of a naked woman. He rose eventually. He unlocked the door again. Open for business. Not that it mattered. In a few hours, business hours were over. He could hear the cold drag races down on lower Sassafras. The drag races were free. The failure mall locked him in for the evening. He was supposed to have access codes for free passage, but the lords changed the codes with great ease and regularity. Even if he could leave, where could he go. He didn't have martial papers. He wondered what it must have been like to raise a family in the Assyrian empire. Surely someone in the Assyrian empire had felt love, it wasn't 24/7 beheadings. Maybe it was. Children had to work or die. What love must have been like when no one would remember you and no one would write about love. Because almost no one could read or write. He had once been Catholic until the church changed their mass back to Latin, cosponsored the drag races with the Pentecostals, and founded the Benevolent Union of Saint Antonin. Any one of those changes pushed him. He didn't know any way to push back. Figurines never pushed.

Every other Thursday they would have an execution at the drag race. Or an excommunication. A killing-one-bird-with-two-stones kind of deal. He remembered how youth used to be different. Races were different. There were no sensory cowls to follow the coverage and feel crashes. He had gone to a drag race with his uncle when he was nine or ten. In some ways things were not much better then. His uncle had worked at Hammermill and had lost two fingers and a thumb in a paper cutter. The noise was noisy. Few had jobs. He, young, had bought a button of his favorite car, number eight. A black car with red trim. He hadn't known why this was his favorite. It made as much sense to him as driving so fast that one needed a parachute to slow down. His uncle died of a brain tumor ten years later, before everything started happening. That didn't make much sense either. He went to high school in the basement of Erie's cathedral. On the way to the cafeteria he could pass by the dead bishop crypt. A windowless, pious room filled with minor diocesan relics. The school had excelled at football and extolling football players. Academics had been a distant third. He wore his clip-on tie on the first day of school. His mother had picked it out for him. Their family eschewed vacations so that they could earn enough indulgence for the cathedral school. That first day, the clouds from the paper mill took a wrong turn and the city smelled like broken-down fish. Within ten minutes of school a senior ripped off his tie. He joined the chess club, which provided him a small measure of exquisite carnage. They would hide in the boiler room and play.

As he slept that night, night slept next to him. He could hear the sound of worms eating books. He ate ramen that night, which didn't sit well. He would have been old enough for Social Security if there had been such a thing as security, for his nonwinning ilk. He didn't know where the worms or the books came from. Before sleeping he encrypted a description of the chess set, through a Senegalese server. Precautions had to be made. In the morning, one prospect was insistent. He double-checked his library and made sure there were no worms there. He called Pepin and arranged a meeting. She didn't want to meet at the store again. He entertained the thought that perhaps she was a spy. Ridiculous. But then again he was desperate. She had to work that day. Presque Isle, she suggested. The last remaining public beach. All right. Tomorrow. Wonderful. See you then. See you. That night he dreamed of vomiting chess pieces. The tiny faces of the chess pieces also vomited out smaller chess pieces. And so on. At the appointed time, he met with Pepin at the appointed place. Old Lighthouse Beach. The lighthouse had been uprooted some time ago. The hole was covered. Tall walls separated this beach from the others, which were used for either private residential and/or military purposes. He wore a sky-blue tie. She had no way of seeing the tie because of the containment suit, but it made him feel better. Egyptian peacekeepers had landed here less than five years before. They didn't get far. The gun towers towered over them. They gleamed even though there was no sunlight. War kites soared above them. The winds lacerated. The beach was empty. Past the breakwalls, the flotillas held guard on the lake. People who wanted supreme protection lived there. One had to have means to live there, of course. The flotillas had no libraries. On the beach, Pepin was pensive. She said things to imply that she was pensive.

For example, she said, Don't worry, the turrets can't hear us. On account of the wind.

And: Even if someone accosts us, and I'm not saying they will, we can pretend we're lovers. Having an affair. We might have to pay a fine, but we won't be stoned.

Wonderful, he replied. He tried not to think of their meeting as a date. He couldn't help it, though. He thought, Maybe she's the black queen.

I work at a Wal-Mart, she said.

Who doesn't, he said, suddenly sullen. It was hard, with the wind, smoke, and sand, to actually complete words.

She grabbed his hand. No, what I mean is, I know how to cut corners, squirrel away, range free without persecution. But listen. At the bowling alley, I'm trying to teach one of the robots to play chess. How great is that. I have two robots, but one is slightly newer and therefore smarter than the other. It has potential. I've taken it home.

He didn't know tedium could be so thrilling. He couldn't feel her skin on account of their mittens, which were retrofitted oven mitts.

Let me tell you about the potential buyer, he said. It's a woman not far from here. Cambridge Springs. Thirty miles south of here.

He knew that the greatest tournament ever on American soil took place in Cambridge Springs. 1904. A long time ago. Many grand masters played at that tournament. He didn't want to bore Pepin, who only inherited chess, with the details. A recessive gene. Cambridge Springs was halfway between New York and Chicago. A refueling stop for the bullet trains. None of the sulfuric springs were left. His handling fee would be worth the entire inventory of his store.

Who is this woman?

She is a collector of chess sets. I've dealt with her in the past. Incredibly reliable, A plus plus plus.

The woman in question—he wasn't really even sure whether she was a woman—had demanded that he tell Pepin this.

How much will she offer?

Like I said, enough to buy a factory. Anything. Live in the flotilla if you want. A sky fortress. Health insurance. Fairy dust money.

Pepin moved toward the green surf. Salamander water danced along her galoshes. I worry about what's inside me sometimes, she said. Whether I'm a dachshund in a world of giraffes. She stopped and stared at a point in the sand. As if she wanted to turn it into glass. He stood next to her.

Pepin?

No, she said. I've changed my mind! I won't!

It wasn't entirely clear who she was speaking to. She ran up the beachhead back to the road, toward his kidney-bean car. A far cry from black number eight. Town criers told him it was his own fault for not succeeding. She didn't have a car. Buses were infrequent. He'd still give her a lift if she wanted one. They could smooth over their differences. He could moor her. He tried to follow. She was fast. He smelled cinder and powder keg. At the road, she turned around to say, I'm sorry, but the chess set is not for sale.

What? Why?

I want to learn how to play. She crossed the road and entered a trailhead opposite the beach shore that he hadn't noticed before. A thicket with a narrow sidewalk running through it. A straight line into the peninsula. He tried to remember the trail—he had lived in Erie his entire life—and couldn't for the life of him. He was about to follow her when he started laughing and said to himself, Fuck it, she's a loon, she's a dachshund. He sat down on a mossy picnic table, shaking his head. He was a little sad at how—when his life was in danger of rupturing with change—softly and quickly everything turned back to the way it already was. He would never talk to her again. He remembered watching videos in science class about African animals, how when a person had an infection, that person would let maggots crawl into the wound and eat the infected tissue. Then, once flies, they would fly away. The table collapsed. Pepin disappeared, toward marshes and miseries. The trees were leafless and scarred with knives' marks and acid initials. She had never asked for his name, not once.

✤

4.

Pepin's floating. He's floating about them. Their time is now, but his is not. He puts his finger into the marmalade sky and doesn't feel any wind. It's windy. He's a lighter-than-air aircraft. Of sorts. They're playing. They don't know the time. They don't know the proximity of adversaries. One chanced a glance at the other. Neither has touched the board. Which means it's white's turn. Soon they will meander. He's not sure what is sensory information and what is realism. On his farm, once, he milked cows and learned to like it. Hills were called mountains in his childhood. He hates chess even more, after what has happened to him. He loves God! However, that is unimportant. His mother's name is Marguerite. She is still farming. She has farming stories that he will never hear. White moves finally. C4. The English Opening. White has made him laugh. Lieutenant Carve—that isn't his name, it has to be Carver—is close. Carver's floating, but in a boat. He will be woken. The English opening lends itself to positional play. Jockeying, and not swift tactics. At least at first. The English Opening can lead to brutal retributions eventually. Pepin sees Black's knife next to the board. Pepin's cold somehow. More than usual. To disavow knowledge of the game, he holds his breath. He came to New France because of a girl. The girl was sixteen. Somewhere she is. She died of smallpox on the Atlantic crossing. He can't hold his breath long enough to reach her. He's forgotten her face. They threw her into the Sargasso. Other women have resembled her, all the same. He lets out his breath. A sulfur trace streaming over the peninsula. No one's living there. Black king and white queen are dead. He didn't see their ashes deposited into Misery Bay. That's what the commodore later calls it. But it fit. It fits. He's deposited, too. Part of him. A safety deposit in a sand bank. He doesn't hate White with all of his heart. Pepin knows he is young. She was not. The young are interruptible. After what has happened to White and Black and the others, he thinks he came away easy. He's floating, after all. He hasn't found anyone else floating. The French fort is ephemeral. They who think they are more than footnotes. So they share the same language. Big deal. Everyone is a footnote. Entrapment isn't so bad. It nourishes broken things and makes them grow big and strong. He would like, at some point, to see one of his loves again. Unlikely. The French fort passes. LeBoeuf lasts a little longer, though he can't see that. The factory has slid into the marshes. It's hard to talk about in the open. No one can see this, as no one can directly see a black hole. Pepin can only see the absences around the factory. There are tricky currents and tide pools within the peninsula's many nooks and moors. It's a good place to hide and hide things. We have met the enemy, and they are ours. The factory continues its production unbeknownst to the Pennsylvanians. Underneath the duckweed. The state buys the lake port when he inhales again. The state needs access. A safe harbor. He sees odd speculative bubbles. America has plans. America, he wants to say, you are one clumsy girl. You are so obvious about your schemes. Winters remind him of past frostbite. He lost a pinky tip on the farm. He was a hard worker in Quebec. He gutted fish. They mixed the fish with potatoes and put it in tins. Meal alchemy. The Cathars, he realizes, weren't quite so fearsome as he had feared or even hoped. Even after all they did to him. They weren't even really Cathars. They liked thought costumes. America would have done them good. A declaration of independence and constitution. The city arrives, sloping to the bay. Burghers want to build a profit fleet. War with the English makes this possible. Pepin thinks of the English Opening again. There is no American Opening. There ought to be. He's contemplated mating with clouds. Albino gulls dive. He has time for historiography. The American fleet sinks an English fleet. *Niagara* monster. The remainders of the American fleet are sunk in Misery Bay. The land bridge floods. Recedes. He doesn't want to mewl over his predicament. The hardest part was when they opened his chest cavity. That's when he fled. That's when holding his breath became more than a way to conquer hiccups. Civil war brought actual factories. He applied for a cabin boy position in Quebec City. He milled around the docks. He was hungry. He didn't know they had only canoes and no cabins for boys. He could read. He was the only applicant. He was on the canoe with the goat, which shit everywhere. No wonder they wanted to kill it when they landed. Once in a while a chips wrapper swirls by, and that's it. He's grateful for litter and nutritional statements. Food pyramids printed on trash. Of course there are always the Eriez to consider. The skunk people. Maybe if they hadn't been eradicated by the Iroquois, things would have been different for him. Or a beheading on the spot, upon landing on the peninsula. Hard to say. Ironworks cast dies, meanwhile. A long era when trains stopped in Erie. The depth's factory felt competition. This was no doubt natural. A kiss is a technology aimed to achieve a desired effect. A kiss is an opening. It's difficult to consider his belly button. He can't look. He first kissed the White Queen while gathering berries with her. Eventually she crushed the berries against her thighs. The passage of their mutual seduction. She would wander through the nascent city nude. Poles, Germans, Irish homing-pigeoned to the city. The gem city, it's called for a while. No one finds gems limning the streets, but at least there's work. Presque Isle is inaccessible except by boat. Mosquitoes hate tourists. There is a lakeside lighthouse. A house attaches to it. Children live there. Pepin watches them get older. They build a trail cutting across the peninsula to the bay side. Dead fish are a language. They gather near the docks as a grammarian's convention. A sidewalk trail past the marshes. Oh, they tore that up. But not for a long time. They use the trail to go to school, to the bay on the other side. A ferry to Erie. The trail seems straight. The children die. The factory's migrating, underwater. Sledging on the bottom, upturning mercury boots and nonrefundable cola bottles on the bay's bottom. He imagines cats in diving bells hauling the factory underwater. He observes pesticides and tourist arrivals and bathhouses and children drowning in undertows. Or straying off the sidewalk trail. Deer shy away. Ticks pounce. Grand masters joust thirty miles away in a tourney. In the early history of chess, the queen used to be a limited piece and could not move far. Anonymous Europeans made technological enchantments to accelerate the game. The queen became the most powerful piece. Aside from the king. Even that was questionable. The king's power rests in his vulnerability. His bones tremble. He sees her at last—and himself—in the eighties. Building a sand castle next to her mother. Her mother stares at the sand. They're both on a beach towel. Her mother cocks her head and starts digging. He's unsure of her dowsing—not of its accuracy but whether he wants to be found. She puts her hand flat on the sand. She tells her daughter to wade. The sand castle's spires remind him of home. Rain ruins and wolves skirting the crop edges. He never understood Cathars and never would.

Wade? the daughter says. A pigeon flies past, out of its habitat.

Practice your doggy paddle, Cleo. Don't swallow the water, it's filthy. Keep your chin up.

This last command, even he can tell, is tactical advice and not encouragement.

He enjoys the linear progression of time. Even though he knows it's kind of a farce. It turns out that the colonists on the peninsula had been kicked out of the Cathar establishment. Loose as it was. For violence and malfeasance. The White Queen told him this a few days before their separation. The girl is dutiful and splashes into the waves. The mother scoops up the bag. He mimics spitting sand out of his mouth.

Much later, the factory comes ashore in a foggy night. Sets up shop in an abandoned warehouse, of which there are plenty. Zebra mussels invade in its wake and win. Much later, Pepin floats above the stucco house and sees recalcitrant spires, gangplanks, chained vats inside the factory. Tractor-sized photocopiers where the cats are penned. Inner ichors. The mother loses the Black Queen! Or rather, the Black Queen escapes. Hard to say which is true. He is over the house. A good view. The mother gives up chess. Cleo senses she should never discuss this. House turned up top to bottom. Arguments over who lost the queen. It's useless, he hears. It's useless. The remaining pieces are squirreled away in storage, and the mother dies. And then everyone is filled with the Lord, and a few people design systems to save and consolidate other, less fortunate people. Much later, he whispers to the girl—now much older—that he will give his breath and breadth, and that she will never have to be alone unless she wants to be. She opens her mouth in the bath. She doesn't move to open the door when she hears knocking.

That's the factory representative, he tells her. He's offering you an eviction notice. Don't read it. That's why I'm here for you now. I'm hearing you.

She doesn't read it. I love you, she says. He sees through the foreman's window the knife. He can shift back, at any time, to feeling Black's knees on his chest and the first fluttering cut across the neck. He doesn't. The churches sadden the streets in bright crosses. Migratory species are shot down with antiaircraft guns. Icarus solutions mean losing track of extinctions. Selling the horns as unicorn horns. Ground to a powder. Satan is a better chess player than God. It doesn't mean he wins. But he has nothing to lose. Operators on abandoned blocks on Eighteenth try to contact like-minded psyches through telepathy and ham radio. Signals bounce off him because they don't reach anyone else. Pepin doesn't correct her. Now go sharpen your teeth, he says, and find the rest of me. I'm in the attic, in a banker's box. Your mother painted it blue.

5.

The foreman went to the failure mall and killed the fence, which wasn't hard. The foreman had been on a business trip. Every trip was a business trip. Afterward, it put the "security" system to sleep and rifled through the fence's possessions. Most of which were poor and worthless. It bit its fingernails in boredom until it found Cleo's dossier in the secret library. The library was in a compartment behind the fence's desk. How original. It was heartless. The secret library was mostly twentieth-century porn and chess books. Bestiality and endgame strategy, mostly. Your boat is floated, motherfucker, it said, standing on the fence's windpipe and providing a small benediction that it thought tender, though it was not. Chess was a way to convince itself not to self-destruct. Between two horse copulation magazines was a slender, stapled volume of anonymous sestinas. It smiled. It had once lent the book to the fence as collateral. The compartment smelled like gobstoppers and semen. It secreted the sestinas into its pouch and left the mall. It needed pieces. Crossing Thirteenth, it started walking to the East Side, toward home. The streets were empty except for police pretending to be homeless. But their ragged jackets were too clean and had too many iron-on sponsorships. The homeless had no sponsors. They didn't bother the foreman. They might have even winked. In the failure mall, it had memorized the sestinas, poems about picking blackberries for the untenable Lord and effervescent failure. Its cogs creaked. It truly had been in Cambridge Springs yesterday, surveying the ruins of the old grand master's hotel. For future development. At some point, no property would be too far away. However, the foreman was not arrogant and was more than willing to admit its own shortcomings. It had thought that Cleo would merely confuse yearning with confusion and let the tensions settle into her. Her ordinary life. And she had, for a long time. But people weren't solvable, unfortunately. Not that it didn't try. The old set had to be acquired. The friendly takeover, however, had broken the deal. Cleo's reluctance couldn't be anything else. This made the foreman faux sad. Crossing State Street, it began whistling the old national anthem. Its favorite song. The one-hundred-year-old peanut and macadamia nut shop was closed. Most recently the store had sold circus peanuts and only that. Circus peanuts were the undead of the candy world and were in a strong market position. The foreman heard waves crashing over Dobbins Landing, half sunk and tilted. Upon reaching East and Tenth it crossed itself at Saint Anne's as a lark. Novenas were held there for a long time. The trick was: go to the church nine days in a row and one would receive a plenary indulgence. One had to appreciate the psychosis needed to perpetuate that worldview. However inelegant an exchange of spiritual capital it was. Much simpler to declare Jesus as savior, enter a Christworld nexus, and invest your annuities in the war futures in paraclete funds.

It speculated on such strategies in the factory. It reached the factory. The lights were turned on at the silent gates, but it kept walking, toward Cleo's house. It could hear the copiers caterwaul. The eviction notice hadn't moved her in the ways it had intended. It needed compliance. The house was empty and lightless. After letting itself in and finding no one, it sat on the elliptical couch. It appreciated, in a way, the venomous quirks of the mother. The gardener had drowned himself. So easy to drown when living next to a lake! It heard patters from the balustrades of the factory. It saw the ukulele on the floor. It stood and took it. It started to pluck at it. A string broke. It smashed the ukulele against the television, shattering the instrument. Inside the ukulele was the skeleton of a small bird. A passenger pigeon. It laughed and plucked the bird out by the wingtip. It could tell the bird was a passenger pigeon by the bone structure and beak size. Poor bird, it said. Where are your children. Where is your flock. The last of your kind died in a zoo. It placed the bird in its pocket with the sestinas and went outside. From the backyard it saw the robot, a classic Walbot, sitting in the cemetery behind the stucco house. The cemetery had a slope and an emptiness. The foreman opened the unhinged gate and walked toward the robot. The robot was nursing a small campfire. Campfires were illegal. The robot was male-like, with beach-blond hair and a Wal-Bowl identification plate on its chest. Anyone with beach blond, finely tuned hair in Erie could easily be recognized as an android. The robot didn't look up and rubbed its hands. The foreman liked to brew tea from black cat blood.

What's your name, son, the foreman said, crouching on one knee.

Nicollette, the robot said. With a French accent.

The foreman smirked. It had learned how to smirk at board meetings of the godly and unimpaired. Do you know you're trespassing on private property, Nicollette? Do you want me to cite code?

The robot shivered and crossed its arms. It knew not sadness in its face, its Ken Zen eyes.

Cleo said I could live here, it said.

And where is Cleo?

Nicollette didn't respond at first. It stared into the fire and its features became blurry, somnambulant.

How about this, Nicollette said. I have an offer for you. A game of chess. I win, and you leave Cleo alone. You win, and I'll deliver her to you. And her possessions.

The foreman could not lose. It had had many years of study for such a competition. It had once carried on a correspondence game with a Maori grand master—a used car salesman in Wellington—for several years. Won handily.

I accept, it said.

The robot produced a board and pieces. *The* board and pieces. Not a cheap plastic set one would buy at Wal-Mart, cardboard board, plastic pieces light enough to float in water. The foreman was nearly struck dumb.

Play here? it said.

The robot pointed to a revolutionary's tombstone that had been flattened by time. It placed the board there.

There's no black queen, Nicollette said.

Of course there is, the foreman said, cracking its knuckles. It's just not *present*.

What do you propose we do, then, the robot said. Your call.

Pretend as if it's there.

Invisible, you mean.

Sure. Why not.

All right, the robot said. If I want to move her, then, I will indicate the proper square.

The foreman stiffened. Unacceptable, the foreman said. I always play black.

Black always moves second. It is not an advantageous addiction.

It is for me.

You misunderstand me. I always play white. The arrangement will ensure that neither one of us will trust our gift too much.

You're not Nicollette, the foreman said.

It doesn't matter, Nicollette said, turning the board so that the foreman was white. Move. The foreman looked up at the moon, spider-webbed with cities. It could call for the tree doctors, its special spies, any second. Or summon white phosphorus from the secret kites, down to end Nicollette. But it didn't. It tried to contemplate an opening. Across the street, it tried to cue up its database of every chess game ever played and recorded. There was a silence. It set its mind to dreaming solutions but only found considerable terror. It wanted to step away, overturn the board. Move, Nicollette said.

The foreman—which wasn't really a foreman any longer, as much as a compilation of inert, powerful ideas trapped in a body—reluctantly moved F4. An oddity.

Bird's Opening? Nicollette said. My. Very brave of you. Very brave.

It remembered her face as she was pulled from the temple roof, how she kept trying to laugh when the captain put a musket in her mouth. The captain refused to let her laugh when he pulled the trigger. He had killed himself a few years later at LeBoeuf.

Does chess have to be about winning and losing, though? the foreman asked, trying to squirm. So single-minded?

Nicollette squinted at the board. Well, there is the draw.

It became exasperated and said, That's not what I mean.

Across the street, noises. It wanted to turn its head. Its memories were caught in a sphere akin to a soap bubble. The foreman had never gone to high school, never kissed anyone, never became moved by anything except other people's capital. Its existence lent credence to the idea that children with medieval ideas of right and wrong ran the show. They grew up. They ran an economy or two. A fiefdom. They never died. They became imaginary. It heard cats escaping from the front gates. Thousands of them. The cats' brains were used as processing power. Which was not to be confused with process and power. It wanted to close the gates. It wanted to sleep. It could never sleep. Cleo must have let them go. Cleo could sleep. The cats scampered onto Dunn Boulevard. Some were as large as elephants, some were as small as field mice. Some had eight legs, and some dragged themselves away on two. Some had cancer, some had bubonic plague, some had dementia, some had agoraphobia but managed to escape somehow. Some could speak French, some could speak Mayan, some could speak Basque, some could think in every language but not speak any. Some could give lectures on industrialism and living wages, some could teach Go. Some had napalm tails, some had rope tails, some had switchblade tails. Some had diamond claws, some had lapis lazuli claws, some had hardened corn syrup claws, some had no claws. The only traits they shared was their catness. And in a way, they weren't even really cats; much as the first Cathars in Erie weren't really Cathars. Whatever their state, the cats turned a hairpin turn and headed south, away from the bay, toward upper Peach, toward the mayoral domes and Christworld. They ran away from their history, which resembled a sestina. They would not have to repeat their well-groomed epitaphs anymore.

6.

Most chess games are casual and therefore too unimportant to record; this one was not, but still no one knows who won or lost. Or who played in the first place, for that matter, or what happened to the pieces placed on a tombstone of the American Revolution. A hand—not at all parental—picked them up and set them down outside the field of play. Outside the confines of the medieval army. Lost or sacrificed, the pieces cannot do anything but fathom their disposability. Which is no small task. Because, at some point, white or black checkmates the other and all of the pieces must be cleared, and the board set again, like a wolf trap. There were no survivors. There are only winners and losers.

Desperately, people try to show others that their lives are not, in fact, desperate. That they aren't spoilt children. And to keep a straight, nonlachrymose face while doing so. One has no choice but to reconstruct everything lost, as if blindfolded. To try, at least, even if the memories are gossamer thin, almost islands, a map unrelated to any territory. This often involves touching amusements. Touching a sweater made in Antarctica. Touching a soldier boy's limbless arm. Touching a chess set missing the black queen—the Cathars ran out of bone, in a way it was that simple—thinking of the mother who gives up what she loves. And yet, the state cannot concede anything, any soft intent. The state takes and makes people happy, despite themselves. The state plays incandescent anthems, ruins stolen kisses and love, and obeys the rules it makes. Which is a small task. Someone in the office turned off its photocopier and its story was no longer copied nor illuminated for others. Someone unauthorized in the factory entered the break room—which had a roof—and left the refrigerator door ajar. For the hell of it. The foreman was happy, in a way. It closed its eyes and felt the passenger's skeleton stir.

No one can say whether anyone lived in Erie or not after the cats were freed. It is inconclusive. The city becomes unimportant to most purposes. Lost in the footnotes of the sun's fog and the moon's fog. Even the fog's fog. It is not its story anymore. The story becomes smaller and smaller. Nicollette—the robot calling itself Nicollette— is lost, and the foreman is lost, and Cleo is certainly lost. They might have existed ever after, but they are still lost. So many stories are lost every day without really anyone trying, and no one is able to dredge them back. But, listen, there are footsteps in the city. The black queen weaves a path through the streets of fog, looking for an opening, looking for a way out and home.

ABOUT THE AUTHOR

Alan DeNiro was born in Erie, Pennsylvania. He received a BA in English (College of Wooster) and an MFA in poetry (University of Virginia). His fiction has appeared in *Crowd*, *One Story*, *Minnesota Monthly*, *Fence*, *3rd Bed*, and *Polyphony* and has been shortlisted for the O. Henry Award. Alan has taught writing at the University of Richmond and the Loft in Minneapolis; written two text-based computer games, *The Isolato Incident* and *Ogres*; founded Taverner's Koans, a poetry journal and resources website; published poetry in *Willow Springs*, *Cimarron Review*, and *Can We Have Our Ball Back*, as well as two poetry chapbooks, *The Black Hare* (A Small Garlic Press) and *The Atari Ecologues*; reviewed for *Rain Taxi*; and cofounded the Rabid Transit series of fiction anthologies. He is currently working on a novel, tentatively entitled *Total Oblivion, More or Less?* He is a proofreader at Fallon Minneapolis, an advertising agency, and lives outside St. Paul, Minnesota, with his wife, Kristin, and three cats. DeNiro's home online can be found at www.goblinmercantileexchange.com.

PUBLICATION HISTORY

Grateful acknowledgement is made to the following magazines and anthologies in which some of these stories first appeared:

Skinny Dipping in the Lake of the Dead, *Fence*, Volume 2, Number 2
If I Leap, *Altair*, 6/7
Our Byzantium, *Polyphony* 3 (Wheatland Press)
The Centaur, *Spoiled Ink*, July 2005
Cuttlefish, *Lady Churchill's Rosebud Wristlet*, 8
The Caliber, *Santa Monica Review*, Fall 2002
The Excavation, *Minnesota Monthly*, June 2001
A Keeper, *Electric Velocipede*, 6
Fuming Woman, *Trampoline* (Small Beer Press)
The Friendly Giants, *3rd Bed*, 4
Child Assassin, *One Story*, 22
The Exchanges, *Crowd*
Salting the Map, *Fortean Bureau*, 17

Acknowledgements

There are too many people to thank, but I'll try to catch as many people as possible: my Clarion '98 classmates and instructors; writing groups that I've been a part of, including the Karma Weasels and the Ratbastards; Haddayr Copley-Woods, Eric Rickstad, Jenny Woods, Midori Snyder, Fred Ollinger, my parents and siblings, my many students over the years, and the editors who have helped hone these stories and made them better. In particular I'd like to thank Barth Anderson and Chris Barzak for their invaluable advice, and Kristin Livdahl, my amazing wife, who has been my incomparable partner throughout the years.

Small Beer Press

Carol Emshwiller · *The Mount* · 1931520038 · $16
"Best of the Year"—*Book Magazine, Locus, San Francisco Chronicle*
★ "Brilliantly conceived and painfully acute."—*Publishers Weekly* (starred review)
—— *Report to the Men's Club* · 193152002X · $16
"Elliptical, funny and stylish."—*Time Out New York*

Angélica Gorodischer · *Kalpa Imperial* · 1931520054 · $16
Translated by Ursula K. Le Guin
★ "Should appeal to [Le Guin's] fans as well as to those of literary fantasy and Latin American fiction."—*Library Journal* (starred review)

Ellen Kushner · *The Privilege of the Sword* · 1931520208 · $35
"One of the most gorgeous books I've ever read: it's witty and wonderful, with characters that will provoke, charm and delight."—Holly Black (*Valiant*)

Kelly Link · *Magic for Beginners* · 1931520151 · $24
"A netherworld between literature and fantasy."—*Time Magazine: Best Books of 2005*
—— *Stranger Things Happen* · 1931520003 · $16
"Best of the Year"—*Salon, Village Voice, San Francisco Chronicle*
—— editor · *Trampoline: an anthology* · 1931520046 · $17
20 astounding stories by Emshwiller, Jeffrey Ford, Karen Joy Fowler, & others.
"No unblinkered, gloveless reader can resist the stream of associations unleashed by Ford's story and the rest of *Trampoline*: influences as disparate as science fiction, magic realism, pulp, and *Twilight Zone* morality plays."—*Village Voice*

Maureen F. McHugh · *Mothers & Other Monsters* · 1931520194 · $16
Finalist for the Story Prize
"Gorgeously crafted stories."—Nancy Pearl, NPR, *Morning Edition*

Jennifer Stevenson · *Trash Sex Magic* · 1931520127 · $16
"This just absolutely rocks. It's lyrical, it's weird and it's sexy in a very funky way."
—Audrey Niffenegger, *The Time Traveler's Wife*

Sean Stewart · *Perfect Circle* · 1931520119 · $15
★ "All-around terrific."—*Booklist* (starred review)
"Stephen King meets Ibsen. Trust me."—Neal Stephenson, *The Confusion*
—— *Mockingbird* · 1931520097 · $14
"Hands down the best novel I have read in 2005, and one of the best I've ever had the privilege to read."—Park Road Books, Charlotte, NC

Ray Vukcevich · *Meet Me in the Moon Room* · 1931520011 · $16
"Vukcevich is a master of the last line....ingenious with the short-story form."
—*Review of Contemporary Fiction*

Kate Wilhelm · *Storyteller: Writing Lessons & More from 27 Years of the Clarion Writers' Workshop* · 193152016X · $16
"Oh, but this is a lovely book.... Wilhelm fills *Storyteller* with lessons about how to write, and just as important, how not to write."—*Strange Horizons*

Peapod Classics

Howard Waldrop · *Howard Who?* · 1931520186 · $14
> Revised introduction by George R. R. Martin (*A Song of Ice and Fire*): "If this is your first taste of Howard, I envy you. Bet you can't read just one."

> "The resident Weird Mind of his generation, he writes like a honkytonk angel." —*Washington Post Book World*

Naomi Mitchison · *Travel Light* · 1931520143 · $14
> A young woman is transformed by a magical journey in a fabulous novel which will appeal to fans of Diana Wynne Jones, Harry Potter, and T. H. White's *The Sword in the Stone.*

> "A 78-year-old friend staying at my house picked up *Travel Light*, and a few hours later she said, 'Oh, I wish I'd known there were books like this when I was younger!' So, read it now—think of all those wasted years!"—Ursula K. Le Guin (*Gifts*)

Carol Emshwiller · *Carmen Dog* · 1931520089 · $14
> "An inspired feminist fable. . . . A wise and funny book."—*New York Times*

> "A first novel that combines the cruel humor of *Candide* with the allegorical panache of *Animal Farm*."—*Entertainment Weekly*

Small Beer Press Chapbook Series

Theodora Goss, *The Rose in Twelve Petals* · Richard Butner, *Horses Blow Up Dog City*
Christopher Rowe, *Bittersweet Creek* · Benjamin Rosenbaum, *Other Cities*
Mark Rich, *Foreigners, and Other Familiar Faces* · Judith Berman, *Lord Stink and Other Stories*
Alex Irvine, *Rossetti Song: Four Stories*

Lady Churchill's Rosebud Wristlet

A twice-yearly fiction &c zine ("Tiny, but celebrated."—*Washington Post*) edited by Kelly Link and Gavin J. Grant, publishing writers including Carol Emshwiller, Karen Joy Fowler, Jeffrey Ford, Eliot Fintushel, James Sallis, Molly Gloss, and many others. Fiction and nonfiction from *LCRW* has been reprinted in *The Year's Best Fantasy & Horror, The Best of the Rest,* and *The Zine Yearbook.* Many subscription options (including chocolate) available on our website.

www.smallbeerpress.com